PRAISE I

'A beautiful... ...ng and accessible

...Hilary Mantel... This is succinct,
...ng storytelling, which casts light on the origins of
...inian conflict. A timely, terrific novel by a writer at
...y top of his game.' DAVID BELBIN

'An historical novel big on romance and contemporary relevance. The Land Agent creates a vivid picture of Jewish Palestine in its original state, when the idealism of socialist settlers competed with the more hardnosed vision of Zionists for how to build the future homeland.' MICHAEL GOLDFARB

'Has the swift fluency of a master storyteller.' IAN STEPHEN, *Northwords Now*

PRAISE FOR *The Credit Draper*
'An odyssey of cultural confusion and survival. Full of hope, honour and sadness.' MCKITTERICK PRIZE JUDGES

'A rare evocation of an earlier genre: the immigrant novel, with a welcome Scottish dimension.' CLIVE SINCLAIR, *The Jewish Chronicle*

'A subtle, beautifully written story... a truly fine debut which heralds bold new voice in fiction.' RODGE GLASS

PRAISE FOR *The Liberation of Celia Kahn*
'A compelling tale with characters who imprint themselves on the streets of Glasgow.' SCARLETT MCGWIRE, *Tribune*

'Entertaining and compelling. Explores so many stimulating political themes.' ALAN LLOYD, Morning Star

'Sensitively rendered... A quietly brilliant book.' *The Skinny*

Novels by J David Simons

THE GLASGOW TO GALILEE TRILOGY:

The Credit Draper

The Liberation of Celia Kahn

The Land Agent

AND

An Exquisite Sense of What Is Beautiful

THE
LAND
AGENT

J David Simons

Saraband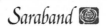

Published by Saraband
Suite 202, 98 Woodlands Road
Glasgow, G3 6HB
Scotland
www.saraband.net

ISBN: 9781908643964
ebook: 9781908643773

Printed in the EU on sustainably sourced paper.

Publication of this book has been supported by Creative Scotland.

ALBA | CHRUTHACHAIL

1 2 3 4 5 6 7 8 9 10

For my friends

'Buy land, they're not making it anymore.'
MARK TWAIN

One

Poland, 1919

EWA KAMINSKY. 'She is a whore.' That was what Lev's uncles, aunts and cousins told him to his face. Even though she was his new step-mother. She had been married once before, she had even been known to apply carmine to her lips from time to time. But surely Ewa Kaminsky was no *kurve*? At the very worst, she possessed ambition. And that was to get Lev's father, Szmul, out of Poland, away from his job in the liquor and tobacco store that he would never own, away from the memory of two sons killed in a war and another run off to who knows where. She wanted to go to America, where lipstick came in push-up metal tubes, where people sat in movie theatres, went roller-skating, visited amusement parks and rode to the sky in elevators. Where Szmul could make something of himself, rather than drink and smoke the stock he was supposed to sell. Where she didn't have to worry about the Soviets and the anti-Semites.

And what was Ewa's passport to this happiness?

A Kanzler 1B.

It was the most beautiful machine Lev had ever seen. If you could call it a machine. It was more like a work of art. A symbol of German craftsmanship at its finest. Apart from two suitcases of clothes, it was the only item Ewa brought with her from her previous marriage. Black, simple, elegant. The maker's name 'Kanzler' scrolled across the top in an elaborate gold script. Two shift keys. Eleven type bars. Eight characters to a bar. It was sturdy. It was fast.

1

It could type up to two hundred words a minute. Ewa proved it to him. She sat down in front of it, inserted a sheet of paper, wiggled her fingers like a concert pianist. One minute later, she showed him:

> *Dear Sir,*
> *Following on from our conversation of the 12th inst., I would like*
> *to order 2 doz. garments in the size and colours we discussed...*

He had no idea what the words meant but he pronounced them as if they were some kind of magic spell miraculously appeared on the page.

'English,' she said. 'And typing. The keys to my success.' She laughed at her own joke. 'A secretary in America.'

'I want to learn,' he said, surprising himself by this sudden ambition.

'Typing is not for a young man. If you want to use your hands, you must build bridges. Or skyscrapers.'

'I want to type.'

She had taken off her shoes to work at the Kanzler. Now she rubbed the sole of one foot with the toes of the other as she considered his request. The noise of the friction caused him to shiver.

'I will give you six lessons. One hour each. You can practise in between. In fact, practice is essential. You will wash your hands and clean your nails before you even look at the machine. I will check them first. And what will you do for me?'

'Whatever you want.'

She did as she promised. Six lessons. First, she explained the mechanics. The unique combination of lever action and swing that created the high speed between type and roller. The friction-feed of the paper. The QWERTZ lay-out of the keys that was very close to the English QWERTY formation except for a couple of letters here and there. She made him memorize the keys, how to work his fingers over separate blocks of letters. And she did all this in a small room during the course of a hot summer, sitting beside him in a thin, cotton dress, thigh against thigh, the warm skin of her bare forearm next to his, her soft fingers touching the backs of his hands, her breath against his cheek, her breasts against his shoulder as she adjusted the paper, the scent of lavender behind her ears and on the back of her neck. Between lessons, he scrubbed his hands into a cleanliness even closer than simply 'next to' godliness. He practised and practised with a nimbleness and frenzy of which even the great pianist Paderewski would have been proud.

On his seventh visit, she pulled out the test sheet from the roller, scrutinised the page.

'One hundred and three words,' she announced. 'Only two mistakes. You have done well.'

'Thank you. You have been a good teacher.'

'Now, come here.'

He approached the desk.

'Open your trousers.'

'What?'

'You heard me. Open your trousers.'

He was grateful for all the typing lessons, for his fingers, despite their trembling, managed to work open the buttons.

'Good,' she said in a matter-of-fact tone. He stared at the ceiling as she pulled quickly at his hardness. It was over in less than a hundred and three words. She gave him her soiled handkerchief.

'Burn it,' she said.

Perhaps Ewa Kaminsky was a whore, after all.

The next day, his father announced they were emigrating to America.

Lev loved Sarah. He had loved her for as long as he could remember. His brothers used to tell him that the first word he ever uttered was 'Sarah', not 'Mama'. Sarah, Sarah, Sarah. Lev loved Sarah. He would have carved that declaration on every tree in the forest if he hadn't been too frightened to go there. For that's where the Catholic farm-boys lived with their pigs, their hens and their cows. Jews weren't allowed to live with animals, although he wasn't sure if that was a prohibition by God or the State. He was always confused on those matters. Especially as his grandfather Gottleib had a dog. Bazyli, it was

3

called. His grandfather had owned several dogs, all of which he called Bazyli even though they were different breeds. To Lev, this series of Bazylis had merged into one grotesque mongrel in his memory.

Lev loved Sarah. Sarah was all grown-up now. Long limbs and small breasts. She went every month with her mother to the ritual bath to do whatever women do. She was exactly six months older than he was. A fact she never let him forget. Which meant he was always following after everything she did. Into children's school, into Hebrew classes, into the choir. He took up knitting, skipping, climbing trees and throwing stones at dogs because of her. And when Sarah decided to join the Zionist Youth, he did exactly the same. Although in his immaturity, he had no idea what the Zionist Youth was all about.

It didn't help he had no-one else to look up to. His mother was long dead from an unspecified women's complaint. His grandfather lived in the woods, his father was either selling or drinking liquor, or spending time with Ewa Kaminsky. His eldest brother, Amshel, whom he adored, had announced one Friday afternoon he was going down to the butcher to collect the meat and never came back. It was the first Sabbath meal Lev could ever remember without a dinner of cooked flesh. His two other brothers were always fighting. Either with Lev, or each other. Or with the Catholic farmboys in the woods. They ended up fighting for Poland in a war they thought would be good for the Jews. It wasn't good for the Jews. And it wasn't good for them, for they never came back.

He quite liked the Zionist Youth, or the Young Guard as they preferred to be called, although he wasn't sure what they were supposed to be guarding. They went on long walks and built fires and talked in Hebrew and sang songs in Hebrew and danced in circles around the fire. As he grew older and followed Sarah into more senior groups within this Young Guard, they learned about the *Yishuv* or 'settlement' in Palestine, they collected money to help people go there, they discussed Zionism and whether it might be better for the Jews to go and live in Uganda. It was all very abstract to him. Until Sarah said:

'I am going to Palestine.'

He looked up from whittling a stick, something he did a lot with the Zionist Youth. 'Why?'

'What do you mean? "Why?" What do you think we've been preparing for all these years?'

Lev hadn't thought he was preparing for anything. He had just wanted to hold hands with Sarah as they danced around the fire and went about collecting money to send other people to the *Yishuv*. It hadn't occurred to him she might actually want to go there herself.

'Will you come with me?' she asked.

He was about to say 'yes' to the idea of the two of them walking arm in arm through a land of date palms and donkeys, eating oranges freshly picked, chatting away in Hebrew about the house he was building in the Galilee where she would milk cows and ride horses and deal with all the other animals they were allowed to own. But then she added:

'There is a group of us going. Our very own *kvutza*. We're going to work on the land together, eat together, live together. All for the purpose of building a Jewish commune in our very own homeland.'

'You're going with a *kvutza*?'

'Nine of us. Will you come?

'I don't know.'

'Of course you will. You always follow me.'

And with that remark, she did something she had never done before. She kissed him full on the lips. Her mouth was so soft, so warm, so tingly, so imbued with everything that felt good in the world. He still felt the taste of her on his lips as he walked home to Ewa Kaminsky and that final typing test.

Lev's brother, Amshel, the one who ran away without picking up the meat for the Sabbath dinner, once told him that their father always looked as if he was carrying an imaginary piece of heavy furniture up a stairway.

'Look at him, Lev.' And here Amshel would hold up a circle of thumb and index finger in front of his young brother's eye to help him focus better on the figure plodding up the street. 'He looks like he's *schlepping* a piano.'

But as Lev stood now waiting for his father to speak, he knew it wasn't the weight of an imaginary piece of furniture that pulled the man down. But the burden of loss of a wife and two sons. Not to mention Amshel who had disappeared.

'Lev. Ewa... your stepmother... my... we... we just want you to know we would be very happy if you decide to come with us to America.'

'Yes,' Ewa said, taking his father's hand. 'We would be very happy. One big, happy family.'

'A new beginning for all of us,' his father continued. 'After all the tragedies we have suffered.'

'The tragedies were terrible,' Ewa confirmed.

'We realize it is a big change for you. But you are old enough to make your own decisions. How old are you?'

'Eighteen, father.'

'Yes, old enough to make your own way in life. You can continue to stay here and work in Mr Borkowski's store. He says he will be happy to promote you to do the selling instead of me. Or you might choose to go to Palestine with the Young Guard – that is up to you. We will understand.'

Sarah was the opposite of his father. She appeared to float in the air as others carried the weight of her life for her.

'It would be so good if you came with our *kvutza* to the *Yishuv*. An even number makes everything so much easier.' He waited for her to kiss him again. But she didn't. And Ewa Kaminsky wasn't repeating her open-your trousers routine either.

Two

LEV WENT TO THE FOREST. He used to go there with his father, his brothers or the Young Guard. But rarely alone. And never in such weather. The snow was falling heavily. He pulled down his cap, pushed his scarf up against his mouth. His feet, he couldn't feel them at all. He had wrapped his punctured boots in old cloths before he set out but the numbness had set in quick. He didn't think it would be this difficult. But each step sank deep into the white mush, sucking his strength. He would have turned back but he was closer to his destination than he was to his home. Why would someone live out here? With the silence, the Catholic farmers, the robbers and the wolves?

He reached the edge of the pine forest, leaned in close to the first row of trees for shelter, twigs breaking off against his upper arms, branches dragging across this back, dropping their icy load down his neck. He searched for the breach in the perimeter showing the trail. Something slithered and scampered through the frozen leaves inside the forest. A wild beast? A *dybbuk* waiting to pounce on his indecisive soul? He picked up a stout branch the length of his forearm, judged its heft in his palm. It would have to do.

He found the path easy enough and turned into the forest. The snow hardly made it in here but neither did the light. Or any sound. He stopped, held his breath, just to listen to the silence. 'Aye, yay, yay. Ewa, Ewa, Ewa,' he called out, listened to the words echo off the trees. He brushed off the snow from his coat, stamped his feet on the hard ground, blew into his gloves. 'Sarah, Sarah, Sarah. Aye, yay, yay.' He hummed loudly as he walked deeper into the forest, brandishing his club, hoping the noise would frighten off the bear and the boar.

Before Amshel disappeared from the family, Lev used to go hunting with him in this vast, dark interior that seemed to stretch on forever. Or at least Amshel would hunt while Lev was left to forage for telltale signs of their prey from the rubbed marks on the tree bark, from the corridors of broken branches or the imprints of hooves on the earth. Together they would build hide-outs from which to spy on the giant hogs that came to languish in the mud pools. Amshel wasn't like other older brothers. Lev could see that when he looked around at his peers, whose senior siblings teased them, bullied them or treated them like personal slaves. Amshel taught him things. How to make a catapult, where to find the wallowing pools, the berries and mushrooms to eat, the best plants to use against insect bites, the sounds of the different birds. He didn't teach him how to shoot though. Their father forbade it, and Amshel would support him by saying: 'There is enough killing in this world without you adding to it as well.' As they stomped these trails, their eyes, ears and Amshel's rifle primed for wild boar, Amshel would talk freely of the village girls he lusted after, the wealth he would accumulate from schemes involving the distillation of alcohol from various vegetables, the grand apartment he would purchase for the family on the Nowy Świat, Warsaw's finest street. And on these excursions into the forest, Lev, unarmed as he was, always felt safe in the presence of his older brother.

He saw the light first, from the flutter of flames reflecting in a window. Then the smell of woodsmoke. A cottage in the clearing, one stone wall where the fireplace stood, the other three made from logs caulked with tar or wood fibre. He looked around for a dog. There used to be a dog. *Bazyli? Bazyli? Where are you, you stupid mongrel?* He rapped the club against the heavy door. Snow fell from the roof. He knocked again. He heard a wooden bar scrape across, a crack of light, a gust of warmth. A woman's voice, harsh like the wind suddenly picked up through the forest. Zelda. He shivered.

'What do you want?'

'It's me. Lev.'

'I don't know Lev.'

'Lev Gottleib.'

'Who?'

'My grandfather. I've come to see my *zeide*.'

The door opened further. Zelda squinted at him. A small woman with a square head on top of a square body. Not someone you could knock over with a feather. She could wield an axe like a man, cleared half the trees to make this dwelling.

'I don't see too good.'

'It's Lev. Szmul's son. Will you let me in?'

'He's asleep.'

'I'll wait.'

Zelda scratched her scalp through hair as sparse as winter weeds. 'I don't know when he wakes.'

'Zelda. It's freezing out here.'

'All right, all right. Come in.'

The room was dim, warm and smoky, with the stink of rotten vegetables, drying wool. The roof leaked in a couple of places into rusted tins on the floor. One wall was shelved to the ceiling with books. Two stools. A table carved from a log. There was a kitchen area with a sink, a few pots and peelings, pelts strewn everywhere. He had heard it was Zelda who had skinned them, laying traps for the wolves, slitting their throats when caught. The townsfolk said she'd even killed a bear, slipped underneath its paws while it stood on its hindlegs, ripped open its stomach, then sliced off its testicles. A delicacy where she came from. Although where that was, nobody knew. She had been his grandfather's housekeeper for as long as he could remember. He had never known his grandmother, who had died giving birth to his youngest uncle. There was only one bed in this cottage, so Lev had to make up his own mind where Zelda slept. The same friends, uncles, aunts and cousins who called Ewa Kaminsky a whore used to say the same about Zelda. But not to his grandfather's face.

'Who is dead?' she asked.

'No-one is dead. I just want to talk to him.'

'He sleeps.'

'When will he wake?'

She shrugged.

'I can wait. I brought him some tobacco from the store.'

She snatched the package from him, sniffed it hard along an edge, then waddled over to the kitchen area, searched out a bowl. From a pot by the hearth, she ladled out some liquid, handed it to him.

'It could be a long time. Sit.' She pointed to a stool by the fireside. He did as he was told. Zelda went over to a pile of skins, laid down and closed her eyes. He watched her as he drank the soup – beans, herbs, bits of bark. More like a potion than a broth. He listened to Zelda's snoring, the spit of the fire, the droplets of water falling into the tins, until he slipped off his stool onto one of the pelts, into his own deep sleep.

The rough shaking woke him. And the rancid hiss by his ear. 'Son of Szmul. Come, come. He is ready.'

'What time is it?'

'What do I know about time? He is awake.'

Lev pushed himself to his feet. His forehead ached. 'Water.'

Zelda nodded to a barrel in the corner. He dipped in a tin cup and drank. It tasted of the forest. A window above his head showed a half-moon high in the sky. He had slept for hours.

'Come, come,' Zelda beckoned. She opened the door to the only other room.

His grandfather was sat up in his bed, wrapped in a prayer shawl, a tattered, black silk *yarmulke* on his head. His beard hung grey and dirty like a hank of raw wool. It had been a while since Lev had last seen him, but he looked the same. Perhaps the old were always just old in the eyes of the young.

'Which son of Szmul are you? Is that you, Amshel?'

Lev looked for a stool. But there was none. Instead, he had to crouch in a half-kneel before the bed. 'There is only one son now, *zeide*. You know that. I am Lev. The youngest.'

'Come closer.'

Lev did as he was told.

'Let me feel you.'

His grandfather's fingers lightly tapped the skin of his face. The touch was dry like parchment.

'Ah yes, now I remember. You are the good son.'

'The good son?'

'Amshel, he was selfish. The other two, what were their names?'

'Hershel and Baruch.'

'Yes, Hershel and Baruch. They only had time for each other. But you, you also look out for others. The name shapes the man, Lev. Your name in Hebrew, it means "heart". But in Yiddish, Lev also means "lion". Do you have the heart of a lion, Lev?'

'I don't think so, *zeide*.'

'You are still young. You have time to find one. Why are you here?'

'My father… Szmul… your son… he is leaving the town.'

'To Warsaw?'

'To America.'

His grandfather sighed, a whispery, papery breath. 'Ah, America.' Then the anger rose, as Lev knew it would. 'With that *kurve* he now calls a wife? Not your mother, mind you. Your mother was a good woman. An angel. Not a whore like this one. With her lipstick and fancy ways. When did he decide this?'

'A few months ago. He is leaving after winter.'

'He sent you to tell me this? After a few months.'

Lev waited for his grandfather to calm. 'He didn't send me.'

'He is leaving without telling me? It is that *kurve*. How she drives a wedge between father and son. So if not to tell me, why have you come?'

'I came to ask your advice.'

'You are going with him?'

'That is what I want to ask. The Zionists want me to go to Palestine. A small group of pioneers. Ten of us.'

'Ah, the Zionists. They think now the British are in control, their dream will come true.'

'They will arrange the papers. Provide some funds. We are going to start a commune. Build an agriculture settlement in a Jewish homeland.'

'They will want you to build roads for Jewish capitalists. When you could walk on streets made of gold?'

11

'What do you say, *zeide*? I should go to America?'

His grandfather started coughing. An awful sound. Zelda was quickly by his side with a cup of water. He sipped from it then waved her away. 'Listen, Lev. To go to America is simple. It is a fresh start. You make no sacrifices. You go, you get work, you make money, you buy a house, you get married, you have children, you die. To go to Palestine. It is not a fresh beginning. It is like grafting new branches onto old vines. It is complicated. The people. The history. The land.'

'I still don't understand. Where shall I go?'

'It is not for me to tell you. You must make up your own mind. Or listen to your heart. But I think it is best you go somewhere. For here they hate us.'

He left his grandfather coughing into the fringes of his prayer shawl. Zelda caught up with him just outside the door.

'He will be dead before winter is out,' she whispered.

'What?'

'I saw it before. This wasting disease of the lungs. One month. Two at the most.'

He rubbed his eyes. So much death in his family. 'I should go back in to see him.'

'No, no. It is just good you came. That is enough. He is very fond of you.' She grabbed his arm. 'What will you do?

'I am following my heart. I will go to Palestine.'

Zelda fished something out of her apron pocket. 'Can you take this?'

A rag. Something wrapped inside. A tiny stone? A jewel? 'What is it?'

She looked at him coyly. 'My tooth.'

'A tooth?'

'From when I was a child. I want you to bury it in the Holy Land.'

Three

LEV WAS THE YOUNGEST of the group. The others treated him like a little brother, their mascot or ignored him completely. They called themselves the Ten Tribes. *Esera Shebatim*. Sarah's idea. The ten lost tribes now found. Six young men and four young women. They might have been found but Lev still felt lost.

The Land of Israel-Palestine Office helped with financial support and the arrangements: the immigration papers and visas from the British, the permission from the police, the train ticket from Warsaw to Trieste, the border permits, the boat ticket to Alexandria and on to Jaffa. Ewa helped him pack his trunk. A suit, work clothes, short underwear, a pillow, dried bread, smoked fish, the handkerchief he never burned. His father gave him several pouches of tobacco: 'For bribes.' A bottle of *schnapps*: 'It gets cold on the train.' A bundle of Polish marks, mixed in with some Russian roubles and Italian lira: 'The lira are from Ewa. You will need to rent a room while you wait for the boat.' His father might have been a sad man, but he was practical too.

They came with him to Warsaw station. All the parents and families and friends did. It was quite a crowd, waving flags and singing *Hatikva*. Ewa kissed both his cheeks and he remembered her smell of lavender. His father shook his hand. Lev followed Sarah onto the train. Along with the other Nine Tribes, he leaned out of the window as the train pulled away. Ewa was waving and blowing kisses. His father looked as if he was holding one end of a large wardrobe. Lev never expected to see either of them again.

The Ten Tribes squashed into a compartment for six. Lev sat on the floor. He would have liked to sit by the window. He'd never been on such a large train before. Never been beyond Warsaw. Now he would travel through the land of his birth without seeing anything of the south. The Tatra Mountains, Lake Solina, the salt mines of Wieliczka. And then he thought – what did it matter? He didn't owe this country a backward glance. In a reflection of his thoughts, a voice shouted out:

'We need new names now.' It was Koppel. The oldest. The son of the ritual slaughterer. He handed out pieces of pickled brisket as he spoke. 'Hebrew names. Not the downtrodden Yiddish of the Polish diaspora. The names of kings and prophets and heroes. From now on, I shall be known as Ariel. The Lion of God.' He roared and everyone laughed.

'And I shall be Shaul,' said Shimmel. 'Shaul Hagadol. Shaul the Great.'

'The great what?' asked Yankel, now to be known as Noam.

'The great boaster,' replied Boaz, the former Zalman.

'I am Doron,' said Hirschel.

'Ahuva,' said Sheina.

'Dalia,' said Libke.

'Ayala,' said Rivke.

'I am not changing mine,' said Sarah.

'What makes you so special?' Rivke asked.

'Sarah is not a name for the downtrodden,' said Sarah somewhat smugly. 'She was Abraham's wife. She was the matriarch.'

'What about you, Lev?' Ariel asked.

'Lev already is a Hebrew name,' he answered. 'Lev means "heart".'

'But Lev Gottleib? You cannot be the heart of Gottleib. Heart of what?'

'I don't know.'

'Heart of a goat,' Shaul the Great suggested.

'Heart of a pig,' said Noam, more cruelly.

'Heart of a sheep,' said Boaz. 'Always following us around. Why are you here anyway? You only ever sat around whittling away at pieces of wood at the Young Guard. Where is your commitment? Your ideals? Your passion for the land?'

14

Lev felt he needed to whittle away at a piece of wood right now. Then he would take it and stab it into Boaz's eye. But Doron, once known as Hirschel, intervened. 'Don't be so self-righteous, Boaz,' he said. 'We're not just travelling towards a new future. Some of us are running away from the past as well.'

An impressed hush fell on these words of wisdom. Lev thought Doron should be a rabbi in their new land, not some fruit-picker or swamp-drainer. Ahuva was the first to speak, a young woman whose beautiful voice was unfortunately not matched by the features of her face. 'What are you running from, Doron?' she asked.

'From the anti-Semites.'

'From a violent father,' added Shaul.

'From oppression,' said Ariel.

'From an arranged marriage,' said Dalia.

'From poverty,' said Boaz.

'From abandonment,' said Lev.

The train stopped just before the border with Czechoslovakia. It was the darkest point of the night, but a full moon lit up the station. Two soldiers with rifles across their backs, white eagles painted on their helmets ordered them to get out, to take all their luggage with them. The platform was covered with patches of ice. A brazier burned near the station master's office. A sign said: *Zebrzydowice*. From a carriage further up the platform, several religious Jews wearing long, black coats and fur hats descended, began to pray inside a halo of moonlit engine steam.

Along with the other Nine Tribes, Lev was asked for his papers and the tag that matched up to his trunk. The soldiers wandered in and out of the group, pressing against the girls, kicking the cases, running their hands along jacket linings in search of coins, pushing their faces up too close when they spoke. One of them took off his helmet, scratched a shorn head covered in scabs.

'The train for Vienna leaves in four minutes,' the soldier said, replacing his helmet.

Lev nodded along with everyone else.

'It is a cold night in Zebrzydowice,' the other soldier noted. He had a piggish face made all the more squashed by the tight helmet strap. 'A very cold night in Zebrzydowice.'

'All our papers are in order,' Ariel insisted, although the leonine roar had gone from his voice.

'Perhaps,' the one with the scabs said. The religious Jews further up the platform bowed back and forth to the rhythm of their mumbled prayers. 'Or perhaps not. The train leaves in three minutes.' A spurt of steam escaping from behind the wheels appeared to confirm this fact. The soldier looked behind him, shouted at the praying Jews: 'Shut up! Or I will shoot.' Silence. 'Two minutes.'

Lev stood quietly with the rest of them, wondering if a blow would be struck. Or if one of the girls would be taken behind the station master's office. Or if a shot would be fired. In the midst of all his anxiety, he found that he had stepped forward. And in a voice sounding remarkably like his own, calm despite the tremors spreading out from his stomach, he said: 'It is a cold night in Zebrzydowice.' The others stared at him. Lev produced his father's bottle of *schnapps* from his inside coat pocket. 'This might keep you warm.'

The soldier with the scabs snatched at the bottle, inspected the label. 'What about my friend?'

'For your friend, I have this.' Lev handed over two tobacco pouches.

The soldiers passed it between themselves, sniffed the contents. 'And for my sick mother in Katowice?'

'I have these.' He gave them the roubles.

A whistle sounded.

'Get on,' the pig-faced one ordered. 'Quick, quick.'

Lev didn't think he was a hero. It had to be some other Lev who had stepped forward, bribed the guards. Where had that courage come from? Was it really courage? Perhaps it was just recklessness? An overwhelming desire to impress? A talent for negotiation? Or perhaps he really did have the heart of a lion?

Back on the train, they had lost their compartment to a group of Czech farmers with a stack of shotguns, a giant food hamper and an Alsatian dog. They now had to stand all the way to Vienna in a freezing corridor. But Lev didn't care. He was in Czechoslovakia now. He

16

had the back-slapping and cheek-kissing to keep him warm.

'You did well, Lev.' Boaz pushed in beside him. 'And you saved me handing over this.' He brought out his own bottle of *schnapps*. 'A toast. To a cold night in Zebrzydowice.' Boaz took a sip, handed it over.

Lev drank deeply. The sweet, burning taste hitting the back of his throat, the liquid warming his stomach. 'Aaachh,' he said, imitating that voice of manly satisfaction he had heard so often outside Mr Borkowski's liquor and tobacco store. 'Yes, a cold night in Zebrzydowice,' he gasped.

'A cold night in Zebrzydowice,' mimicked Noam.

'A cold night in Zebrzydowice,' shouted Shaul the Great.

And that was the battle cry of the night as the *schnapps* was passed around and they ate the last of the brisket and they sang the songs of the Young Guard. Sarah squeezed along to stand next to him. 'It's not easy being the youngest,' she said.

The train jolted their bodies together. His head was dizzy from the brandy. It was no longer a cold night in Zebrzydowice.

By the time they reached Vienna, Lev felt he was part of the *kvutza*, one of the Ten Tribes. After all, he had stood with them for hours on the train, slept against them, shared food, tobacco and *schnapps* with them, made communal plans and eternal promises, kept guard while they urinated between carriages. In Vienna, they were met by Noam's uncle, a fat little banker with a wet moustache who took them to a coffee house. Lev had never sat on velvet before, drunk coffee from a glass, eaten rich pastries made from ingredients he never knew existed. What was that flavour? Vanilla. And that? Apricot marmalade. Noam's uncle declared them all mad. 'What is this craziness about communal settlements? You won't last a month, a year at most.' He stretched his arms behind two of the girls so that the buttons of his waistcoat strained to bursting point. 'Now, do you know what I would do with my time and money in Palestine? Invest in cement. They are talking about building a port in Haifa. What will they need? Cement. A power station in the Galilee. What will they need? Cement. So, nephew, if you hear about any opportunities involving cement, telegram me. With just one word. Cement. And I will come running.' It was hard for Lev to see Noam's uncle running anywhere. But he was a generous man. He took them to a market, bought them bread, cheeses, tins of Portuguese sardines and cured meats for those who didn't keep *kosher*. He took them back to the train station, paid off a guard so they would have a compartment all the way to Trieste, waved them off with one last word. Cement.

In Trieste, they rented two rooms in a boarding house near the port. No-one wanted to go out for fear of being attacked or robbed. They played cards into the night. Ariel woke them early the next morning. They walked ten abreast, arm-in-arm, to the harbour in an early morning fog. Lev had never seen a ship before. It was called *Dalmatia*. It left three hours later.

Tragedy struck at sea. Not as in the sinking of the Titanic or the Lusitania. But a personal tragedy. Lev didn't see it coming. After all, up until then, it had been the ten of them all together. The Ten Found Tribes. A *kvutza*. Bound together by shared dreams and common urination.

There were no cabins in immigrant class. Just rows of benches lined up below deck. Lev picked one out, stashed his trunk underneath, laid down on the thin, stained mattress. Boaz's feet were at his head, Doron's head was at his feet. Within two hours of setting off, everyone was on the top deck, throwing up over the side. Everyone except Lev. The tossing of the ship, the smell of engine oil mixed in with vomit, the dip and rise of the horizon, none of it affected him at all. As others retched and staggered back to their benches, only to get up, stagger and retch again, Lev wolfed down sardines spread across hunks of bread. As others moaned about having thrown up every inch of their stomach lining along with their liver and intestines, Lev savoured the taste of *vursht* accompanied by a raw onion and pickled cucumber. As he enjoyed the strong, tangy flavour of a hard Tyrolean mountain cheese as recommended by Noam's uncle, he pondered upon why he might be immune to this swaying motion. And he concluded that such had been the inner turmoil of his life up to that point, any external rocking motion was unlikely to have an effect.

But when the ship entered calmer waters, the situation changed. Where there had been the Ten Tribes, now there were Eight and Two. Lev was part of the eight. The other two consisted of Sarah and Shaul the Great. He observed their pointless promenading together for hours around the upper decks. He watched as they stood by the railings, staring out to the Mediterranean, wasting their precious supplies of dried bread on the following seagulls. He spotted them laughing and chattering away together under the lifeboats when they could have been part of the Zionist discussion groups. He cringed at Shaul's insincere smile when he saw him buying Sarah a trinket from a rowing-boat trader in Brindisi harbour. It was now his turn to lie moaning on a bench on the lower decks, feeling as if his whole insides had been gutted. He was too ill to surface. He didn't see the dolphins running off the prow. He missed the full moon party when the Jews danced the *hora* to the music of a Romanian *klezmer* band. He didn't smell the aroma of the bitter-sweet olive groves of Kalamata. He would never know the dazzling white villages of the Aegean coast-line. Or the cosmopolitan crowd gathering at Alexandria harbour, where Europe met Africa met Asia. But these exotic attractions no longer mattered. Sarah was his life. The reason he did everything. He waited until she was alone.

'Have you been sick?' she asked. She plucked a thread from her cardigan. She had knitted it herself. He had helped her unravel the wool. He moved her towards the railings so the breeze could whip away the stink from the piles of excrement and rubbish scattered around the deck.

'Yes, I have been sick. Ill from seeing you together with Shaul.'

Her cheeks reddened, making her even more beautiful. 'I like him.'

'You never liked him back in Poland when he was Shimmel Feldman, the moneylender's son. With a high-pitched voice and a head full of lice. How we used to laugh about him.'

Sarah laughed now. 'He's changed. He's grown into a man with grand ideas.'

'I have grand ideas too.'

'What ideas do you have?'

'I want to marry you. And we can build a house in the Galilee where you can rear chickens and ride horses. And I will... I will...'

'Yes, Lev. What will you do? You don't know, do you? Because you've never given yourself a chance. You've just copied everything I've done.'

'But I love you.'

'I'm sure you do. And I love you too, in my own way. We've grown up together. We've shared so much. But you are like a little brother to me. Not a prospective husband.'

'And Shimmel, the lice-ridden moneylender's son, is?'

'You know he doesn't have lice any more.'

He knew that. He was aware of Shaul's glossy, black curls and the deep voice that sang the bass parts in all their songs. 'I can't live without you,' he whined.

'But you're not going to live without me. We're all going to be together in one happy *kvutza*.'

Two days later, the ship dropped anchor off the port of Jaffa. Lev could see palm trees and minarets, camels strutting across the beach, fishing boats, clusters of two-storey houses with their domes and their verandas rising up the hillside from the port. People all over the ship were praying and singing and wailing and dancing. How happy they were, this ragged, stinking bunch of immigrants. He wished he had gone to America.

His *kvutza* assembled. The eight tribes and the two lovers. He handed his trunk down to one of the Arab porters who had pulled alongside in the longboat that took them to the shore. A British official examined his papers, a doctor questioned him.

'Mentally ill?'

'No.'

'Infectious diseases?

'No.

'Criminal?'

'No.'

Broken heart? Yes.

He went off to the bath-house with the other males, put his luggage into quarantine, held up his hands while he was searched for

20

weapons, then stripped off his clothes. In the shower room, everyone sang Hebrew songs as they washed away with carbolic the filth of the voyage and the dirt of the diaspora. Lev found himself standing next to Shaul.

'Look at us, Lev,' Shaul shouted as he scrubbed away. 'We have arrived. A new land. A new life. Look at us.' Lev did look. And now he understood why Shaul was called Shaul the Great.

Outside the bath-house, he was given a clean set of clothes courtesy of a London-based Jewish charity and waited for the group to assemble. Ariel, Shaul, Noam, Boaz, Doron joined from the women's washrooms by Ahuva, Dalia, Ayala and Sarah. Shining, smiling faces, all except Lev's. The Nine Found Tribes and One Lost Soul. Bound to spend a life together. They walked out of the shade of the port buildings towards the wire fence.

At first, Lev couldn't see. The light so bright it stung his eyes. And the noise. People shouting in Polish, Yiddish, Hebrew and other languages he didn't recognize. 'Post?' was the predominant cry. Post from Vilna? From Warsaw? From Kalisz? From Odessa? Faces clamouring at the wire. Holding up signs: *Bluma Fischel from Gorzkowice. It's Max.* British soldiers beating them back with sticks, Arab police with camel-whips. *Room to let. Fresh water tap. Four can share.*

'Over here, Lev,' Ariel said, pointing to someone bearing a placard: *Palestine Welcomes the Young Guard from Poland.*

But Lev's attention was somewhere else. Another sign. In Hebrew and English. It read: *Palestine Jewish Colonization Association. Can you type?*

Four

Palestine, 1924

'I WAS LOOKING FOR a really attractive girl,' Mickey Vered would explain to anyone who asked, usually a couple of young women at the fashionable Casino coffee house in Tel Aviv. 'A knock-out. From Kiev. Because the girls from Kiev are the most beautiful in the world. Just like you. You are from Kiev, aren't you? No? Really? Hard to believe. Well, anyway. Walk down a street in Kiev, and you will fall in love a hundred times. And instead… what did I end up with?' And here Mickey would point to Lev. 'I was strolling down a Haifa street looking for my Kiev girl, when I stopped this stranger here to ask for a cigarette. Five years we are together now. A married couple couldn't be happier. Who would've thought a Polish immigrant possessed a pouch of such fine tobacco? Eh, Lev?'

Lev would smile shyly, stare down at his glass of lemon tea. He had heard the story many times before. The part about Mickey asking for tobacco was true, for he never bought his own, not because he couldn't afford it but because he didn't want to admit he was a smoker, that there was an element of his life he could not control. But Lev also knew that Mickey had never walked down a Kiev street in his life. For Mickey was Michael Rosenblatt. From Manchester, England. Mickey had lied about his age to join the British Army which had then shipped him to Palestine to fight the Turks. Mickey told Lev he had drunk mint tea in the desert with T.E. Lawrence, that he had helped Allenby liberate Jerusalem. 'Look, that's me there. Right beside the

General's horse at Jaffa Gate. With my hand on the pommel. I know you can't see my face, but those are my fingers, Lev. Those are my fucking fingers.' Mickey liked to swear. Mickey liked Palestine. He liked the opportunities it afforded him. He liked the sun. He liked the light. He liked the girls from Kiev.

Mickey eventually confessed to the Army he had signed up as a minor, making his enlistment null and void. So they had to let him go. Mickey Rosenblatt became Mickey Vered, 'vered' meaning 'rose', he thought he'd forget about the 'nblatt' part. And here Mickey stayed. In a spacious house in the Jewish area of Haifa known as Hadar Hacarmel. Or 'Glory of the Carmel' in Mickey's English, Carmel being the mountain around which the town was built. After their fortuitous meeting in the street, Lev moved out of his hostel dormitory and into a rented room in the same house. The property was owned by a Madame Blum, a widow with no children. Husbandless, childless Madame Blum was the opposite of Mickey. She hated Palestine.

'I curse the day my husband ever brought me here,' she told Lev at least once a day. Herr Blum, a dealer in raw cotton, was killed when he was run over by the Haifa to Damascus train. No-one knew how the accident happened. Whether he was drunk, his foot got caught in the track, or even if he were pushed. It was a strange demise. Especially as the train didn't run that often. Madame Blum was left to hate the dust and the sun and the heat and the noise and the sweet coffee and the pitta bread and the olives and the *halva* and the dates and the almonds and the British and the Jews and the French and the Arabs and the bad manners and the lack of efficiency and the bad time-keeping and the young harlot who steals your husband when your back is turned. Mickey had a remarkable patience for Madame Blum. He would listen to her constant complaints with interest, he would light her Russian cigarettes, make her tea, massage her shoulders.

'She is a childless widow. I am like a son to her,' Mickey explained to Lev.

'Even so. Your compassion surprises me.'

'This is a nice house. Bright, well-proportioned rooms. A European-style toilet. Conveniently close to the harbour. Close to my office.'

Lev was never sure what exactly Mickey did for a living. Mickey told him he traded in this and that, wheeled and dealed, imported and exported, called himself an entrepreneur. Sometimes there would be an excess of grapefruit on the table at Madame Blum's, or almonds, or bananas or grapes. In the kitchen, there might be crates of wine, boxes of stockings, buckets full of artificial teeth. Outside in the small garden, ploughshares, an electricity generator, bales of cotton.

Although they generally spoke Hebrew together, Lev began to learn a little English from Mickey, who, in turn, practised his Yiddish. To Lev's surprise, it seemed the Jews of Manchester spoke that hybrid of higher German and Hebrew quite fluently.

'*Vas ist de vetter heinte?*' Mickey would ask him over breakfast each day.

To which Lev's reply was always: 'The weather is bloody hot. But I believe it is raining in fucking Manchester.'

It was on Mickey's hectoring that Lev finally changed his own name. Or, at least, his surname. 'Everyone must have a new name in Palestine,' Mickey declared. 'Look at me. Look at Abraham, our forefather.'

'What about Abraham?'

'God changed his name from Abram to Abraham. From "great father" to "father of all nations". Father of Arab and Jew alike.'

And so Lev changed his name. A new name for a new Lev. No more Lev Gottleib. But Lev Sela. Lev meaning 'heart'. Sela meaning 'stone'.

The offices of the Palestine Jewish Colonization Association in Haifa faced the sea, with a view of the harbour that was always being built to turn it into a proper deep-water port. The construction work was a constant reminder to Lev that he should have taken that early advice from Noam's uncle back in Vienna and invested in cement. Not that he ever had much money to invest. But the breeze into his office was fresh and free. And he earned enough money to live on.

The Palestine Jewish Colonization Association was commonly abbreviated to PICA. 'Because it was always PICA-ing up land here and there,' according to one of Mickey's English puns Lev could never understand. PICA bought land that it would long-lease to Jewish individuals or collective settlements. It also invested in factories, mills and wineries. The organization was funded by a wealthy benefactor who preferred to remain anonymous to the point it was forbidden to say his name either in public or in private. This person was known simply as the 'Anonymous Donor'. But everyone knew he was a famous banker, an elderly French aristocrat, one of the richest men in the world.

While this Anonymous Donor provided funds in support of PICA's offices in Palestine, Lev knew the real talent behind the Association's acquisitions and investments, especially when it came to land, lay with his employer and only other staff member at the Haifa office. The man who had once held up the placard advertising for a typist at the Jaffa docks. Samuel Ziv. Otherwise known affectionately as Sammy the King.

Sammy the King was in his mid-fifties but had all the energy, both physical and mental, of a man thirty years younger. Sammy came from somewhere in Russia, he would never admit to exactly where. He could speak Yiddish, Hebrew, Arabic, English and French as well as Russian. But it wasn't of languages that Sammy was the king. It was of the soil.

Sammy knew everything about alluvial deposits, levels of acidity, what was good for cereal crops, for vegetables or for tropical fruits. Just by smelling a handful of earth he could tell whether it came from the Upper Galilee, the Valley of Jezreel or the Maritime Plain. A taste licked from a wetted finger would inform him whether it lacked potassium, nitrogen or phosphorous. When he unfurled a map across his desk, he didn't see uncultivated land. He saw its earthly potential. He imagined ploughed fields, orchards and plantations. He saw oranges, grapefruits, dates, almonds, melons and bananas. He heard the hiss of the barley tickled by the breezes from the north, the crack and crinkle of the tobacco leaves drying in the desert *hamseen*. His mind's eye squinted to the yellow of the sesame fields. Sammy the King was PICA's man on the ground in more ways than one.

In the five years Lev had worked for PICA, he had come to love Sammy. He didn't think of him as a king, more as a prophet, a wise man like his grandfather in the woods, a kinder, happier, more sober version of his own father, a protector like his long-lost brother Amshel. He admired Sammy's great understanding of how a person could be attached to the land. 'Land is land is land' was Sammy's answer to everything. For Sammy appreciated what it was like to work the soil, to catch the earth under fingernails, to have it ingrained into the skin, to smell the mulch in the turn of the hoe. He saw how men and women cultivated the soil to survive, how they returned to the same place year after year to feed their flocks, how they saw beauty where others saw only limestone and dust. All this made Sammy a tough but fair negotiator, a man with compassion for those who lived on the land, a man who possessed an even temperament, which was a valued commodity in this hot-tempered country where attachments to land were so complex.

But Lev learned there was always one subject that could be relied upon to upset Sammy's equanimity. And that was the mention of the organization which, like the Anonymous Donor, should never be named in his presence. The KKL. The *Keren Kayemeth LeIsrael*. The Jewish National Fund. Or as Sammy the King called them: Those Bloody Zionists.

According to Sammy, Those Bloody Zionists had a more zealous approach to land acquisition than PICA. Once the target area had been identified, Those Bloody Zionists would go all out to purchase the land, then worry later about the funding, the infrastructure, the resettlement of the tenant farmers – the *fellaheen* – already living there. PICA, on the other hand, operated in the image of its founder and backer, the Anonymous Donor. PICA was more French. It was more bureaucratic. It was more cautious. It wanted the proper financing to be in place, budgets to be drawn up, compensation agreements worked out. All of which gave Sammy more time to deal sympathetically with those whose lives might be affected by PICA's acquisitions. To many, Sammy might have been a king, but Lev also knew that to his detractors, he was seen, as with the haemorrhoids he so often complained of, as a pain in the bloody *toches*.

Five

ON HIS FIRST DAY AT WORK, Lev had been presented with an Adler 15, also a German machine but not as elegant as the Kanzler 1B of his Polish youth. Like the Kanzler, it had four rows of keys, but with a single rather than a double shift. He had sat down in front of it, rested his chin on clasped hands, quietly thanked Ewa Kaminsky. He wondered how life was treating her in America. Whether she had found her lipstick in the push-up tubes. Whether she had taken his father to visit an amusement park. Or whether it was possible for his father ever to be amused by anything. He had then fluttered his fingers over the casing, felt the pads tingle in anticipation of their contact with the keys, breathed in the ink on the fresh ribbon, lined up the PICA-headed paper and began.

His job had been to type up letters written in Sammy's scrawl. These letters could be in English, German or French. Since Lev couldn't fully understand any of them, it made no difference. There were letters to benefactors and agencies all over the world. There was an ongoing correspondence with the British administration in Jerusalem. Then there were negotiations with Arab landowners in Damascus and Cairo. Letters came in and letters came out. Their subject matter? Always land. The ten thousand square miles that constituted Palestine, of which PICA owned or had concessions to about 240 of them. There would be issues about maps and surveys and certificates and the title deeds known as *kushan*. The Turks had their version of the legal ownership of Palestine, the British had theirs, the Zionists and the Arabs had theirs. Sammy the King had his.

'There are only five words you need to know,' Sammy once told Lev, as he counted them off on his fingers. '*Mulk, Miri, Waqf, Metruke* and *Mewat*. They are like the Arabic version of the Five Books of Moses. These are the real laws of this land.'

Sammy stood up from behind his desk, lit a cheroot. And as he paced, so the lesson began.

Mulk. The absolute ownership by a private individual of non-agricultural property. 'Just as I have bought a house here in Haifa,' Sammy explained.

Miri. Agricultural land owned by the State but granted in perpetuity to an individual for cultivation. 'But stop farming for three years,' Sammy warned with a wag of his finger, 'and the land goes back to the State.'

Waqf. Land that has been handed over to an institution for charitable or religious purposes. 'For example, to build a mosque.'

Mertuke. Common land owned by a village. 'For example, for roads or pasture.' Sammy sat back down. 'There you are.'

'You said there were five words. What about *Mewat*?'

'Yes, *Mewat*.'

'You didn't tell me what *Mewat* is.'

'*Mewat* is complicated. I don't know if your pebble of a Polish brain can grasp such legalistic concepts.'

'Sammy, just tell me.'

'Why does a typist need to know such things?'

'You know I want to learn.'

'You won't believe me.'

'Please, Sammy. What is *Mewat*?'

'All right, all right.' Sammy's eyes creased at the prospect. 'Imagine. You and I, we visit an Arab village. Let's say somewhere between here and Tel Aviv. I stay in the village but you start walking away from it. Into the desert. Across the plains. Along the sand dunes. It doesn't matter. And you start shouting as you walk away.'

'What am I shouting?'

'What do I care? As long as you are saying something. And you keep on shouting and you keep on walking and you keep on shouting until the moment I can't hear you.'

'How will I know you can't hear me?'

'I'll make a signal. Wave my hands.'

'Then what?'

'You look around.'

'And?'

'Whatever land you see that's not already *Mulk*, *Miri*, *Waqf* or *Mertuke*, that's *Mewat*. For *Mewat* is dead land.'

'Dead land?'

'Yes. Waste land. Swamps. Desert. Unused. Uncultivated. Unpastured.'

'What's so special about that?'

'It means you can start to cultivate this land without permission. And if you do, you acquire rights to that land. You might have to compensate the owner, almost always the government, for the value of the original uncultivated piece of wasteland. But the land becomes yours.'

'Is that a problem?'

'It is to the British. They can't stand the idea of someone acquiring land this way. Just by cultivating it. They are trying to change the law. They don't think *Mewat* is very British. Instead, they think it's barbaric. This idea you can own something by improving it. They think it's uncivilized. Uncivilized? Were the Romans uncivilized, Lev?'

'I don't think so.'

'Of course they weren't. The Romans were one of the most sophisticated cultures on earth. And do you know what they believed?'

'They worshipped lots of gods.'

'I'm not talking about gods. I'm talking about art.'

'You are?'

'Yes. The Romans believed that art was more important than property. In Roman times, if an artist came along and saw a blank wall and he painted a mural on that wall, then the rights to the wall vested in the artist. That was Roman law. *Lex Romanus*. Do you know why, Lev? Because the painting was more important than mere bricks and mortar. Art was more important than property. And it is the same with *Mewat*. Cultivating the land is the essential thing. Bringing the soil to life, planting seeds, growing crops, trees, cereals. That's what matters. Not the ownership of some barren wasteland. And the British cannot see that. They want to change the law. They are so uncivilized.'

Apart from learning these laws of the land, Lev also discovered he had a talent for languages. Like the southern desert plains soaking up the seasonal rains, he realized he could absorb the various grammars and vocabularies that fell all around him without too much effort. On top of his native Polish, his understanding of Yiddish, the English he picked up from Mickey, he also learned Arabic from Sammy while improving his Hebrew until he became fluent. Sammy recognized Lev's talent as well. Not only with languages. Sammy taught him about proof of title, certificates of registration, how to reconcile the various land surveys, dealing with the landowners, mediating in disputes. Lev even thought of becoming a lawyer.

'A bloody lawyer,' he said out loud in English as he stretched out his legs so his heels rested on the sill of the open window. 'I could be a bloody lawyer. Isn't that right, Sarah? You didn't realize that, did you? Before you ran off with that lice-ridden Shaul. That I had a brain. That I could be a bloody lawyer.'

He loved this view of the sea, the town and the harbour. How did a Polish boy from the *shtetl* end up here? With a Mediterranean sun warming the soles of his feet, the wind blowing in warm and dry from a blue, blue sea, the aroma of coffee and cardamom from the Arab coffee shop below, the bleached white buildings crowding the bay. He picked up his binoculars as supplied to him from one of Mickey's many ex-British Army stock deals, looked out over the harbour at the almost permanent line of emigrants waiting to be rowed out to the next west-bound ship. As he focused on each bedraggled and beaten-down figure, he wondered if one day, it would be Sarah's face he saw.

For Lev knew he had been one of the lucky ones. Life had been tough for the other pioneers. During his first few years here, there had been more Jews leaving than arriving. He had seen that from his own work, from the land purchased for groups of settlers who discovered they were unable to survive on idealism and hard work alone. There was the unforgiving nature of the land. The heat. The failed crops. The successful crops that couldn't be harvested for a lack of hands in the field. And then there was the malaria from the undrained swamps. Half the workforce could be out at any given time with the disease. Not to mention trachoma, dysentery and just sheer fatigue.

Sarah's Nine Tribes would probably have started out on a road gang, helping to build the country's infrastructure while strengthening the solidarity of their group through the sheer hardship of their labour. They would have lived in tents by the side of the road, survived off a diet of bread and soup, quinine tablets and sweet tea, spent the day hammering rocks into gravel. When one section was finished, they would strike camp and move off to another part of the country. Once they had proved themselves as a *kvutza*, they might start to look around for a piece of land to start building their own settlement. Lev would have noticed the Nine Tribes in any proposal for any land that PICA owned. And he knew enough of Those Bloody Zionists too to have them check their records if he had wanted to. Yet he never did.

But recently, the number of Jews leaving had been on the decrease. There was more work around, especially in Haifa with its train station, its port that was always being built, the talk of bringing oil here all the way from Iraq. A university for science and technology had just opened its gates. Buildings were going up everywhere, spreading along the beachfront, crawling up Mount Carmel.

'As long as everyone has work, there won't be any trouble,' Mickey said. They were sitting on Madame Blum's veranda, Mickey with his hands in a clasp behind his head. Not a smidgen of sweat staining his shirt. For Mickey never perspired. Even now in the hottest part of the afternoon, the air hardly stirred by the lacklustre efforts of an onshore breeze. 'But don't pretend to yourself there is a great mix between the two cultures.'

'You do business with the Arabs,' Lev noted.

'Aha! But we merchants do not know of cultural, religious or ideological boundaries. We do not care who controls access to Jerusalem's Western Wall. We do not see any difference between a penny and a piaster, a pound Sterling or a pound Palestinian. Business is business, Lev. It makes no distinctions. Business even likes conflict, it flourishes on conflict. But once the trade is done, the Arabs go to their areas and we go to ours. We're like chalk and cheese. Oil and water. Milk and meat. The British and the French.'

Lev knew Mickey was right. The two peoples kept apart. The Arabs in the *shuk*, sitting under the shade of blankets propped up with poles, surrounded by baskets of olives, figs and almonds, cloths laid out with bananas, watermelons, cobs of corn. Or hard at work on the construction sites, or unloading the crates off the harbour boats. From his office window, he watched the merchants at the grain market in their stiff *tarbushes*, the officials striding in and out of their administrative offices just along the street. He passed them outside their coffee houses, sitting on tiny stools, playing cards, smoking their strange pipes, the smell of burning charcoal in the air, always men, never any women. At night-time, he would see some of the young men, migrants from the outlying villages, asleep on rooftops or on the beach. They seemed to move at a different pace from the Jews. They were less frenetic, they had a different attitude towards time, they worked according to the cooler parts of the day. There was a rootedness about them that Lev envied, an ability to sit still and observe. Who were these people? What did they think of us? What did they think of him? 'Look at that ambitious Jew,' they might say. 'Rushing around in the heat of the day in those tight clothes. Always rushing. Always pushing. Taking our land from underneath our noses. At extremely exorbitant prices, of course.' A smile and a cough into a hand at that last remark. 'Why not sit down, sip a little coffee, light up a pipe?' Perhaps this is what they thought. He had no idea. He had no Arab friends.

Lev. Lev Sela. Heart of stone. Always pining for Sarah. Mickey had tried to introduce him to other women. He took Lev to social events at the British club where Army daughters smoked cigarettes, laughed confidently and ignored him. He took Lev to Tel Aviv, a town that appeared to be sprouting out of sand, where every third person operated a soda stand. There, Lev would spend his weekly earnings on a glass of milk and a slice of cake at the Casino coffee house while Mickey pretended he was a British officer and danced the foxtrot with girls from Kiev. Lev would walk the beach while he waited for his friend to do whatever he had to do with them behind the dunes.

Lev could never understand why Mickey was so lucky with the girls. After all, he never considered his friend with his fleshy face and pock-marked skin to be particularly good-looking.

'That's because I've never been in love,' was Mickey's response.

'What's that supposed to mean?'

'You and that childhood sweetheart of yours. What was her name? Sharon? Shoshana?

'Sarah.'

'Yes. Sarah. Well, she's spoiled everything for you. Now every time you meet a girl, you are searching for another big love. And you feel disappointed if you don't find it. Girls pick up on that. It's like a sixth sense. A female phenomenon. Like a dog pisses on its territory, they know your heart has already been claimed by another.'

'Fine. You've explained the reason for my failure. But you still haven't told you me why you are so lucky with the opposite sex.'

'What makes you think I'm the lucky one?'

Back in Haifa, Lev typed away, learned his languages, studied the property laws, corresponded about land that he never saw. For it was Sammy who did all the fieldwork, who tested the soil, met with the owners and the prospective purchasers, carried out the negotiations, sealed a deal over a cup of thick coffee and a slice of orange. Until one day, Sammy called him into his office:

'How long have you worked here?'

'Almost five years.'

'You realize when I advertised at the docks for a typist, I imagined a pretty young woman from Warsaw or Riga?'

'I realize that.'

'And you were the only person to come forward.'

'I realize that too.'

'And all I wanted was for you to type, to file and to make tea.'

'I know.'

Sammy smiled. There was a sweetness in the man that Lev loved. Even when Sammy was angry, the gentleness of his nature could not be hidden from his eyes, from bursting out of the rosiness of his lips. Which Sammy smacked together now in anticipation of what he was about to say. 'I am delighted you took the initiative to learn beyond your duties of typing, filing and making tea.'

'Thank you, sir.'

'Your apprenticeship has been served.'

'What? You are dismissing me?'

'Don't be ridiculous. I am telling you that your time has come.'

'My time for what?'

'Time to be a proper land agent.'

'What do you mean?'

'Take a look at this.' Sammy passed him a file. 'A *kibbutz* is after an additional plot in the Jordan Valley. It's only about 250 dunams. I was supposed to visit them tomorrow. But I have a meeting with Those Bloody Zionists in Jerusalem. I want you to go and see what matters are like on the ground. The area is probably mostly swampland anyway. Find out who owns it, if there are any tenant farmers working on it.'

Lev read through the correspondence with the same excitement and concentration as if they were letters from his long-lost sweetheart. The name of the *kibbutz* was Kfar Ha'Emek. Village of the Valley. 'Can I negotiate a settlement?'

'Don't run ahead of yourself. This is a reconnaissance trip only. Get a sense of whether the owners want to sell, an idea about price, how much the *kibbutz* needs this land in the first place. But keep your cards close to your chest until we know all the facts.'

Mickey clapped his hands together when he heard the news. 'This is your big chance, my young virgin,' he said with an inhale of one of Madame Blum's Russian cigarettes. 'These *kibbutz* girls are like Jezebels. Sharing work, sharing food, sharing beds. Your one night in the Galilee will be a night of bliss.'

Six

Take the morning train on 25th from Haifa to Damascus. Descend al-Dalhamiyya. We will meet you. Rafi Melamud.

Lev had seen from a map that al-Dalhamiyya was a small Arab village but he now discovered that its eponymous station wasn't a station at all. It didn't even have a platform. Just a signpost in the middle of nowhere with its name scrawled in both Arabic and English lettering under the words 'Palestine Railways'. But neither Rafi Melamud nor any of his comrades were to be seen. Lev looked around, shielding his eyes from the white light bouncing off the bleached earth, expecting to see the kicked-up dust of an approaching horse or wagon. Nothing. Just waves of heat blurring the horizon. He walked around the sign, finding it hard to believe this place could be a scheduled stop. He laid down his cardboard tube of rolled-up maps, stacked the crates that had been unloaded with him in a way that provided some shade, sat down on his small suitcase.

He was situated somewhere in the middle of the Jordan Valley rift. There were ranges of hills to the east and west of him but the immediate landscape was bare except for this railway track and a few hardy shrubs. Somewhere off to the north-east was the village of al-Dalhamiyya. Somewhere in between was the tiny settlement of his destination – Kfar Ha'Emek.

He scraped his fingers into the ground, dug out a handful of chalky dust, let the particles sift through his hand. Why would anyone want to live in such a place? Why here, when the breezes of the coastal plains were only a few hours journey away by train? But he could already hear Sammy's words of response in his head. 'Land is land is land.' He flipped the cap off his trench-watch, a gift to himself bought off a British soldier with his first pay packet. Rafi Melamud, if he were coming at all, was thirty-three minutes late.

He had felt so buoyant when stepping down from the train. After all, he was now a young man filled with responsibility and purpose, dressed smart in his freshly-ironed shirt and a fancy tie borrowed from Madame Blum's late-husband's wardrobe. But his self-esteem was deflating with each passing moment, as were the creases of his shirt as he roasted in the heat. He recalled a ruse his father employed with the customers at Mr Borkowski's alcohol and tobacco store, pulling Lev back from his eagerness to serve. 'Let them wait, son,' his father advised through a stink of liquor. 'Make them uncomfortable, let them know who's in charge.' His grandfather, on the other hand, took an entirely different view of tardiness. 'According to Jewish law, to make someone wait is a sin,' he told Lev. 'For you are guilty of theft, guilty of stealing their time.' Between his father and his grandfather, his upbringing had been a bundle of contradictions.

His time was being stolen now, yet he could not help but marvel at the silence. He closed his eyes. It had been a long time since he had experienced such a void of sound. He had to go back to his snow-bound village when he and Sarah would go out to the edges of the forests, look back across the wintry fields, hold hands and hold their breath, listen to nothing. So unlike Haifa with its metal grinding of the seabed in the dredge of a harbour, the screeching gulls above the fish baskets, the shouts of the traders within the grain houses, the *muezzin*'s insistent call to prayer from the minarets.

He dozed in the swollen heat, then woke to slap away at the flies and the mosquitoes, took a sip of water from his canteen, shook the contents next to his ear. Less than a third full. He either stayed where he was and baked to death or found his own way to the settlement. He eased back against the crates, hands behind his head, brought to mind the location of Kfar Ha'Emek without having to unroll his map. He had a talent for that, conjuring up images of words and objects in his head. That was what had helped his learning of languages, holding mental pictures of vocabularies before his eyes until he could learn them by heart. He pictured the geographical position of the settlement as being about a mile directly north along the railway track in the direction of the Sea of Galilee, then off to the north-east for another mile towards the hills lining the far-side of the valley. A forty-minute journey at the most.

He counted the railway sleepers as he walked. And as he built up a steady rhythm to his gait, he found himself thinking again of his grandfather. His *zeide* had been dead for more than five years. Zelda had been right. The wasting lungs had killed him before the winter was out. She had then gone into the village, found Mr Borkowski at his alcohol and tobacco store, dictated a letter for him to send to Lev at the headquarters of the Young Guard in Jerusalem. The envelope, adorned with a list of scored-out addresses, was eventually forwarded to him at the offices of PICA in Haifa. The message was short. *Grandfather dead. Where is my tooth?* He had forgotten all about Zelda's dental request. Her tooth was not buried under some olive tree overlooking Haifa bay as desired but lay where he had tossed it, not far from his grandfather's cottage.

After what he calculated roughly as a mile, he turned away from the railway line, leaving the tracks to head north on their journey to the Sea of Galilee, then all the way to the French sitting in Damascus. The distant hills that had been a shade of purple only twenty minutes or so before had changed to pink. The sun was at its peak now, he could feel it scorching his back as he walked. But it was an arid heat so that whatever moisture bubbled up from his body, evaporated as soon as it sweated to the surface. He began to feel dizzy. And in his heated imagination, he started to muse upon Sarah. Perhaps she had ended up at this very settlement. She could be feeding the chickens or hoeing the ground or draining swamps or sewing up holes in mosquito nets. She would look up from her task, wipe the sweat from her eyes as she observed Lev approaching and ask herself: 'Who is that handsome young man? That prosperous-looking fellow who could be a lawyer or a respected land agent if only he were given the chance. That vigorous chap with a working knowledge of several languages and a decent amount of savings with the Workers' Bank of Palestine. That young man who reminds me of Lev Gottleib from my hometown, the only boy I truly loved.' And as the figure grew nearer, her heart would drum faster against the damp cotton of her blouse at the dawning recognition that this young man was indeed the Lev Gottleib of her dreams, come to rescue her from the hardship of her life, from her misguided relationship with the lice-ridden Shaul the Great. A relationship that had been as parched as the land she had tried to eke a living from with her blistered fingers and aching back. 'Here is Lev, come to save me.'

Lev stopped, put down his case. He was all worked up now. He poured some precious water from his canteen onto his handkerchief, bathed the back of his neck, then drank the rest. The heat on his body, the heat within his body, the heat within his imagination, he thought he might explode. He stamped his feet, kicked down at his sealed-up passion, waited until the fervour had subsided. Then all he felt was despair. This had to stop, these obsessive imaginings about Sarah. It had been over five years since he had last seen her. When would he cease to yearn for her? He picked up his case, stared off to the horizon as if it were a future free of his childhood love he was searching for. In the distance he saw what he thought could be rough signs of cultivation and civilization. Was that shimmering mass a plantation of young citrus trees? Was that vague row of bushes actually a line of tents? And that gust of dust hurtling towards him? Was that a wind storm? Or was it finally the horse and wagon of Rafi Melamud?

It was a horse and wagon. He waved his arms at its rapid approach. The dust cloud continued to move towards him. He watched and waited. The wagon pulled up beside him. It was not Rafi Melamud who sat at the reins. But a young woman. For a moment, he thought his obsessive desires had conjured up the real-life Sarah. But this was not Sarah. This woman's features were narrower, her figure taller and leaner. Her hair was tied up under a head-scarf, she wore a sleeveless blouse, cotton skirt hiked up to her knees, her bare legs and arms deep-tanned, muscled and white-dusted. Her breathing still laboured from her exertions with the reins, her dark eyes flickered at him with impatience.

'*Shalom*,' he said, his first word for hours coming out hoarse and dry.

She leaned forward on the wooden plank that made up the wagon seat, looked him up and down. Her horse, a compact, sweating beast, panted at his ear. She shook her head, said nothing.

'Rafi Melamud was meant to collect me.'

She shrugged. 'That's not my business.' Her own Hebrew was slow and deliberate. He tried to place the accent. It wasn't Russian or German or Polish.

'I am looking for Kfar Ha'Emek.'

'For what reason?'

'I have business there.'

'It is far away.'

'It can't be far way.'

'You don't believe me?'

'My map says...'

'Maps can be wrong.'

He decided it was better not to contradict her. 'You can take me there?'

'You came from the train?'

'Yes.'

'There are boxes?'

'Several.'

'You left them there?'

'What was I supposed to do?' he said. 'Guard them?'

'That would be a good idea.'

'They're not my responsibility.'

'Someone could take them.'

'Who?' he said, stretching his arms out to the empty landscape. 'Who is there to take them?'

She ignored his protest. 'Was there post? Letters? Packages?'

'I didn't see any.'

'There must be post.'

'I told you. I didn't see any.'

'There is always post.'

She spoke so harshly that he held his hands away from his body, as if she should search him. 'Look, no post. Now, can you take me to Kfar Ha'Emek?'

'First, I must collect the crates. Then I will take you.'

She slid to the side of her bench, indicated with a tilt of her head for him to get on board. He climbed up beside her, his suitcase and map tube by his feet, his hands grasping the plank. She yanked at the reins and they were off.

She didn't say a word for the few minutes it took to get back to the station that was no more than a signpost. She didn't look at him either, just stared straight ahead, her eyes squinting against the light and the dust, her lips sucked in tight in concentration. But he watched her from the edge of his vision. For although beneath the film of dust, the tired eyes and prickly demeanour she might not have been Sarah, she was still very beautiful.

As soon as they reached the station sign, she pulled up the wagon quick, jumped off, ran to the pile of crates. She checked the ends of each of them, until she found what she was looking for. Slid into one of the binding tapes was a pile of letters he hadn't noticed before. She flicked through them, extracted a couple, tucked them into the waistband of her skirt. She waved the rest at him.

'See?' she said.

He dropped off the wagon, walked over to where she stood, tapped his foot against the side of a crate. 'What's inside?'

'Necessities.'

'What exactly?'

'So many questions. Tools. Pick handles. Ropes. Perhaps some books.' She pronounced the words slowly as if they were vocabulary newly learned. 'Mosquito nets. And most important – quinine.' She bent down, picked up one end of a crate. 'Well?'

He helped her load up the crates onto the back of the wagon. With the letters received and the work done, she seemed more relaxed. They returned to their seats on the wagon bench. She offered him some water from her canteen, shook hard at the reins and they were off again.

He asked her name. She turned to look at him, scrutinized his face as if to assess whether he was worthy of such information.

'Celia,' she said.

He thought she wasn't going to ask him his but eventually, as if she were doing him a great favour, she said: 'And you?'

'Lev.'

'Lev what?'

'Lev Sela.'

'Really?'

'Yes.'

She glanced at him. 'Lev Sela.' And then in English: 'Heart of stone.'

'So you speak English?'

'Of course.'

He noted her tone had softened slightly. 'Where are you from?' he asked.

'Scotland.'

'I know about Scotland.'

'Oh yes? What do you know?'

'It is near Manchester.'

'Two hundred miles is not so near.'

'Perhaps. But it always rains in Manchester.'

She gave a slight laugh. Which surprised him as he hadn't meant the remark to be funny. He felt a desperate need to make her laugh again but as he tried to remember some more of Mickey's English sayings, he noticed some tents up ahead, a few outbuildings, a livestock enclosure, smoke from a fire. 'What is this place?' he asked.

'Kfar Ha'Emek.'

'You told me it was far away.'

She smiled at him for the first time. 'I needed help with the crates.'

Seven

CELIA DROPPED LEV OFF by a low, partly plastered, brick building. 'Give these to Rafi,' she said, handing him the bundle of letters. 'I must take the medicine to the sick tent.'

Lev let the dust settle from her departure, looked around. The brick building was surrounded by tents, ten of them, patched-up, sandy-coloured affairs, he guessed they had been acquired on the cheap from the British Army now that the desert campaigns were over. It was the kind of deal Mickey might have brokered. Behind the tents, there was a stone byre fronted by a fenced-in area where half-a-dozen skinny cows chewed on some sparse gorse and a few chickens roamed. Beyond that, a rusted anvil, a wagon, buckets of tar, a couple of wooden sheds for storage, stalls for the horses, a covered area for the hay. Further off, a remote tent where Celia had already pulled up the wagon, gone inside. The compound reminded him of the small farms back in Poland. He recognized the sense of struggle and sadness about the place. Jobs half-completed, repairs needing to be done, improvements to be made. He picked up his case and tube of maps, entered the brick building.

The dining room was laid out with six long, trestle tables, assorted chairs and benches. At one end there was a cloth partition beyond which he guessed was the kitchen area from the sound of pots being washed and scrubbed. At the other end of the room, a solitary figure sat bent over some spread-out sheets of paper on the table.

Lev called out to him. 'Rafi Melamud?'

The man looked up then his voice came out deep and fierce. 'Who wants to know?'

'Lev Sela.'

'Who?'

'From the Palestine Jewish Colonization Association,' Lev said as he approached the table. 'From PICA.'

Rafi Melamud was a solid boulder of a man with a thick neck and round head, hair cropped short. As he leaned back in his seat, his short-sleeved work shirt stretched tight around his powerful chest, as if it were a piece of child's clothing on an adult's body. He didn't get up. 'I expected you tomorrow,' he said, waving his hand over his papers. 'These accounts are for you.'

'No, today. It was definitely today.'

'Definitely tomorrow.'

'I have your telegram.'

Rafi's steady look challenged then quickly softened. 'What does it matter? You are here now.' He motioned to the chair opposite. 'Sit.'

Lev did as he was told.

'Hungry?'

Lev nodded.

'The midday meal is finished.' Rafi called out to the kitchen: 'Shoshana.'

'*Yah*,' came a cry from behind the cloth partition.

'Is there soup?'

'There is always soup.'

'We have a guest.' Rafi clasped his hands in front of him, the knuckles on his thick fingers were grazed, his fingernails filled with dirt. 'You walked from the train stop?'

'Celia brought me.'

'Ah yes, Celia. Were there boxes?'

'Yes.'

'Good. The new tools. And post?'

'Yes, yes. I almost forgot.' Lev handed over the bundle.

'Letters are always good. They are our only hope.' Rafi flicked through the envelopes until his eyes clouded over in disappointment. 'Ah, here is your soup.'

Shoshana waddled in. A stout young woman with large, bovine eyes, an enormous bosom, a filthy apron and a stink of sweat about her. 'Here,' she said, handing Lev a tin cup with one hand, a chunk of bread with the other. 'It's all there is.' She glowered at Rafi. 'Until I'm permitted to kill another hen.' She turned her back on them, returned towards her kitchen.

'You are my little chicken,' Rafi shouted after her. 'You want that I should kill you?'

'I want I should cut off your dirty tongue for my soup,' Shoshana called back, before disappearing between the folds of the cloth partition.

Lev sipped at the hot liquid. It was thin and salty with some slithers of tough meat. He soaked it up with his bread and ate.

'From Poland?' Rafi asked, flicking away some flies from his paperwork.

'*Tak.*'

'Polish is for the weaklings in the diaspora. We speak only Hebrew here. Where is Sammy the King?'

'I thought only PICA called him that.'

'The four kings of Israel. Saul, David, Solomon. And Sammy. King of the Land. Where is he?'

'He had a meeting in Jerusalem.'

'You can help us?'

'That's why I'm here.'

'You look too young.'

'I've been with the organization for a number of years.'

'You can lend us money? We need a tractor. More tools. More food. More everything.'

'I have no authority in money matters.'

'Bah! Then what do you have authority in?'

'I am here to discuss the land.'

Rafi grunted. 'Ah yes, the land. The land is simple. There is an area down in the valley. About 250 dunams. Half is occupied by a Bedouin family. They have a large vegetable plot, the rest for grazing. The other half is swamp. The Bedouin use it for watering a few buffalo, goats, horses, a small herd of sheep.'

'What do you need it for?'

'If we have the land, we have access to the River Yarmuk, a tributary

44

of the Jordan. That is the most important matter for us. Then we can draw off water, then we can irrigate, then we can bring life to this dried-up place. Sammy knows all of this.'

'I had a look at the maps before I came. I can't see the plot you're talking about.'

'Show me what you have.'

Rafi moved his papers, Lev extracted the maps from the tube, rolled them out on the table. 'One is from the time of the Turks by the Palestinian Exploration Fund,' he explained. 'It's about sixty years old. This other one we made with the help of the British from campaign maps they produced during the last war. We used these when we first bought the land for your settlement. Where is the piece you want?'

Rafi twisted the maps around, peered in close, ran a dirty-nailed finger down from the Sea of Galilee. 'I don't see it,' he said. 'It should be here but I don't see it. Where the hell is it?'

Lev went round to Rafi's side of the table. 'Where should it be?'

'There. Outside this pink boundary. What is this boundary?'

'Inside that is the land we lease to you now.'

'No, it cannot be. This shows your pink boundary as going right up to the River Yarmuk. I told you we don't have land to the river.'

'You do according to the maps.'

'Damn the maps. I know my own land. Our boundary is this ridge, not the river. The river flows below the ridge. Your pink line shows the ridge and the river as if they were the same line. But the river does not go like this. It twists to the east, then back again to make a bulge. And inside this bulge is the land we want.'

'I don't understand. How can both maps be wrong like this?'

Rafi sniffed hard. 'What does it matter? Just alter them.'

'We can't do that. According to official documents, the land doesn't exist.'

'I can assure you it does. It's got a swamp full of malaria and a family of Bedouins on it.'

'I need to see for myself.'

'It is not far to the ridge. From there you can look down on this land that does not exist. I'd take you myself but I have to finish these accounts now you are a day early. Come, I will point you in the right direction.'

Rafi took him outside, indicated a rough dirt road rutted with the grooves of wagon wheels. 'Down there. Straight line for a half-mile or so. Until you come to the ridge. We call the place the Centre of the World. You won't need your maps to show you why. We can talk again later. After supper. After supper is the time for talking.'

Lev headed off east along the track, passed rows of citrus saplings, a field of wilting wheat, another of sorghum, a line of eucalyptus trees shedding their ribbons of white bark. Then as he reached the ridge, the land suddenly opened out before him, the width and depth of the view taking him by surprise.

He needed a few moments for his eyes to adjust to the vast space, the brightness. Before him a valley that stretched eastward for miles to the pink ridge of hills he had seen earlier. These hills would be part of Trans-Jordan, then beyond to Persia and Arabia. To the north, there would be Syria and Lebanon. To the south, Jerusalem then on to Egypt and Africa. Behind him was the Mediterranean, then Poland and the rest of Europe. Rafi was right. This really was the Centre of the World. And below him in the valley was the Yarmuk River, not flowing parallel to the ridge on which he stood but meandering eastwards to take in its grasp a piece of land that did not figure on any map. He could make out the Bedouin encampment dotted with black tents, flaps raised against the sun and for the capture of any breeze. He cupped his hands over his eyes. A man on horseback moved among the goats, children were playing in the dirt, a cluster of women watching over them from the shade of a tent. Part of the land had been cultivated with a few rows of vegetables. But a large section was just swamp, a couple of figures bent low with their baskets among the reeds.

Eight

THE DINING ROOM was surprisingly quiet for a group of over thirty people. No laughter. No strident voices. Some dull-toned conversations, that was all. Mostly men, perhaps about ten women, all about the same age, in their mid-twenties, even younger. Lev sat beside Rafi, feeling very much the city boy in his long trousers and shirt, although he had given up on the tie. Those sitting close by barely acknowledged him. Not, he felt, out of any rudeness but rather a weariness that excluded the burden of conversation with a newcomer. Everyone seemed caught up in their own islands of existence. He noticed Celia over at another table, reading a letter while she ate. A few lucky others did the same with the post they had received. He spooned up the same soup he had eaten earlier except for a few beans added to fill out the broth. Bread, jam and honey on the table, this was the evening meal after a hard day's work in the fields.

He realized he could have been one of these young pioneers. If God or Fate or Love had dealt him a different hand. Or if Ewa Kaminsky had not taught him how to type. One of these weary souls trying to build a community here with barely the strength left at the end of the day to lift a spoon to their lips. He was never as exhausted as the members of this group, his hands were not calloused, his clothes were not in need of a launder and a stitch, there was always a fine meal waiting for him at Madame Blum's.

Here, after supper, everyone washed their own dishes, dried them, stacked them away, sat back down at the tables. He noticed the mood immediately pick up. Conversations were louder, chairs were shifted closer, pots of tea were poured, cigarettes were rolled, pipes were lit, a couple of the women took out their knitting, another started to sing to herself, pages of a newspaper were passed around.

He watched on as Celia continued to read her letters, unconcerned about the activity going on around her. She paused only to look up in irritation if someone should block out the light from the nearest lantern. The headscarf she had worn when Lev had met her earlier had been abandoned to reveal a mass of dark curls. A young man squeezed in beside her. There was a slick-haired confidence about him that reminded Lev of the British police officers strutting around Haifa with their Webley revolvers. Celia turned away, shielded her letter from the intruder, bit down on her knuckle as she concentrated on her reading. What was she doing here, this young woman from Scotland?

Rafi stood up, held out his arms for silence. 'Comrades,' he shouted. It took a while for everyone to settle. 'Comrades, comrades. We have a visitor.'

Lev felt himself flush to the attention, raised his own hand briefly in acknowledgement.

Rafi continued. 'Lev is here from PICA. I asked them to have a look at the land down by the river. As noted in the minutes of previous meetings, there is a long-standing need for us to–'

'You had no authority to do that,' called out one of the pipe-smokers. He was a thin, bespectacled young man with pointed, ferret-like features, a peaked worker's cap tilted back off his forehead. 'No authority whatsoever.'

Rafi struck his fist on the table. 'For God's sake, Amos, we agreed all this. We agreed access to the river was important. Look at the wheat. It's dying in the fields. We haven't seen rain for weeks. Hardly a drop in months.'

'We agreed in principle *at some later date*,' Amos countered. 'We didn't agree to any negotiations with the Anonymous Donor and his beloved PICA.'

'I am the *kibbutz* secretary. I have the authority to take the initiative. It is important PICA understands what we want.'

Amos pushed himself slowly to his feet, confidently surveyed the audience. 'Understands what we want?' he snarled, shaking the stem of his pipe at his listeners. 'We can't even work the land we have. We already have to bring in cheap Arab labourers from al-Dalhamiyya and Tiberias. That land down there is just more work. It's just another swamp to be drained.' Amos placed his hands on his hips, swivelled his puffed-out chest in defiance. 'It's not more fields we want. What we need is money for a tractor. And a thresher. And another plough to work the land we already have. Can PICA give us that?'

'And what about the Bedouin?' This question came from a blonde, red-cheeked man with piston-like biceps bursting out of his short-sleeved work shirt. He represented what Lev thought of as the 'New Jew', the kind of scythe-bearing figure he used to see back in Poland on posters advertising the joys of agriculture to the Zionist Youth. All that was missing was a twinkle of light flashing from this New Jew's blue eyes. 'Have you told Zayed we want his land?'

'We don't know if it is his land,' Rafi said.

'Of course it's his land,' said the New Jew. 'His family have been coming here for centuries.'

Rafi sighed, his own face red now with rising irritation. 'There is doubt regarding his ownership.'

'What doubt? If it is not his land, then who's is it?'

'I'll let our friend from PICA explain,' Rafi said.

Lev looked around at the expectant faces. This was his moment. When he had to step forward, take control just as he had done on that cold night in Zebrzydowice on the Poland-Czechoslovakia border. He gripped the table edge, pushed himself upwards onto his feet.

'The land under discussion...' He was pleased to hear his voice had emerged both calm and even. He glanced at Celia but she was still engrossed in her letter reading. He pressed on. 'The land under discussion does not appear on any map in our possession.'

'What the hell does that mean?' Amos asked.

Lev sucked in a breath, looked over at his questioner. He sensed something self-righteous and smug about the man, marked him as one of those Russian socialists full of noble ideals that would come to nothing. He had seen plenty of them from his office window, wearing those very same peaked worker's caps, lining up to catch the next boat out of their Promised Land. 'It means I don't know who owns it,' Lev admitted. 'It could be this Zayed you talk about. It could be the British. It could be the French. It could be some Arab landowner sitting in a villa in Cairo. I just don't know.'

'Well, if it doesn't feature on any map,' someone called out, 'it must be no-man's land.'

'No-woman's land, comrade,' Shoshana from the kitchen corrected to roars of laughter.

'No-woman's land, then. Why don't we just take it?'

'It's not that simple,' Lev said. 'There are laws, ancient property laws that are likely to apply in the absence of any documentation. I need to make enquiries, take advice. I should also like to talk with the Bedouin. Who is this Zayed?'

'He is the elder,' Rafi informed him. 'He speaks on behalf of the tribe.'

'Can I meet with him?'

'What will you tell him?' New Jew called out. 'That you've come to steal his land?'

'PICA does not steal land,' Lev countered, trying to keep his voice steady against remarks he was beginning to take personally. 'You reside here now on land PICA bought properly and fairly.'

'But there was no-one living on it at the time,' New Jew said. 'What will you do with Zayed and his family once his land has been purchased?'

'It is not PICA's policy to displace tenant farmers unnecessarily. Zayed and his tribe can come and go as they have always done. Once properly drained, this land is only needed for access to the river.'

'We don't need the land at all.' It was Amos again, still on his feet with his poking pipe. 'I keep saying, we can't even drain the land we already have. We should only take what we can work with Jewish labour. That is a basic principle. If we have to bring in Arabs to work for us, we are no more than colonialists.' Amos spat out the last word with contempt, before adding with even more bitterness: 'And capitalists.'

'And when Rafi here wants to start damming the river,' New Jew continued, 'what will happen to Zayed's pastures then?'

'Enough, comrades,' Rafi said. 'Enough. I still don't see any reason why Lev cannot meet with the Bedouin. It is, after all, only a preliminary talk.'

'I will need a clear mandate from the group,' Lev added.

'I will ask for a show of hands,' Rafi said. 'Against?'

Only three hands were raised.

Amos sat down defeated while New Jew shuffled in his chair, folded his thick forearms against the victors.

'Good,' Rafi said. 'Now who is free to take Lev down to see Zayed?'

'I can.' It was the young man with the slick-backed hair who sat beside Celia. 'I have to go there tomorrow anyway.'

'That's settled then,' Rafi declared. 'Jonny will take him. Now let's move on to other matters. We have much to discuss.'

Who should work with the children now Ahuva was sick? Could Shoshanna kill another hen? Was there money available to buy more vegetables from the Arab farmers? Who could work on building a children's house? What to do about the mice? Avi needed help to tar the wagon wheels. Chaim wanted to keep bees. Tools shouldn't be left in the fields. Where could they get more books? Could Tsur keep the stray dog he found in the valley? Some of the married couples wanted their own tents. Where was last week's newspaper? Yes, where *was* last week's newspaper?

The talking went on and on until everyone was tired of it and a wind picked up, causing the lanterns to sway. The discussions subsided and one of the women started to sing, quietly at first until the melody was taken up by someone else, then another and another. Lev recognized the tune from the country of his birth. He began to hum the melody. And then there were more songs, again in Hebrew or in Russian or Yiddish, songs of *der heim*, of the homeland. The group drew closer, the lamps were turned down save one, there was clapping and finger-clicking, one of the members returned with a battered accordion, a few people got up, held hands, began to dance in a circle. Celia was one of them. Lev watched her carefully as she played out the familiar steps. Her eyes closed, a few paces to the side, dipping her body then pulling back, arching upwards, forcing out her breasts, throwing back her head, caught up in her own private passion, as she retraced her movements in rhythm with her partners. He heard his own voice soar to the melodies accompanying the dancers and somewhere deep within himself he felt a yearning for something he could not name. But just as the intensity of the music reached its zenith, the dancing broke up, people started to leave, still singing as they filed out of the door, their melodies spilling into a star-filled night.

He was to bed down in the dining room. He was brought a cot, a pillow and a blanket. Everyone else had gone to their tents. The last lantern was left burning at the far end of the room for when the night guard came in to make tea. Lev lay awake on his back, staring at the corrugated roof. It had been a long time since he had felt so much a part of something. He would have to go back to his time spent with Sarah and the rest of the Ten Lost Tribes. Since then, his existence in Palestine had been a lonely one. He had his relationships with Mickey, Madame Blum and Sammy but beyond that, he had no family here, no other friends, no connection to any community. The singing, the dancing, the camaraderie, it had deeply moved him. He turned restless in his cot, was about to get up to make himself some tea when he heard someone enter at the far side of the room. He looked up. The figure moved into the light of the lantern. Without thinking, he called out her name. 'Celia.'

'Who is that?' she said, moving towards him, peering into the darkness.

'Lev. From the station. From PICA.'

'I didn't realize you were here.'

'It's all right. I couldn't sleep.'

'I'm just going to sit by the lantern. I want to write a letter.'

'At this time of night?'

'It is the only time I have.'

'I was just getting up to make tea.'

'Stay. I will bring you some.'

Her sudden kindness surprised him. He propped himself up on his cot, watched as she worked, firing up the charcoal in the samovar, testing the temperature of the water, filling up the teapot. She poured out two cups, brought them over. He saw that she was wrapped in a blanket, her body in the bathe of the lantern casting strange shadows around the room. He felt excited by her presence as she crouched by him, passed him his cup, then again surprised when she pulled up a chair, sat by him, placed her own cup on the floor. He watched as she stretched her neck, massaged the nape with her hands, the movement causing her blanket to drop slightly to reveal a glimpse of her upper breasts. He realized she might be naked underneath.

'So?' she said, with a quick smile as she recovered her cup. 'Can you solve our land problem?'

'It could be complicated.'

'Everything is complicated here.'

'Land is an emotional issue in Palestine.'

She sipped at her tea, staring at him over the rim of the cup. Then she closed her eyes, blew on the liquid so the warmth rose up to massage her face and she relaxed into the feeling of the heat. She opened her eyes again. A soft, dark brown, like smooth leather freshly shone. He saw a hidden warmth in her gaze, but an insecurity resting there also.

'Since we are talking about land,' she said, 'where is your land?'

'I come from Poland. A small town. Not far from Warsaw.'

'And what brought you here?'

'I came with a *kvutza*. A group from the Young Guard. The plan was to build a settlement together. Probably something quite like this one.'

'And now you are a land agent for PICA.'

He took a sip of tea. It was bitter and lukewarm. 'Everything changed.'

She nodded. 'It often does.'

'And you?' he asked.

'I wanted a fresh start. But I've learned you can never really do that. You're always building on what is already there. Either within yourself, or within others. And within the land itself. There is so much ancient history here.'

'My grandfather told me the same thing. Coming here is like grafting new branches onto old vines. He said if I really wanted to start from the beginning, I should go to America.'

'I don't know about America. All I know is life in this community can be extremely hard. But it can also be very beautiful.' She rocked the base of her foot against the leg of his cot. 'I saw the way you sang along with us. Perhaps you should try this way of life again.'

She held out her hand to take his empty cup. Instead of giving it to her, he grabbed her wrist. It was such an instinctive move, surprising himself with his own boldness. For a few moments, they both looked at where he held her.

'Not now,' she said, pulling her arm away. 'I have to write.'

Nine

Kfar Ha'Emek, Jordan Valley, Palestine

My dearest Charlotte

*I am replying to your letter number six, which I received this morn-
ing. It took three months to get here. This delay between our corre-
spondences confuses me in the details of what we already know
and don't know about each other when we write. I also fret as to
whether letters may have gone missing. I try to keep copies of my
previous letters but carbon paper is very difficult to get hold of.
Please send me some with your next parcel.*

*I wish you were here beside me so we could chatter away into
the night as we did in the old days back in Glasgow. I miss our flat
in the West End, the gas lamps and the tree-lined streets, especially
now as autumn approaches and the leaves turn yellow and gold.
Here we have very few trees, except for some boring eucalyptus,
which stay the same all year round. Those times in Glasgow seem
so far away from me now, it is hard to believe the Celia who sits
here in the deepest Galilean night writing this letter is the same
Celia as the one you knew.*

*It doesn't surprise me to learn you have now become a
campaigner for the temperance movement. I can just imagine you
handing out your leaflets on the trams, on the trains and at football*

matches. All these posters for abolition plastered everywhere. Glasgow must be awash with temperance propaganda on every hoarding and lamppost. But even if you can't get people to vote for abolition, at least you're getting the drink trade to take notice. We always used to say what a disgrace it was that public houses were only places for manly drunkenness and petty violence rather than somewhere women like ourselves could go for entertainment and light refreshment. I remember someone telling me back in Glasgow: 'It's not your capitalism or your socialism you need to be worrying about in this city. If you're looking for "isms", it's alcoholism you need to be concerned about.' I cannot help but agree with that statement. Here, we have almost no alcohol – there is no money to buy any. But sometimes the Arab farmers give us bottles of their local drink. It is called 'arak'. It tastes like liquorice out of a Glasgow sweetshop. They don't drink it by itself but along with their food. It is very strong. One sip makes my head swim.

Jonny and I are no longer a couple. I am sure you have already guessed that outcome from my last two or three letters – if in fact you received them. I think I knew in my heart we would not end up together from the moment I arrived here. On our very first day, he took me out to a ridge and showed me what we call 'The Centre of the World'. It is a viewing point that looks east to Persia, north to Syria, south to Jerusalem and Egypt and west to Scotland. I remember how excited Jonny was to show me this place, all the hopes and plans he had for us, but I remember thinking even then that I didn't want to be a part of it all. Oh, I know you probably consider me cruel for leading him on, to let him bring me all this way with dreams of a life together. Yet I really did try. We shared a tent for several months. But it was clear to both of us we were not becoming closer but moving apart. We talked about it so much, trying to convince ourselves of something we weren't really feeling underneath. I think he is happier now we are apart. These kind of couplings are not really encouraged anyway. Of course, there are those who arrived here already as man and wife. And others who paired off to share a tent together and eventually had children. There are five children here now and oh, how we adore them. But there are some people who feel that to be paired off in a couple is against the principles of equality. That it is not fair a man and woman may enjoy conjugal rights while others may not. But who has time for such things anyway? We are always so exhausted. And even if you are sharing a tent, there are always other people there, behind a strung-up blanket, pretending they are asleep but still listening. It is better to be alone, don't you think? To be a strong, independent woman.

I am writing this letter in the dining room. It is very late, I don't even know what time it is. There is a young man asleep in a cot at the other end of the room. Or at least he is pretending to be asleep, for I believe he is watching me. His name is Lev. I think he likes me. He grabbed my hand a while ago when I took him over a cup of tea. I pulled it away, of course. Yet I could feel all my feminine wiles coming to the fore just because there was a new male in the camp. How fickle I am after everything I have just written above. At the same time, it is hard to believe I can still be attractive when my clothes are so dirty, my hair is stiff with dirt and I stink for lack of a good wash. If he had come on the Sabbath, at least then I make a little bit of an effort. But what does it matter? As I just wrote, perhaps it is better to be alone.

In the meantime, this Lev has come here from the organization that owns our land to help us acquire some more. More land. We cannot even take care of what we have. But it is essential we get this plot as it will give us access to the river. For there is one thing that is just as important as land here in Palestine, and that is water. Our crops are dying in the field and there are severe restrictions on the amounts we can use for bathing or the laundry.

At tonight's meeting, I believe Lev began to realize what a nest of vipers he was sticking his hand into. This piece of land is a symbol of all our differences in this little group of ours. When we talk of land, what we are really talking about are all the tensions that lie beneath our relationships, all the things we are too frightened to say to each other face to face. Some people in our group are against acquiring the land for ideological reasons. For socialist reasons. For Zionist reasons. For practical reasons. For personal reasons.

For spiteful reasons. At the meeting tonight we ended up discussing it all over again. Discuss, discuss, discuss. That is all we do here when we are not working. That is what socialism is, Charlotte. Discussions and committees and meetings. We discuss everything. In the end, it is not the one who is right who wins, but the one who can last longest. I feel I can't even spend a penny here without a damn discussion. If I just lift up my skirts in the fields and go there and then, perhaps there should be a discussion about that too. I know it is important to talk about things as a group. That we should all feel equal. That we should give according to our ability and take according to our needs. But sometimes I am just sick of it. Sometimes I just yearn for a dictatorship (a benevolent one, of course, run by a woman) when someone just tells me what to do without any talk, talk, talk.

Look at me, talk, talk, talking away. I am sorry, Charlotte, I must stop chattering on like this. I am so very tired. There is so much more that I could tell you but I must finish this letter so I can get this Lev to take it back to Haifa with him tomorrow. That way it should arrive with you more quickly. What price the grasping of my hand? Why, a postage stamp to Great Britain, of course.

All my love

Celia

Ten

'NOT NOW.'

Lev turned over in his cot, watched a pink lizard, its skin almost translucent, slither along one of the beams, disappear into a crack. He listened to the scratch of Celia's pen across the paper. He heard the tiredness in her sigh. He couldn't believe he had grabbed her hand like that. The last time he had held a female hand was when he had danced the *hora* around a campfire with Sarah and the rest of the Young Guard. His palm had been so sweaty then, he feared she would slip from his grasp. With Celia, his hand was as dry as parchment as it was propelled towards her wrist by some hidden force outside himself. Until he heard those two words that had filled him with just a little hope.

'Not now.'

He remembered visiting his grandfather in his cottage in the woods, he must have been eight or nine years old at the time. It had been springtime, and they sat outside on a rough bench in the strengthening sunshine. His *zeide*'s dog, Bazyli, lay in a flea-ridden, wheezing heap at his feet, a woodpecker drilled away at some linden tree in the forest, there were butterflies in the air, poppies sprouting all around the rough grass. His grandfather had an arm around him, his ancient beard tickling his cheek as he read to him the wisdom of the great sages.

'Hillel is my favourite,' his grandfather told him. 'For his teachings are simple and true. They speak profoundly of love.'

Lev was not interested in these teachings of Hillel. He was just wondering if he could find a way back through the woods to his home without being set upon by the Catholic farmboys. Or chased by the *dybukks* that haunted the forest in search of young boys under the age of ten. He therefore had little attention for the words of the great Hillel and the Golden Rules he was supposed to live by. As for love, he knew even at that young age he would love Sarah more than the words of any ancient Jewish sage.

'I know you are young, Lev,' his grandfather continued, smacking his wet lips together, a motion Lev knew signified the advent of a serious talk on the Torah. 'But if you remember just a few words out of all that I tell you, just a few words, then your life will be the better for it. I promise you.' Smack, smack, smack. 'These words come from the *Ethics of the Fathers.*'

And his grandfather droned on. Lev watched the slanting light through the trees, the flick of Bazyli's ear to a blood-sucking insect, a butterfly caught briefly in the tangle of his grandfather's beard. But in all the dreaminess of that lazy day, he did remember a few of his *zeide*'s words. There were only five of them. And he recalled them now as he drifted into sleep. To dream of a cottage in the heart of a Polish wood where for a few moments he had dwelt in an intense happiness only possible in the innocence of childhood. '*Eem loh achshav... eh matai?*' If not now... then when?

It was still dark when Lev woke to the first of the workers coming into the dining room for a hot drink before going out to the fields. He rose quickly, folded away his cot, wrapped a blanket around his shoulders, went outside to the covered pit toilets. He couldn't remember the last time he had been up this early. The dew, the hiss of the crickets, the low-flying bats with their leathery wings disturbing the air above his head. He entered one of the huts, held his nose against the stink of excrement mixed with disinfectant, emptied his bladder into a deep shaft. For a few moments, he considered his forefathers who might have urinated on this very same spot, stopping off with their camel train as they passed through this valley en route between Damascus and Jerusalem. The uncircumcised Abram before he had made his covenant with God, marking out his territory for future generations. He shivered, shook himself off, returned to the dining room. He made himself a cup of thick coffee, sat quietly in a far-off corner watching the young men and women as they shuffled in, then disappeared back out into the darkness. He looked out for Celia. But she never arrived.

'*Yalla*.' Jonny rose up off the wagon seat, whipped up the reins. '*Yalla*.' Then, in English: 'Come on, for God's sake.' The skinny beast wriggled in its halter, picked up pace, kicked up some more dust. Lev gripped the seat with one hand, tried to continue eating his breakfast of a half-rotten banana with the other. A bunch of the same blackening fruit slid around on the boards behind him. Perched on the seat between them, a Gladstone bag, its leather worn and sagging. He asked Jonny where he was from.

'Glasgow,' was the reply.

Lev thought Glasgow sounded like some town in Poland until Jonny added: 'Glasgow, Scotland.'

Of course, Scotland. How stupid he had been. He tossed the banana peel into a field of young citrus trees. 'The two of you,' he said. 'From Scotland.'

'You've met Celia then?'

'She gave me a ride from the train-stop.'

'I hope she was pleasant to you.'

'Pleasant enough.'

'Good. She runs hot and cold does Celia. Especially with strangers. But she's certainly a natural with the wagon and horses. Hard to believe she was a city girl.'

Lev tried to imagine Celia as a city girl. With a fancy hat pierced by a peacock feather, a long coat trimmed with fur, like the elegant women he once glimpsed strolling along the Nowy Świat in Warsaw. He wondered if she had worn carmine on her lips like Ewa Kaminsky. He wondered if she and Jonny were a couple.

Jonny meanwhile said nothing more about her. Instead, he went on to tell Lev how he had been a medical student back in Glasgow before interrupting his studies to go off to fight in the Great War. Lev noted that unlike his own brothers, who had fought in the same war but on the opposite side, Jonny had managed to return alive. He had resumed his studies, graduated as a doctor yet had never practised until now.

'I came to work on the land. That was the plan. I was going to be the great socialist farmer. But there's so much need for medical care here. Not just in our little settlement. But among the Arab villages too. Malaria, of course. Then there is syphilis, trachoma, chronic diarrhoea. Sometimes, just sheer bloody exhaustion.'

They had reached the ridge at the Centre of the World. Jonny pulled the wagon to a halt, extracted a ready-rolled cigarette from his shirt pocket, struck up a match. 'Sorry, it's the only one,' he said, spitting some loose shreds onto the boards at his feet.

'I don't smoke.'

'I prefer a pipe myself. But I'm scratching the bottom of my allowance.'

'Tobacco is rationed?'

'We share out everything. Food, clothes, books, tobacco.'

'Clothes as well?'

'We throw all our clothes into the laundry, pick up what more or less fits from the clean piles. We've got one good suit that does for everyone when we have an official meeting to go to. Haven't you noticed what a bunch of misfits we are?'

Lev did recall Rafi almost bursting out of his too-small workshirt during their first encounter. 'And if I am not a smoker?'

'Each according to his needs. No need to smoke, no need for tobacco. But I'm sure you've got needs others don't have, Lev. Or you have something others need.' Jonny stretched out a hand, grasped at Lev's wrist. 'Like this nice watch. It all balances out in the end.' Jonny dragged hard on his cigarette as if to prove his point, then tipped his chin in the direction of the valley. 'There are your Bedouin.'

'I saw them from here yesterday.'

'Do you speak Arabic?'

'Not much. And you?

'Enough to get by. Zayed's son, Ibrahim, will probably speak with you. He knows Hebrew. A bit of English as well. Have you done business with the Bedouin before?'

'My first time.'

'Really? I thought you boys from PICA were well-versed in these matters.'

'Sammy is the expert, not me.'

'Well, I'll take the lead, then. We'll be invited to eat, of course. That is part of their tradition. But we must politely refuse. Which will be a relief for them as they can hardly manage to feed themselves. They will then invite us to drink with them, an offer we can accept. And remember no discussion of business inside the tent. You must go outside for that.'

'What are they like, this Zayed and Ibrahim?'

'Typical Bedouin. Don't say much. Too many years wandering around the desert with only camels for company. But don't under-estimate them. There's a shrewd intelligence lurking there behind the silences. Zayed is more traditional, of course, but Ibrahim can be quite modern in his outlook. We have a good relationship with them. We buy their vegetables. We give them medicine. They provide us with a few bottles of *arak*. Some extra hands at harvest time. Or help with draining the swamps. Even though there are some among us who don't want to employ them.'

'I heard all the arguments last night.'

'The irony is if we argued less, we'd have all the time in the world to do our own farmwork.' Jonny stared out across the valley. Lev followed his gaze. The sun had come up from behind the hills, the same range he had seen the day before as pink was now a shade of dark purple. A hawk swooped over the rift, then stopped to hover above the reeds in the marshland.

'I thought she would love it here,' Jonny said, tossing his cigarette into the dust. 'I really did.'

Eleven

A RIDER CAME OUT to meet them. He wore the traditional dress – grey robe, dun sleeveless jacket, a matching *kufiya* around his head held in place with a black *aggal*. Lev used to wonder why the Bedouin wore such dark clothes when surely white or khaki was best against the sun. It was Sammy the King who told him it was the looseness of their clothes, not the colour that kept them cool. Across this man's back, a rifle. And running alongside him, the most beautiful dog Lev had seen. A sleek, tan-coloured beast, long ears swept back close to its pointed face as it ran, a greyhound's spindly limbs but full-chested, coat slightly feathered on the back of its legs and its curved tail. Lev had heard of these desert hounds before, but never seen one up close. A saluki.

Jonny brought the wagon to a halt. The horseman pulled up beside them, shortening the reins to wrestle the lurching steed into his control. 'Haahgh,' the man rasped. 'Haahgh.' And the beast calmed. The rider, breathless, smiled at them, revealing a mouth of gaps and twisted teeth. His face was lined deep, sun-beaten, a frosting of stubble around the jaw. '*Assalaamu aleikum*, Doctor Yonny,' he rasped with a desert-dried throatiness. '*Assalaamu aleikum*.'

'*Wa-Aleikum Assalaam*, Zayed. And this is my friend. Lev.'

'*Assalaamu aleikum*, Lev.'

'*Wa-Aleikum Assalaam*.'

Zayed bent over toward his hound. 'Run,' he shouted. 'Run. Run into the sun.' And then on returning upright: 'I must set him free. Or he becomes restless.'

64

Lev watched as the dog raced eastwards away from them, pawing up dust as it ran towards the river. Its grace at speed was remarkable. But then it had to be fast to chase down the desert hares and gazelles it was trained to kill.

'Do you hunt, Lev?' Zayed asked.

'I used to go into the forest with my brother. He was the hunter.'

'And what did you find there?'

'Deer. Boar.'

'Boar?'

'Wild pigs.'

'Hah! I envy you. Here I find only a skinny hare, if I am lucky.' Zayed turned to Jonny. 'My youngest son…'

'I know. I received your message.'

'Good. But first you must eat.'

'We have no time to eat, Zayed. Allah did not make enough hours in the day to complete all the work I must do.'

'So be it. But you must let me invite you and your friend Lev for coffee.'

'Coffee will be good.'

'Then come. Follow me.'

The large tent was made of woven goats hair, the flaps lifted to allow what little breeze there was to pass through. Lev sat quietly, sipped from a small cup of sweet coffee flavoured with cardamom as he watched Zayed and Jonny in murmured conversation opposite. Directly outside the tent opening, two women made butter by shaking a skin-sack of sheep's milk that hung from a wooden tripod. They spoke quietly as they swung the sack between them. Lev selected a dried date from a brass plate by his side, bit down on its tough sweetness. He was glad to see his host had left his rifle outside. For he had no idea how Zayed would react to their imminent discussion. After all, this was supposed to have been a quiet chat with an Arab landowner willing to sell off a malaria-infested swamp at an inflated price. Not a discussion with an armed tribesman occupying land that didn't appear to officially exist. He flicked away a fly, chewed on another date, as he pondered on how to best approach his host. He felt his eyes heavy in the heat and the slow-paced atmosphere of his surroundings. Only for his mind to shudder back into alertness when Zayed clapped his hands and called out: 'Rafiq. Bring Rafiq.'

One of the women, who had been churning the butter, got up, came back with a young boy. He must have been about seven years old. His eyes were swollen, almost completely sealed up with a crusty discharge.

'This is Rafiq,' Zayed said. 'My youngest son.'

Rafiq clung to his mother's robes.

'Stand up straight,' Zayed commanded.

The boy did as he was told.

'I will need to see him outside,' Jonny said.

'Go with the doctor.'

Jonny took the boy to the opening of the tent. There, he prised open one eyelid then the other, twisted his head one way and then the other, as the boy winced against the pain and the sunlight.

Back inside, Jonny said: 'It is good you asked me to come.'

'He will go blind?' Zayed asked. 'Like his uncle?'

'I don't think so. It is early in the disease.'

'What can you do?'

'I will squeeze the lids to see if I can get rid of the poison. Then I will add some drops into his eyes.'

'What is this medicine?'

'It's a plant extract. I don't know the word in Arabic. We call it "witch hazel". I will leave you the bottle.'

Zayed muttered the word back to himself.

Jonny went on: 'The most important thing is to keep the boy's face clean. Boil water and when it cools, bathe his eyes with a clean cloth, then add some of these drops. Everything must be as clean as possible, Zayed. Tell the women not to wipe the boy's eyes with spit and the hem of their robes. And keep him away from the other children.'

'Is that all?'

'No, there is one more thing.'

'What is it?'

'He must not rub his eyes.'

'Do you hear that, Rafiq? No eye-rubbing.'

'I suggest also you tie his hands behind his back.'

'Tie his hands. All day?'

'All day. And all night. I will come back in a week to see how he is.'

'But to have no hands for one week?'

'It is better than to have no eyes for the rest of his life.'

As Jonny had predicted, it was Zayed's eldest son, Ibrahim, who appeared for the discussions. He was a broad-shouldered, proud-looking man who, with hands on hips, swept his torso from side to side as if to impose his dominance on all those present. They went outside to sit in the shade of one of the open flaps, Lev on a rolled-up blanket that stank of horse, Ibrahim cross-legged in front of him, Zayed further back in the shadows. Holes in the overhead matting meant rays of light played on all three of them. The saluki hound had returned to lie close to its master. Jonny had gone off to treat Rafiq. Coffee beans roasted on the embers of a nearby fire. The dog sneezed. Swollen flies moved lazily through the air. Zayed lit up a water pipe. Ibrahim added several teaspoons of sugar to his coffee, stirred slowly. Lev waited, shifted uncomfortably on the blanket.

'Rain will come soon,' Ibrahim said, without a glance upwards.

Lev did look up. There was not a cloud in the sky.

Ibrahim continued stirring. 'What do you want with us?'

'I am from the Palestine Jewish Colonization Association. PICA. Do you know of PICA?'

'You are like the Zionists.'

'No, we are different.'

'How?'

'We try to work with our Arab neighbours.'

Ibrahim snorted, then gave a kind of half-laugh, looked back to his father. Zayed said nothing, sucked on the *nargile*. The water gurgled in the glass bowl.

Lev went on. 'Kfar Ha'Emek is a PICA settlement. It is a good example of our cooperation. If we improve the land for ourselves, we improve it for you too. We drain the swamps together, we stop malaria together.'

'This is true.'

'We give you work.'

'True.'

'We buy your vegetables. We give you medicine.'

'This is all good.' Ibrahim narrowed his eyes, waited, as if he knew already what was coming.

Lev waited too, slapped at a mosquito on the back of his neck, tried to calm himself as he prepared to let out the words he had come to say. Ibrahim sniffed at the air, no doubt searching for signs of the rain he had predicted. A piece of wood shifted, sparked on the fire. The hound stretched and yawned.

'PICA would like to buy this land,' Lev said eventually. He held out his arms as if to indicate the scope of the proposed purchase.

Ibrahim didn't give any indication of surprise. 'Why?' he asked calmly.

'We would drain the swamp for the settlement.'

'And my father? And our tribe? What will happen to them?'

'The land you use now for your vegetables and your cattle, your goats and your sheep, you can still use. Your father and your tribe can remain as tenant farmers of PICA. As *fellah*.'

'But we are not *fellah* now.'

'What are you, then?'

Ibrahim shrugged. 'We are Bedouin.'

'I know. But who do you pay to rent the land?'

'We pay no-one. Every year in the summer, my father brings his tribe and animals here from the south. Just like his father and his father before him.' Ibrahim made a beckoning motion with his hand to indicate all the past generations of his tribe. 'In the last few years, I have stayed on with my own family, to cultivate some of the land. We do not need permission. This is the land of our fathers. Why should we pay?'

'But who owns this land? Who is the *effendi*?'

'The same person who owns the mosquitoes in the swamp.'

Lev smiled at the remark. 'What about the Turks?'

Ibrahim turned sideways, spat into the dried earth. 'They have gone.'

'And the British?'

'Ah yes, the British. What about the British?'

'Have the British been to see you?'

Ibrahim turned, asked the question of his father. Zayed shook his head.

'Why would the British come to see a poor Bedouin?' Ibrahim said.

'They control a lot of the land round here,' Lev said. 'Land they took from the Turks then gave to the Bedouin.'

'No British gave us any land. We already have this land.' Ibrahim smiled over the lip of his coffee cup. His teeth were remarkably white for a tribesman. 'Why don't you just say? Instead of all this talk.'

'Say what?'

'Water. It's the water you want.'

'Yes. The water is important.'

'Water is power. I know that. You know that. Your PICA will know that. The Zionists will know that. The Arabs in the hills over there in Trans-Jordan know that. If you control this river, you control the Jordan River, you control all the lands to the south. You can turn the tap off and on at your will.'

'We just want to irrigate the fields.'

'Yes, it starts like this. Then you put in a little pipe. And then a bigger pipe. Then you build a little dam. Then a big dam. Until all this land here is covered in water. Then where will we go?'

'It will not be like that.'

Ibrahim slapped his thigh. 'Then forget about buying this land. You have my father's permission to come here, take as much water as you like. But no pipes. No dams.'

'Your father is not the *effendi*. He cannot give such permission.'

'But neither can you. It seems you do not know who the owner is. So my father is as good an owner as anyone else. He must have rights after all these years. The other tribes around here have rights.'

'Perhaps. But first, I need to make more enquiries. To find the legal owners.'

'And then what will you do?'

'PICA will try to purchase this land from them. And if we do, you can come here just as you always have.'

'You can write that down in your legal documents?'

'I will see what I can do.'

'You promise me that we can always come here?'

Lev looked closely at the man opposite, the eyes wide open in anticipation of his answer. He then looked beyond to Zayed, sitting quietly, smoking his pipe. He wondered at their lives, wandering across these vast lands with their families and flocks, knowing nothing of boundaries or laws of possession or title deeds, travelling where the seasons and the pastures took them. He and Zayed and Ibrahim. They were half-cousins, after all. Children of Abraham. 'I have no authority to make such a promise,' he said.

Ibrahim turned his body from one side to the other as if he were taking in a consideration of all the land around him. 'It is time for you to go,' he said.

Twelve

Lev sat at his desk, sifted through the letters he had brought back with him from the Jordan Valley until he found the one destined for Scotland. It was addressed to a Charlotte Maxwell in a script written by Celia's very own pen. It was a rather bold handwriting, not what he might expect from a female hand. But then again, Celia was a bold young woman. He could, if he wanted to, steam the letter open, read the contents, return it and re-seal the envelope. No-one would ever know it had been tampered with. He faced the window, held the letter up to the light as if the white of the Mediterranean glare might miraculously reveal its contents. That he might find his name written within in a favourable manner. After all, Celia was a single woman. He had found this out from Rafi, that she and Jonny were no longer a couple. Or 'had stopped sharing a tent together', as Rafi had put it, with a smirk that had embarrassed Lev. He turned his chair back to the room where Sammy was speaking his concerns out loud as he paced the red and blue dyed threads of the Persian carpet lying across the wooden floor.

'This should have been simple,' Sammy said. 'Simple, simple, simple. Are you listening?'

'Of course I am.'

'Well, put those letters down.' Sammy continued: 'That whole area. It's always been a bloody headache. What with Emir Abdullah over in Trans-Jordan, the French poking their nose in from Syria, the British with their mandate on the Palestine side. And now this? A piece of land that's not even on any map. With a family of Bedouin living on it.'

It was hot even though the window was open. The ceiling fan spun and rocked at full blast, ever-threatening to abandon its housing and decapitate the occupants of the room. Lev tried to cool himself by waving the letters under his chin, Sammy was a soaking mess of concern as he went on.

'And if Those Bloody Zionists find out, they'll be after it like a...' Unable to think of the appropriate metaphor, Sammy slapped his damp forehead. 'The Zionists must not find out about this. They must not find out. This will be PICA property... What was the name of our settlement there?'

'Kfar Ha'Emek.' Then in English, for no other reason than to impress his employer: 'Village of the valley.'

'*Kopvaitik tol*,' countered Sammy in Yiddish. 'Headache of the valley, more like it.' And he slapped his forehead again as if to confirm the fact. 'PICA must purchase this land immediately.'

'Not everyone in the settlement is behind the acquisition,' Lev thought he should point out. 'They've got Zionists there who only want to own as much land as they can work with Jewish labour.'

'Don't worry about the Zionists on Kfar Ha'Emek,' Sammy said, back to his pacing again. 'They're just the Little Zionists. The tiny, tiny, little ones.' He brought his thumb and finger close together in a pincer movement to illustrate his point. 'I'm worried about the Big Zionists here. The *ganze machers*. The big shots.' And then Sammy launched into his favourite well-honed rant. 'Those Zionists who think they are the successors to Theodore Herzl. Those who want the land as a foundation for a state. Those who say Palestine is a land without a people for a people without a land. Those who will plant a few Jews and a few trees on it and worry about all the details of housing, infrastructure and economy later. The Big Zionists aren't interested in the finer points of Jewish labour for Jewish land. They'll worry about that afterwards when they're drawing up the conditions for the new title deeds. Believe me, once they hear there's land available right up to that river, they'll be tripping over themselves to purchase it.'

'What about the Bedouin?'

'The Big Zionists won't care about a little detail like the Bedouin either,' Sammy said. 'They will assume they will just disappear. By sheer political will or as part of some Zionist miracle. Pouf! Just like that. That is why we have to stop them.'

'So who do we buy this land from? If it's not on any map.'

Sammy stopped his pacing, stroked his chin. 'This is what to do. I want you to go to Jerusalem. Pay a visit to the British. Take a quiet look at their maps, double-check whether they really don't know anything about this land.'

'Me? Are you sure?'

'It has to be you. If I approach them with some kind of inquiry, they might suspect something. But if it comes from you – a junior clerk – they'll probably think nothing of it. That it's some minor technicality that needs clearing up. It definitely has to be you.'

'When do you want me to go?' Lev asked, somewhat chastened by the term 'junior clerk'.

'As soon as possible. I want to sort out this mess before our important visitor arrives.'

'What important visitor?'

'The Anonymous Donor himself is coming.'

Lev wasn't sure what he thought about the British. Mickey, being from Manchester, was of course one of them. But his friend and co-tenant displayed none of the arrogance or right to rule the natives that the British civil administration possessed. If anything, Mickey sometimes behaved like a native himself, wrapping his head in a *kufiya* before going off to do his deals at the local Arab coffee house. What confused Lev was that he wasn't sure whether or not the British liked the Jews. After all, he had grown up thinking of the British as his enemy, a nation that had sided with Russia against Poland in a war that had killed two of his brothers. However, he was prepared to dismiss the Anglo-Russian alliance as a political one rather than an anti-Semitic one. But here in Palestine the situation was far more puzzling.

He knew it was the British who had come up with the Balfour Declaration, the document much cited by the Zionists as the basis for a Jewish homeland in Palestine. He also knew that the recently replaced Herbert Samuel, the first High Commissioner of British-mandate Palestine, had also been a Jew. He had even seen Samuel once when he came to Haifa to review the possibility of constructing the deep-water port that was now being built. The man arrived at the harbour dressed in a simple grey suit but with a white military pith helmet that made him stand out like a beacon of colonialism among his entourage. All Lev could think of was what kind of wonderful country this Britain must be that would allow this stiff-backed Jew with his neatly trimmed moustache to rise to such a high-ranking position in Imperial government. But even with all these pro-Jewish credentials, Lev still wasn't sure where that nation's true sympathies lay. Of course, the Arabs thought of the British as pro-Zionists because they were creating an infrastructure of roads and services designed to help Jewish industries and settlements. On the other hand, the Jews were convinced the British were pro-Arab, providing them with welfare services through the collection of Jewish taxes, dividing up Palestine so Emir Abdullah could walk away with Trans-Jordan, handing over huge tracts of land to the Bedouin. Lev once asked Sammy for his opinion.

'I don't even know why the British are here,' was Sammy's reply. 'Palestine is of no strategic interest to them. It stretches their resources. It isn't even a colony for them. Its inhabitants are not part of their Empire or their Commonwealth. It is an administrative nightmare with Zionists on one side and Arab nationalists on the other. I can only imagine they feel some spiritual gain from including the Holy Land within their protectorate. But whether they favour the Jew over the Arab? Or the Arab over the Jew? For the moment, I truly believe they are trying their hardest to favour neither. They make the same empty promise of statehood to either side. But I'm sure the time will come when Those Bloody Zionists will drive them to distraction.'

So in the end, Lev still didn't know what the British felt. All he knew was that whenever he had to approach a member of the civil administration in their offices in Jerusalem with their 'hello chaps' and 'jolly good fellows', he always felt more Jewish than ever. Which was how he felt now as he pushed open the door that bore the sign: *The Department of Land Registration of Palestine.*

The chief clerk of maps and surveys bounded out from behind his desk while Lev was still trying to get used to the light, or lack of it. Despite its large windows, the map room was a dim place, all natural sunlight being blocked by the closeness of a neighbouring building. Lev could make out the long tables with their slim, wide drawers underneath that no doubt housed the various maps. And then the earnest, pale face of a thin stick of a man, probably in his mid-thirties, introducing himself as Douglas Raynsford, and shaking his hand with all the enthusiasm of a castaway on some desert island meeting his rescuer for the first time.

'Ah yes, PICA,' Raynsford said, motioning for Lev to sit down at one of the map tables. 'We like PICA. We like PICA very much. We wish everyone was like PICA.'

'Why is that?'

'Because PICA is precise. PICA prepares. PICA submits the proper documents. PICA respects the process. PICA adheres to the rules and regulations as laid down by the Department of Land Registration of Palestine. PICA appreciates that topography is a serious business.'

Lev barely understood half of what Raynsford was saying, this was English at a far higher level than he was used to. But he appreciated nevertheless that his reception was a positive one. He nodded and the chief clerk went on.

'So, what is it you're after, Mr Sela? A map of this ancient and holy city with its population of zealots, thieves, beggars and prostitutes?'

'No, no. I wanted to check one of your other maps. The area of Palestine just south of the Sea of Galilee.'

'That is a very intriguing part of the world, Mr Sela. Very intriguing, indeed. It is where Palestine meets Trans-Jordan meets French Syria. Why would you like to see a map of that particular tangle of a triangle?'

'I completed the appropriate application form downstairs.'

'I'm sure you did. But you see, said application form has not yet arrived on my desk. So perhaps you could give me the reason for your application.'

'PICA bought some land for one of its settlements there a few years ago. I just wanted to make sure our understanding of the boundaries were the same as yours.'

'And why would they be any different, Mr Sela? If Sammy the King registered the deeds in the proper way, which I am sure he did, there is no reason to assume this Department's record of the facts would be different from PICA's.'

'As you said, it is a very complicated area. I would just like to see that our borders are precise.'

'Very well. It will only take a few moments. After all, Palestine is merely a small plot compared to other places where Douglas Raynsford has served. Uganda, for example. Or most recently Tanganyika.' Raynsford bent down to open one of the long map drawers. 'Do you know of Tanganyika, Mr Sela?'

'I don't even know where it is.'

'East Africa, Mr Sela. East Africa. It is a land of mountains, great lakes and a furious ocean. A land thirty times bigger than the one on which we are now situated, Mr Sela. Yet, paradoxically, it is here that I have witnessed the most disputes over land, its borders and its ownership. Can you believe that, Mr Sela? Can you believe that?'

'Yes, I can believe that.'

'Good. Now here are the two most recent maps I have of the area.' Raynsford placed the maps on the table, switched on a desk lamp. 'This first one is by the Palestinian Exploration Fund from the 1860s. And the second is a British one made up during the Great War.'

Lev looked from one to the other. They were exactly the same as the copies already in PICA's possession, the ones he had taken with him to show Rafi at Kfar Ha'Emek. He checked them anyway but there was no sign of Zayed's piece of land. The British really didn't know it existed.

'Have you satisfied yourself, Mr Sela?'

'Yes, I am satisfied. I was on a field trip to our settlement there a week ago. I just wanted to make sure what I saw on the ground was the same as on the maps.'

'I had no doubt it would be.'

'Good. I thank you for your time.'

Raynsford carefully placed a large brown envelope on the table alongside the maps. 'I thought you might like to inspect these also. They have just come into our possession.'

'What are they?'

'As we both know, this is a very sensitive part of the country. Very sensitive, Mr Sela. Very sensitive, indeed. Especially when we British handed over Trans-Jordan to the Emir a couple of years ago. So the Royal Air Force in Amman – Number Fourteen Squadron, I believe – were instructed to take some reconnaissance photographs. To make sure from the air that everything was hunky-dory on the ground. You may wish to peruse the results.'

Lev opened the envelope. There were twelve large aerial photographs of the area. It took him a while to arrange the proper sequence, lay them out in a four-by-three format on the table. He quickly located the southern tip of the Sea of Galilee, then further south to the Yarmuk River – and there it was… Photograph Number Eleven. Zayed's piece of land. Why shouldn't it be there? The maps might be inaccurate but the photographs wouldn't be. He made a show of comparing the aerial photographs to the actual maps, nodding studiously at their supposed similarity. He then very quickly gathered the photographs together, slipped them back into the envelope.

'Have you looked at these yourself, Mr Raynsford?'

'Just a cursory glance. As I said, these photographs were just received. I haven't even had a chance to index them properly. As you can see' – Raynsford nodded towards his desk where large stacks of maps, deeds and envelopes lay – 'there is much to be done. Now, in Uganda–'

'Well, these photographs were as expected. Please let me put them back for you.'

'That's kind of you, Mr Sela. As I said, it is always a pleasure to do business with PICA. Yes, just there. On top of that mountain of paperwork.'

Lev placed himself between the desk and his host. 'You were telling me about Uganda…?' he said as he slid the envelope into the very bottom of the pile.

The ancient buildings on either side were high, densely packed, closing inwards. Washing hung on lines, tarpaulins were draped across the lane against the rain, but still the sun managed to push its way through, picking out passers-by in beams of coloured light. The effect was biblical, Lev thought, like those auras surrounding Jesus in the paintings for sale in the Christian Quarter.

He sat outside Uncle Moustache's café in the Arab section of the Old City. There was no mistaking the owner, a big-bellied Egyptian with a magnificent drooping moustache. Lev had come here on Mickey's recommendation, for the café boasted the best fava bean stew in the whole of Jerusalem. Inside, men at tables played cards or clicked away with their dice and counters at *shesh-pesh*, others smoked water pipes. He was the only one to submit to the traffic in the lane. The packed mules, the '*Yalla, yalla*' of the barrow-boys, the constant bell-ringing of the bicycle riders half-on, half-off of their saddles, the flies, the dust, the smell of dung, the people pressing by, always in a hurry.

Mickey had been right about the stew, Lev's stomach was stretched full of it. He now sipped on his thick coffee – *hel* the Arabs called it, flavoured with cardamom, the taste of the spice drowning out any taste of coffee. The sweet, sticky pastry that came with it was delicious, coating his lips with honey and sugar. He felt calm in the middle of all this busy-ness. His job was done. He had a few minutes to sit down before his bus back to Haifa, to enjoy his accomplishment, to imagine the days if not weeks it would take Douglas Raynsford to reach the bottom of his stack of maps. He had bought a newspaper. He would now sit here quietly, reading about worldly matters. Like a man of the world.

Someone poked at his shoulder.

'Jew?' a voice said.

Lev looked up. A skinny, pallid youth stood before him dressed in the black medieval garb of the Orthodox. A seminary student. With his skullcap and sidelocks, his eyes squint from too much Talmudic study, thick black coat despite the heat.

'Jew?' the boy asked again.

'Yes,' Lev said wearily as he waited for the request for a donation to some seminary cause. Instead, a leaflet was pressed into his hand.

'What is this?'

The youth spat out the words in a stale breath: 'The Jews of the world must unite.'

'Unite against what?'

'This injustice against the Jewish people.'

'Everywhere there is injustice against the Jewish people. I can't fund every single one.'

'I don't want your money,' the student said with disgust. 'Read, go on, read. Read about the Wailing Wall.'

'I don't need to read on. I am not a religious man.'

'Pah! This is not about religion. This is an insult against our people. The tears of our nation have washed these stones for two thousand years. Two thousand years. The Wall must be restored to us. So that we can pray in peace.'

'If I want to pray in peace, I can do so in the quiet of my own room.'

'What kind of Jew are you?'

The question caught Lev off-guard. What kind of Jew was he? He looked up at the sickly youth. He certainly wasn't like this Jew in front of him, who must spend each second of God-given light crouched over in detailed examination of every letter of the Torah.

'Read it,' the student continued to insist.

But the youth's pleas had alerted the attention of Uncle Moustache, who waddled out to the front of his shop, barked at the student to move on. The youth ran off, one hand to his skullcap, his coat-tails flapping behind him, shouting, 'Jews of world unite.' The café owner swore, wiped his hands on his dish-towel, went back inside. Lev looked down at the leaflet. It bore the headline: *If You Wrong Us, Shall We Not Revenge?*

Thirteen

LEV HAD JUST BROUGHT his employer his customary eleven o'clock glass of black tea alongside a bowl of sugar. With head bowed, Sammy stirred in his usual helping of three cubes with his teaspoon. This tap-tap-tapping of metal on glass was the only sound in the room now the ceiling fan had finally given out, having relentlessly served not just PICA but decades of Ottoman administrators before it. On the hat-rack behind Sammy's desk hung the variety of headgear that made Sammy the stand-out character he was on the streets of Haifa. The panama hat (his head-covering of choice), a red velvet tarboosh, a khaki pith helmet, a *yarmulke* on the holiest of days, a *kufiya* on the hottest of days, and even a bowler hat on special occasions. Sammy would doff his headgear at whomever he happened to meet before spouting forth in his greeter's native tongue. It was this remarkable ability to speak Yiddish, Hebrew, Arabic, English, Russian and French that was so impressive. Sammy's body would also adapt to the language of the conversation – he would straighten up in English, swagger in Hebrew, bow slightly in Arabic, hunch slightly more in Yiddish, become agitated in French. The combination of language and hats also had its comic side. He could be a Yiddish speaker in a tarboosh, a skullcap-wearer chatting in Arabic, a Frenchman in a bowler. But it was without any hat that Sammy now raised his head, and said: 'You should have stolen it.'

'The envelope?'

'Just that one photograph.'

'And if Raynsford had caught me?'

'A slight embarrassment, that's all.'

'I would have been arrested. For theft. For treason.'

'Don't be ridiculous. A mere misdemeanour. The British would have made a formal complaint to PICA. I would apologize and promise to punish you appropriately for such destructive behaviour.'

'What destructive behaviour?'

'I would expect you to have destroyed the photograph before you were arrested.'

'I thought I showed enough initiative by hiding the envelope.'

'And for that you are to be congratulated. But Douglas Raynsford is a fastidious man. His suspicions were probably aroused by your enquiry alone.'

'If Raynsford was so fastidious, he would want to go through his pile in the order the files appeared to him.'

'Perhaps. Perhaps not. But these photographs have arisen at an awkward time. They provide documentary proof of the land's existence where previously there was none. We need to register the owner as quickly as possible.'

'But who is the owner?'

Sammy smiled, sipped on his tea. 'You tell me.'

'I don't know. I assume the British can claim it as part of their Mandate once they know it exists. Perhaps even the French in Syria for the same reason. Or Emir Abdullah in Trans-Jordan. Or some absentee Arab owner that we don't know anything about. The Bedouin have no lease, they pay no rent, they don't know who the owner is either.'

'So? What is the answer?' Tap-tap-tap. Sammy's teaspoon on the side of the glass insisted on a reply. 'Come on, Lev. If you want to be a good land agent, you need to find solutions.' Tap-tap-tap. 'What can we do here? What have I taught you?'

And then he had it. 'Of course. *Mewat.*'

'Exactly. *Mewat.*'

'The British don't like *Mewat.*'

'The British hate *Mewat.* But to hell with them. *Mewat* is the simplest solution. As long as these Bedouin are out of earshot from the nearest settlement then the land is *Mewat.* Dead land. This Zayed and his tribe? Have they actually cultivated the land, not just pitched their tents?'

'They have vegetable plots. They graze some livestock.'

'Excellent. Then *Mewat* allows them to register their ownership. I suggest we help them do just that. On condition they sell us back the part that is swampland. At a nominal price, of course, considering our efforts on their behalf. They will have title to their land, we will have access to the river. Everyone is happy. And Those Bloody Zionists won't know a damn thing about it.' Sammy raised his glass of tea in self-congratulation. 'What do you think?'

'I think you are a bloody genius.'

'Good. Because this bloody genius needs you to find out if the land is indeed out of earshot.'

'You want me to go back to Kfar Ha'Emek?'

'As soon as you can.'

Lev tried to hide his delight. 'I will send them a telegram immediately.'

'Do that. But say you are coming in a private capacity, nothing to do with PICA. The place is probably a hotbed of Zionist spies.' Sammy rose from his desk, put on his panama hat. 'And get someone to fix this damn fan.'

Lev skipped back through to his own office where he discovered to his annoyance that he had a visitor. The man was seated with his back to him, his dark hair greasy and long over his collar. There had been an attempt to buff up the shoes but Lev noticed the sole of one was split along the side of the upper. As he drew closer he could see the man's hands placed on each of his long thighs, stretching the too short sleeves of his suit even further up his arms. There was a genuine lack of hygiene about him too. It was not unusual for destitute Jews to turn up here. Sammy usually gave them a few coins, sent them on their way. Despite being funded by one of the richest men in the world, PICA's office in Haifa was a land agency not a charity.

Lev moved around to his desk. Before he had a chance to say anything, his visitor had jumped up from his seat.

'Lev,' the man cried out. 'Yes, Lev. It is you. I would recognize you in a thousand years.'

'Who are you?'

'Who am I? You don't recognize me? You don't recognize your own brother? Lev, it is me. Amshel.'

Lev looked at the tall, skeletal figure standing in front of him. The dark, sun-blasted skin of his bearded face. Or was it just ingrained dirt? The stained trousers tied up with a worn-out leather belt, the dirty vest where the shirt was open for want of a button. This man with his wound-up body dressed in a tight, ragged suit, his hands in a twisted clasp as if he were begging for his prayers to be answered. This was Amshel? He tried to remember how many years it had been. Twelve? Fifteen? Amshel, who showed him how to use a catapult. Amshel, who revealed to him all his secret hiding places in the woods. Amshel, who had wiped his bottom, tied his shoelaces, licked down his hair for lack of a mother to do the same. Amshel, who taught him how to read, who took him hunting, who could distil alcohol from a variety of vegetables. Amshel, who went down to the butcher for the Sabbath meat and never came back. Yes, this was Amshel. He stepped forward into his brother's stinking embrace. 'Amshel. What has happened to you?'

Amshel clung on to him. Lev could feel his brother's bones through the worn cloth, the spasms that caused the ribs to lift and fall. Lev realized his brother was crying, then he was crying too.

Amshel pulled away, sat back down. He rubbed the palm of one hand over and over again across his brow. 'I know, I know,' he kept on saying. 'I am a mess.'

'We need to get you cleaned up,' Lev said, kneading the tears from his own eyes. 'Cleaned up and fed. Then we can talk.'

Lev took Amshel back to Madame Blum's. She wasn't sure how to react to this beggar who had turned up at her door claiming to be Lev's brother. But her maternal instincts took over and she was soon ushering him into the shower room. She looked out a suit from her late husband's wardrobe as well as a clean shirt, socks, underwear, a pair of shoes. She then called Lev into the kitchen where she was now having to prepare her second breakfast of the day.

'I know he is your brother, Lev,' she said, holding up a knife smeared with cream cheese, 'but a few days, that is all. He can sleep on the floor in your room. I only want you and Mickey as my two lodgers in this house. You understand? Just you and Mickey. After a week, you must find him a hostel.'

Showered down and dressed in his new clothes, Amshel began to look something like the brother Lev remembered, but a reduced, thinner, less confident version. Lev watched him eat, how he tried to hold back from stuffing the food down his gullet even though he must have been terribly hungry. In between mouthfuls, Amshel would smile back at him through broken, blackened teeth, saying 'My little brother' before forking up another portion of scrambled egg. After he had eaten, Lev took Amshel to his room where he immediately stretched out on the bed, fell asleep. Many hours later, Lev had to make do with the floor, listening to his brother's heavy breathing as he tried to find his own sleep.

Fourteen

A HALF-MILE NORTH out of the town of Haifa, away from the market, the harbour and the olive oil factory, through clumps of skinny palms, a broad beach stretched along the curve of the bay, bordered by the smooth wind-sculpted slopes of the white dunes and the occasional tufts of tussock grass. It was here Lev took Amshel to talk. Lev walked barefoot, but Amshel kept his shoes on. The fact that Amshel's shoe size matched exactly that of Madame Blum's late husband augured well for the future of his brother's feet.

There was so much to say, to find out, to remember, it was difficult to know where to start. From the beginning, where his brother had walked out on their family? Those lost middle years? Or here at the end, as to how Amshel had managed to track him down?

'Who could have imagined this scene?' Amshel said. 'The two Gottleib brothers walking along the sand in the Mediterranean sunshine. Who could have imagined? In the Holy Land.' Amshel lifted his head back to the sky. 'All this sun and glorious warmth. What about the old winters? You remember them? When we had to hammer out the water from the barrels. When our piss would freeze mid-stream. When the snow reached past the rooftops.'

'We would go skating at the lake.' Lev recalled slipping and sliding hand-in-gloved-hand with Sarah, her cheeks red like a painted wooden doll, the smooth slice of the blade on the ice, the laughter, the mingling steam of their breath, these images frozen in time.

'And our old *zeide*. What happened to him?'

'He died about five years ago. A disease of the lungs.'

Amshel stopped walking. 'I am sorry to hear that. He was a wise man. A righteous man. I liked him a lot. And that woman he lived with in the woods? What was her name again?'

'Zelda.'

'Ah yes, Zelda.'

'Our brothers too.'

'What about our brothers?'

'They went off to war. They never came back.'

'What? Hershel and Baruch? Dead?'

'Yes, both dead. You abandoned us. They were killed. In the end, it was just Papa and me.'

Amshel looked down at his feet, at his newly inherited shoes. He ground the toe of one of them into the sand, then the heel. Lev watched him stand like this, rocking this one foot back and forward in a quiet meditation of grief and grinding sand. A light breeze arose, causing the palm branches to creak, stirring up the beach, billowing out their shirts. The smell of citrus in the air. Amshel sniffed hard, slapped Lev across the back. 'Come on. I'll race you to the top.'

Amshel was off first up the face of the dune but Lev was sure he could catch him. The headway wasn't too tough on the lower slope but as he climbed, his legs dug in deeper, dragging him down into the sand. He was surprised at how quickly he began to tire. He could hear the heavy wheeze of Amshel's breath up ahead but he still couldn't catch up with his older brother. Surely he would start to tire too, slowed down by the sand in his shoes if not by his poor health? Yet Lev had underestimated his brother's fitness. Amshel pulled away from him just as he always used to do, almost skipping up the higher slopes until he reached the top where he let out a loud whoop. Lev finally made it to the summit, Amshel grasped his shoulders, pulled him down on to a grassy clump.

'Still can't beat your old brother?'

'Get off,' Lev gasped. 'I let you win.'

His brother laughed. 'I doubt that.'

'I was feeling sorry for you.'

Amshel relaxed his grip, pushed himself to his feet. 'I've had some bad luck recently. That's all.' He pointed down to the shoreline. 'Hey, look at that.'

Stretched along the beach was a camel train, heading north. Ten of the beasts, each laden down with jute sacks draped over their single humps. Riding in between them were the Arab drivers, sitting sideways across their mules, tiny in comparison to their load-carrying counterparts.

'On their way to Acre,' Lev said, raising himself on to his elbows.

'Or Damascus.'

'Or Beirut. Or Persia.'

'Hey, we should wave to them.' And that's what Amshel did, got up on his feet, started flapping his arms about. And Lev remembered that was what he had always loved about his brother. That exuberance. It warmed him to think it had not disappeared.

'Let's slide back down,' Amshel urged.

'No. No. Sit down and tell me what happened.'

'Look. They're waving back.'

'Amshel. Why did you leave us?'

Amshel sat down, reached out for a piece of dried wood, started to dig deep grooves in the sand. 'I met a girl, Lev. I met her by chance, simple as that. By God's divine hand.' He drove the stick even deeper into the dune. 'I was driving the horse and wagon over to Rzeczyca, making a delivery of crates of vodka for Mr Borkowski. And there she was on the road with two of her friends. I gave them a ride. A simple deed. A simple deed that changed my life. Her name was Theresa. A beautiful girl. Dark and vital. As if she were sucking up all the energy of the earth through her toes. I fell in love with her, Lev. Who wouldn't? And the wonderful thing? She fell in love with me too.' Amshel looked up from his digging, his dark eyes clouded over with sadness. 'But what could we do? A Jewish boy and a Catholic girl.'

'You could have stayed.'

'Papa would have killed me if he had found out. Her father would have cut my balls off, fed them to their dogs. I had no choice. We had no choice, but to leave both our families. We travelled south to Wieliczka. I found work in the salt mines. We lived as husband and wife. These were the happiest days of my life, Lev. The happiest.'

'So what happened?'

'She died. Two years later. Typhoid fever. She was just twenty years old.' Amshel stopped talking, scraped a hand across his beard, a raspy, manly sound. *I should have lent him my razor*, Lev thought.

They both looked out to sea for a while. The camel train had gone, leaving just the waves to break along the broad shoreline. Amshel tore up some long grass with his stick, tossed away the clumps and continued: 'I stayed on at the mines. It suited me, working underground, away from the world. It is quite a beautiful place. Miles and miles of passageways of salt. So white. So quiet. It is like working in snow and ice. The miners have carved sculptures and friezes into the rock. There is even a cathedral. There is also a statue of Theresa. It took me three years to make. When it was finished, I left.'

'Why didn't you come home?'

'I didn't think Papa would still have me. So I came here. For a while, Palestine was good to me. The sun nourished my miner's pale skin, healed my salted wounds. I was strong, good with my hands, good with a pick and a spade. I found work easily. I built railroads, hammered metal, planted trees. And then I got sick. Fever, vomiting. Malaria probably. It became harder to keep a job. I ended up on a road gang. That's when I met Sarah.'

'Sarah?'

'Sarah from back home.'

Lev felt a sudden twinge grip his chest like the pain of an old wound. 'My Sarah?'

Amshel laughed. 'Yes, your Sarah. That pretty little girl you used to follow around. With your tongue hanging out like a lost wolf cub. How she made you do things for her. Run for this, Lev. Bring me that, Lev. Yes, yes, Sarah. Woof, woof, woof.'

'Enough,' he said, pushing his brother hard on the shoulder. 'Just tell me about her.'

Amshel sighed a long breath with a bout of coughing at the end of it. When he had recovered, he said: 'It was about three or four years ago. She was with one of those Zionist youth groups. Socialists building roads for the capitalists. What a joke. What idiots. I vaguely remembered some of them from our home town. But they were only children back then. Sarah, I remembered, because of you. They had plans to start a settlement, I don't know where. I only worked with them for a few days. Then I got sick again.'

'What was she like?'

'The same as most of them. Exhausted. Skinny. Disillusioned. Her hair was darker than I remember. Still pretty though. It was good to talk to her about home, about the people we knew.'

'Did she say anything about me?'

'She told me you abandoned the group as soon as they reached Palestine.'

'Was she still with Shaul?'

'I don't know any Shaul.'

'He was called Shimmel back then. Shimmel Feldman. The money-lender's son.'

'I don't remember her with anyone in particular.' Amshel turned over on to his back, closed his eyes, offered up his face to the sun. 'It's best you forget her. You know what it is like with these socialist groups. Everyone is sleeping with each other. Sharing a bed, sharing food, it's all the same to them.'

Lev pulled at some clumps of tussock grass. He didn't toss them though. Just made a little pile of dead weeds. A pyre to his dead love. Killed finally by the thought of her sleeping with all these different men. Not just Shaul but possibly others from his original *kvutza*. Ariel, Noam, Boaz, Doron? 'You knew I was here four years ago?'

'Yes.'

'And you didn't try to find me?'

'I didn't know you had changed your name. It wasn't easy to track you down.'

'So why now?'

'I'm sick of this place, Lev. It's a hard life. And I don't mean physically, although that as well. Everything is a struggle. With the Arabs, the Zionists, the British. Every day is like a fight. It tires me out inside. In my soul. I want to leave.'

'Is that what you want? Money to leave?'

Amshel turned to face him. 'Sarah told me Papa emigrated to America. Is that true?'

'Yes.'

'Do you know where he is?'

'I have heard nothing from him. He went to start a new life. With his new wife. Did you know he married again? Did Sarah tell you that? Do you care about any of us?'

'Calm down, Lev. Yes, she did tell me about the new wife. Do you know anyone who has his address?'

'You can't just turn up in America like before, Amshel. Immigration is tougher now. There are restrictions. You need papers. You need money.'

'Papa could sponsor me. He might be a millionaire by now.'

'Even if he was, why would he want to see you again?'

'Do you know anyone who has his address?'

'Borkowski at the liquor store. When *zeide* died, I got a letter from him. He had news of Papa then as well.'

'Good. That is very good. I will write to Borkowski. Can you help me do that?'

Lev nodded.

'I shall have to wait here for his reply.'

'You can't stay with me.'

'Why not?'

'Madame Blum won't allow it.'

'I could charm her into staying.'

'You would be wasting your time.'

'Lev, I am your only brother. I am family. I have nowhere to stay, no money, no job. It will take weeks for Borkowski to write back. You have to help me.' Amshel pushed himself to his feet then bent to take off his shoes. He poured the sand out of one, then the other. 'Well?'

'I know a place.'

'Where?'

'In the Jordan Valley. One of the new settlements.'

'A *kibbutz*?'

'Don't worry. You won't have to become a socialist. This place is desperate for help. You have the skills they need. I'm sure they'll take you on a temporary basis. I'm going there myself in a few days.'

Amshel tied his shoes together by the laces, slung them over his shoulder. 'It could be a plan.'

'It's a good plan.'

'As long as I don't have to sing the *Internationale*.'

'Only Yiddish folksongs.'

'Even worse.' Amshel held out his hand, pulled Lev to his feet. 'Can you lend me some money?'

'What for?'

'To drink to the health of the Gottleib brothers.'

Fifteen

Kfar Ha'Emek, Jordan Valley, Palestine

My dear Charlotte

It is now two weeks since I last wrote but I have not received any letters from you in between. I imagine you must be busy with all your temperance campaigns. I just hope you haven't got yourself into trouble. The idea of banning the sale of alcohol in parts of Glasgow is bound to raise tensions in the city. I know you are a brave and fearless young woman but you must be careful not to place yourself in danger. I worry for you. But, at the same time, I have so much admiration for you too. It is so important to bring an end to the desolation caused by drink. If I were back in Glasgow, you know I would be at your side.

I am well but very weary. You may recall in my last letter I mentioned the possibility of our little settlement acquiring land to give us access to a nearby river. Water, water, water – it never stops raining in Glasgow, yet here we crave the slightest drop. However, for some of us the idea of taking on more land is a horrible prospect. We just don't have enough workers or hours in the day to start thinking of draining more swampland, digging irrigation ditches and so on. We work so hard already just to survive, it is difficult for me to see how we can do more. My bones ache, the skin on my hands is as tough as old boots, I feel dried up inside and out. We need more help but new settlers do not come. They are not stupid, they know the conditions are harsh, they know there are probably better opportunities in the towns like Tel Aviv and Haifa.

I realize I paint a grim picture of life here. You are probably asking yourself – why doesn't she just pack her bags and come back to Scotland? After all, her relationship with Jonny was what took her there in the first place and now that is over. Well, Charlotte, these are excellent questions. I ask them of myself at least once in a day. But there are good times here as well. And when they come, they fill me up with such happiness and joy, I believe all the hardships are worth it.

Today was a good example. A group of us went out together to pick olives. We inherited a small grove here of about thirty ancient trees and some of the Bedouin from down in the valley came to help us. There was Zayed, who is the elder of the tribe, and some of his sons and grandchildren. He has so many wives and children I think some of his grandchildren are the same age as his youngest sons so it is difficult to work out who is who. I also believe I saw the handsome Arabian prince you asked me to find for you. His name is Ibrahim. However, I do not know if he is married. Even if he is, perhaps you could become one of his harem.

These Bedouin made fun of us because we chose to pick the olives by hand from off long ladders. Zayed said they just use sticks to beat the branches until all the olives fall off onto the ground. But one of our group – Benny is his name – who comes from Greece and claims to be an expert on olives (as if the Bedouin haven't been around olives for thousands of years), he says doing that damages the crop for the next year so better to pick by hand. All afternoon I am at the top of a ladder, drawing my grasp along each branch so the olives peel off and slide into my bucket. It is a bit like milking a cow. Not that you would know how that feels like, my dear city girl. At the end of the day, I am atop my ladder and I have a clear view across the valley to the mountains of Trans-Jordan and the sun is setting behind me, and there are all these rays of light spread out through some passing clouds. I can just make out a shepherd with his flock on the hillsides, the Bedouin tents in the valley. I can imagine this place as the land of my forefathers, Abraham, Isaac and Jacob. For a few moments, I feel there could be a God and I realize why this land is so important to so many. My heart stirs and all the tiredness drains away from me and I feel this deep joy within me and I realize that there is nowhere on this earth I would rather be. Until your handsome prince Ibrahim starts shaking my ladder and shouts up at me, laughing in a friendly way – 'Yalla, habibi' – 'come my friend'. 'Yalla, yalla.'

Such is my life on this settlement in the Jordan Valley. Please write soon – I long to hear from you.

All my love

Celia

PS: Do you remember I told you about the young man who came here to help with the land negotiations, the one who grabbed my hand? I received a telegram from him this morning, asking if he could come to visit. He gave instructions for the postal clerk to wait for my reply. My message was we don't accept visitors here, only those prepared to come and work for a few days without pay. How is that for a test of this young man's affections? I doubt I will hear from him again.

Sixteen

THE WINDOWS AND DOORS of the dining room lay wide open. Flies crowded the table-tops for the sticky spills and wedged crumbs of the recent meal. Rafi Melamud sat at the same seat where Lev had first met him. His bald head shone with moisture, the open neck of his blue work-shirt revealed sodden curls beneath. The man looked tired. It wasn't just the large pouches under his eyes, all the skin on his face appeared to sag with the weariness of a senile hound.

Lev guessed Rafi had once been an officer in some distant army, a man used to letting his subordinates wait for their orders. For Lev was being made to wait now. As was Amshel sitting beside him, flicking at flies, constantly shifting his position, hands in and out of his pockets. Standing opposite, next to Rafi, was Amos. Ferret-faced Amos wearing the same peaked worker's cap and arrogant look as he did at the *kibbutz* meeting where he had so vehemently opposed the proposed land acquisition. It was Amos, not Celia, who had arrived with the wagon at the al-Dalhamiyya train-stop, not to meet them, but to pick up another delivery of crates. It was Amos who had told them on the way back how much he hated PICA with its pen-pushing European financiers imposing capitalist values on pioneering socialists. Lev had asked him why he bothered working on a PICA-funded venture when he could move easily to a more communist-minded settlement. Amos had been affronted by the question: 'I have no intention of ending up as a victim of mass murder and torture,' he had replied bitterly.

Rafi tapped the fingers of one hand on the table-top, displacing a squadron of flies in the process. Lying in front of him, a pile of thirty-six cans of the best Norwegian sardines.

'Your gift...' Rafi said. 'Our members will be grateful.'

Lev accepted the gratitude with a dip of his head although it was Mickey who had helped. Lev had asked him if he could come up with a suitable token to take to the settlement. It emerged as a choice between these tins of sardines or sets of false teeth.

'You want to stay a couple of nights?' Rafi asked.

'As a visitor. Not in any professional capacity as a PICA representative.'

'You're happy to work?'

'Yes.'

'I'll be your sponsor then. Amos here will second you. Isn't that right, Amos?'

Amos nodded, stretched his lips into a condescending smile as if to say: *I might hate everything you and PICA stand for but I am generous enough to support you in this matter.*

Rafi went on. 'Good. I'll inform this evening's meeting as a formality. Tomorrow morning, five o'clock, I will have a hard day's work for you. As for your brother...'

Amshel pulled in his outstretched legs, wriggled upright. 'Yes, sir... comrade.'

Rafi smiled. 'You can build houses, comrade?'

'I can make you a palace for a king.'

'There are no kings here. We just need something simple for our children.'

'Whatever you want.'

'You will be on your own most of the time.'

'I can manage.'

'We can provide you with meals. But you will have to sleep where you work.'

'The sky shall be my roof,' Amshel said. 'Like Jacob, our forefather, with his pillow of stones.'

Rafi chuckled. 'Well, unlike Jacob, the children's house will need a roof.'

'Of course.'

'You will not be able to vote at our meetings,' Rafi said. 'Or even speak at them.'

'You are merely an unpaid guest worker,' Amos added. 'It is a concept I do not approve of...'

'...but we have to be practical too,' Rafi continued. 'We can give you two months on this basis. Can you finish within that time?'

'If it's not a king's palace you want then I don't see why not,' Amshel said.

'Good. I shall also notify this arrangement to this evening's meeting. Amos, I assume, will not second the proposal on a matter of principle. Isn't that right, Amos?'

'That is correct.'

'Amshel, I will therefore ask Celia to support the motion since she has met your brother.'

'I doubt Celia will be at the meeting,' Amos said. 'She is sick.'

The thick stench of disinfectant stung Lev's eyes as soon as he pulled aside the tent flap. He slid inside, closed up the doorway. Cracks of light stole through the tent seams, exposing a round interior partitioned off by ropes and blankets to create three separate cramped living spaces. Celia, or at least the prone figure he assumed must be Celia, lay on a cot under a mosquito net in one of them. The other two cots were empty. He took a couple of paces forward, placed the workclothes he had just picked out from the communal laundry on a vacant chair, then steadied himself with a grip on the centre pole.

'Who is it?' strained a weak voice from the cot.

'It's me. Lev.' And then, just in case she had no idea who he was: 'Lev from PICA. I sent a telegram...'

Celia raised herself up slightly, looked in his direction, then flopped back down on her pillow. He fumbled with the netting until he found the gap, crouched inside, sat down on the stool by her cot. Celia lay on her back wrapped tightly in a sheet from the waist down like some mythical fish-creature. Her upper body was dressed in a plain blouse translucent in patches where her moist skin soaked the cotton. Her hair was flattened damp to her skull, yet her lips were dry and split. The heat coming off her body was tangible. He felt his own forehead bristle with sweat.

'You came,' she said.

'Yes. I am here.'

After the meeting with Rafi, Lev had gone over to the hospital tent. There he had found Jonny, the doctor from Scotland, who told him there was nothing to worry about. A fever was just a fever. Most likely a mild form of dysentery. It was only if the temperature broke, then came back again a few hours later would there be a concern about malaria. She just had to rest, drink lots of fluids, Jonny would monitor her condition. No need to move her to the medical tent either. Let her recover in her own cot. She shouldn't be disturbed.

Lev decided to go see her anyway, to make sure she was drinking, to bathe her hot brow. Which he did now. He poured out some water from a jug into a cloth, she let out a slight moan from the coolness pressed on her forehead. He was disturbed to find himself aroused by the sound. He lifted away then dabbed the cloth lightly into the dryness of her mouth. Again she moaned. He pulled away, sat back on the stool.

'You have a fever.'

'I have malaria,' she insisted.

'Jonny said you have mild dysentery.'

'Jonny, Jonny, Jonny. Always looking after me.'

'That's what doctors do.'

'Even when I don't love him, he still looks after me. Did he tell you I broke his heart? I let him bring me all this way so full of hope for both of us. That we could have a life together here. And then...' Her voice drifted.

'You need to rest.'

'It is so hot in here. So hot. Water. I am so thirsty.'

He poured some water into a tin cup, brought his hand under her slippery neck, lifted her head to the rim until he could tip the liquid into her mouth. She coughed slightly to the first touch of the water against her throat, then gulped at it greedily. When she was finished, he let her head fall gently back against the sodden pillow.

'In Scotland, it isn't hot,' she said. 'Everything there is cold and wet and green. Jonny and I went picking blackberries once in Perthshire. It was a grand day. We met a gypsy woman who sold us a tin bucket and there was a man with a dancing bear. Can you believe that? A dancing bear. In the middle of Scotland…'

He leaned over, gently pressed her lips closed with the damp cloth. 'You should sleep,' he said.

'Why am I sick? I am never sick. Even in cold and wet Scotland. When the whole world was dying from Spanish influenza, I was fine.' She tried to raise herself from the pillow again but failed. 'I don't want to have malaria, Lev. I am scared.'

'Please. Try to rest.'

'This is what it must be like to die. To close your eyes so that the darkness swims in front of you and you fall deeper and deeper into it until you finally drift away. Will I know that I have died? Will I know?'

'You are not dying. You have a fever, that's all.'

'Take my hand. Here, hold it, talk to me. Please. Tell me about yourself. And I will listen. I am too tired to talk about bears and buckets…'

He felt her hot fingers grasp his own. He watched as she closed her eyes, as her lips twitched into a silence. He spoke quietly, telling her of his small town in Poland, how his mother had died not long after he was born, how he and his three brothers had been raised by his father. He spoke of his father as a sad man, bowed down by the early death of his wife, the hardship of bringing up a family on his own, the pain of never understanding why his eldest son had disappeared, then the tragedy of losing his next two sons in a war. He told her how his brother, Amshel, had suddenly returned into his life and that he was here now, sleeping under the stars, charged with building a house for the children she was yet to have. And even though she was now asleep, he told her about Sarah, how she also had asked him to come with her to Palestine. How she also had broken his heart. And he wondered whether Celia would do the same.

Seventeen

THE SUN WAS NOT YET UP when Lev rose from his cot, crept over to where Celia slept. Inside the blackness of the tent, it took him a while to find his way through the mosquito net, then he followed the sound of her laboured breathing to the top of the cot. He laid the back of his hand on her still-hot brow, convinced himself her temperature was down on the day before. He made sure there was enough water left in the jug, then moved back out of the netting, to dress quickly into his workclothes. A chorus of screaming cicadas accompanied his short walk over to the dining room, the occasional scent of frangipani in the dew. Rafi was there already, as was Jonny, Amos and a short, fair-haired muscleman Lev knew as Barak. They were all clustered around the one table, warming their hands on glasses of coffee.

'Our final member has arrived,' Rafi said. 'From where, we can only guess.'

Lev flushed at the comment but it appeared to go unnoticed by the others. He poured himself a coffee from a pitcher at centre-table, sat down. He looked around for milk, saw none, decided not to ask.

'I was telling the others about the truck,' Rafi informed him. 'It arrived last night.'

'What truck is that?'

'From Iraq. It came in with our young date palms.'

'How many?' Amos asked.

'Eighteen off-shoots.'

'That's more than we expected.'

Rafi went on: 'I thought we'd put six of them in a nursery for a few weeks until more roots are formed. We'll take our chances with the rest and put them straight in the ground.'

'What did the Iraqi suggest?' Barak asked.

'Nothing. He's just the middle-man.'

'We should have grown them from seeds,' Amos grumbled.

'It takes too long,' Rafi countered. 'It would be ten years before they gave fruit. This way we'll be eating sweet dates within four.' Then to Barak: 'Go hitch up a wagon. Bring it round to where the truck unloaded.'

The plants were about five feet tall, each weighing about sixty pounds and boasting a cluster of strong, spiky leaves bagged into a tied-up jute sack by the Iraqi seller. It was a tricky job to load the first batch of six onto the wagon. Lev found himself paired with Jonny, the two of them grappling clumsily with the weight and awkward shape of the young trees in order to slide them on board. Barak and Jonny then drove the wagonload out to the planting site before going off to hook up the horses to the water-truck. Lev walked out to the site with Rafi and Amos, a shovel over his shoulder, his clothes wet and muddy, his back already aching from his endeavours.

Rafi wanted the young trees planted either side of a rough track leading from the perimeter gateway into the settlement so that in a few years the entrance way would be marked by a grand avenue of palms. 'Like a French boulevard,' he said, although no-one had ever seen one of these tree-lined Parisian streets before. Two holes had already been dug – about three feet wide, the same measure deep.

Working with knives and wearing heavy work gloves, the three of them stripped the spikes off the branches of the young trees, careful to avoid the poisonous tips. Once Barak and Jonny had returned with the water-truck – essentially a couple of wooden barrels tied horizontally to a wagon bed – the next task was to fill up the holes with water.

'Ground's too dry,' Amos said. 'It'll just soak everything up.'

'Then we'll just have to keep pouring,' Rafi said, motioning for the rest of them to pick up buckets.

They filled up from one of the barrel taps, poured the water into the first hole. Amos was right. They ended up using half a barrel just to reach half way.

'Now unload an offshoot,' Rafi commanded.

Lev positioned one of the plants on the wagon for Barak and Amos to take and place in the muddy hole. Jonny and Rafi then took over, shovelling in earth to fill in the gaps. When the tree was properly embedded, the area around it was soaked with some more water. The process was repeated for another offshoot in the second hole. It was only then they stopped working. With cupped hands, they drank water from the barrels, sat down against the wagon. Lev closed his eyes. He was exhausted and there were still four more trees to plant from this batch alone.

'I'm worried about the water,' Amos said. 'We can't keep using our supplies like this.'

'I agree,' Rafi said in an unusual consensus with his comrade. 'We'll take from the river next time.'

'We can't do that,' Barak said.

'Who's to stop us?'

'Zayed won't like it,' Amos insisted.

'So what?' Rafi said. 'We don't even know who owns that land anymore. Soon it will be PICA land, then our land. Isn't that right, Lev?'

It had been a quick stop at the dining room to pick up a couple of fresh-baked loaves and a clutch of boiled eggs, while Jonny went quickly to check on Celia. Then it was off down to the river. It was just three of them, Rafi and Amos staying behind to argue and to dig more holes. Lev clung on to one of the barrels at the back while Jonny sat beside Barak up front. The wagon jumped all over the place but Barak didn't seem to care, happy to whip away at the horses, let the wheels tip off the ground on the bends as they raced to the Centre of the World, then down a twisting track into the valley. Lev wasn't happy about the situation, thinking this was not the right time to start irritating Zayed and his tribe, but there wasn't a lot he could do about it. Amos and Barak had already protested, but Rafi seemed to always get his way. He was glad at least to see they crossed Zayed's land as far away from the tents as possible without driving the wagon into the swamps. He looked back towards the encampment where he could make out various figures and livestock but no-one on horse-back. Perhaps Zayed and his sons were out hunting with the saluki. Barak pulled up the wagon level with the riverbank. Lev stood up, unscrewed the tops off the two barrels, the others jumped down with the buckets.

They worked in a line. Barak, now stripped to the waist, scooped the water out of the river, handed back to Jonny, who twisted round, held up the bucket-load for Lev to take and pour into one of the barrels. Lev then threw the empty bucket onto a bed of reeds close to Barak and the process continued. Once they had found a rhythm, Lev started to enjoy the work. The task was hard but shared equally it went quickly. After one barrel was filled, they took a break. Lev sat on the wagon seat, Jonny leaned against a wheel and smoked, Barak lay on his back on the ground a few yards away, his feet soaking in the river. The sun was high in the sky now, bleaching the valley into a dried-up stillness. It was strangely quiet, the only movement being a twist of smoke rising from a single fire over at the Bedouin camp. As he looked around at his co-workers Lev felt they could be figures in a painted landscape rather than in a real one. He glanced at his trench watch. Just after eleven o'clock. Almost six straight hours of work with hardly a break or a bite to eat in between.

'You visited Celia.' Jonny spoke into the distance without a turn to look up at him.

'I went to see her last night.'

'I told you to let her rest.'

'I just gave her some water. She slept most of the time.'

'Doctor's orders. Do not disturb.'

Lev stayed quiet. Jonny kicked out at one of the buckets. They both watched it roll down to the river until Barak put out a hand to stop it.

'I'll give you a piece of advice,' Jonny said.

'What's that?'

'Don't build up your hopes.'

Lev wasn't sure how he was supposed to respond but his attention was distracted anyway by a dust-cloud across the river. At first, he thought it might be the wind blowing up a minor sandstorm over on the Trans-Jordan side. But as his eyes strained to see what was happening, he saw four figures emerge on horseback from the centre of the cloud. 'Someone's coming,' he shouted.

'Zayed?' Jonny asked.

'No. On the other side. Arab horsemen.'

Both Barak and Jonny were up quick on their feet, eyes fixed on the horizon.

'It could be nothing,' Jonny said.

'Or it could be trouble,' added Barak. 'They've got rifles.'

'What do we do?' Lev asked.

'We're not on their side of the river,' Barak said. 'We're not doing anything wrong.'

'Apart from stealing their water,' Jonny said.

The horsemen reached the opposite riverbank, pulled up their breathless steeds. The beasts strained at their reins, half-circled, pawed at the dust as they settled. Sat up by the barrels, Lev noticed the two wagon-horses snort and shiver in their harness in some kind of equine response.

'Ha!' one of the riders called out. As with the others in his group, his head and the lower part of his face was covered by his *kufiya*. His rifle remained in a strap across his back. 'Ha!' the man called again.

Barak stood with his legs apart, hands on hips, bare chest stuck out towards his adversaries.

'Stop it, Barak,' Jonny said. 'Come on. Start packing up. Slowly. No sudden movements.'

Lev continued to watch the men as he screwed the tops back onto the barrels, collected the buckets from Jonny and Barak. The horsemen talked quietly among themselves, then split into two groups, rode off at a gallop in opposite directions along the bank.

'What are they doing now?' Lev asked.

'As long as they keep their rifles on their backs,' Jonny said, 'I don't care.'

'They're just showing off,' Barak muttered, as he handed Lev another bucket.

After about a hundred yards, both sets of horsemen turned, then raced back to the centre where these faceless riders re-grouped, then sat calmly in their saddles, staring across the river. Lev eased himself onto the wagon seat, Barak was up beside him, slowly gathering the reins. Jonny meanwhile had tucked himself in beside the barrels.

'Go, Barak,' Jonny shouted. 'Get the hell out of here.'

Barak stood up quickly, punched the air with one hand, shook the reins with the other, and the wagon moved off and away. Lev looked back over his shoulder. The Arabs had moved closer to the bank, the heads of their horses drooped to drink from the river.

'What was that all about?' he asked, once they were a safe distance.

'Probably Emir Abdullah's men staking out their claim,' Jonny said.

'Bah!' Barak said. 'Nobody's disputing their claim to the east side of the river.'

'It's not just the land, Barak. It's the water too.'

'I thought they were going to shoot us,' Lev said.

'We should have guns,' snapped Barak. 'How the hell can we live here without guns?'

Eighteen

LEV KICKED AT Amshel's feet.

'What?'

'Time to get up.'

Amshel had been fast asleep, sprawled out against the trunk of an olive tree. A few yards away were the pegs and string set out to mark the foundations of the children's house.

Amshel spoke without opening his eyes. 'Go to hell.'

'I need your help.'

'It's the middle of the day. I'm asleep. Everyone's asleep.'

'That's why we have to do this now.'

Amshel slapped at his cheeks, then looked up. 'Water.'

Lev tossed the canteen, which Amshel caught in one hand, uncorked with his teeth, then drank heavily. 'What do you want?'

'I'll tell you when we get there.'

Amshel held out his hand. Lev took it, hauled his brother to his feet. Amshel was stripped down to a grey vest and a pair of long shorts held up by his own braces. His work-shirt was tied around his head like a turban. His skin had gone even darker from the sun. Unlike Lev, who was sunburnt and blistered.

'You look like death,' Amshel said.

'It's been a long day.' In the end, they'd managed to plant nine date palms. What with that and the fear of being shot at, he was exhausted. All he wanted to do was go to sleep himself. 'Come on.'

'Where are we going?'

'I'll explain later.'

Amshel tripped along beside him like some persistent beggar.

'Where did you sleep last night?'

'I found an empty cot.'

'Are you sure it was empty?'

'I promise you.'

'Who is this Celia then?'

Lev stopped abruptly. Amshel almost bumped into him.

'Someone I like,' Lev said.

'I'm happy for you.'

'I don't want you to be happy for me. I want you to keep away from her.'

Amshel held out his arms. 'Trust me.'

Lev looked at his brother. Life might have been tough on him, thinned out his features, dabbed his hair with edges of grey, messed about with his teeth, but he was still a good-looking man. 'I hope so.'

'Now, can you tell me where we are going?'

He took Amshel out to the Centre of the World. It was only about a mile down the track but the heat of the sun was relentless, and what little water they had taken with them was gone by the time they got there. A clump of young eucalyptus trees offered some meagre shade. Amshel sat down by one of them. Lev remained standing.

'What are you up to?' Amshel asked as he picked away at the white bark.

'I can't tell you.'

'PICA business?'

'It doesn't really concern you.'

'If it doesn't concern me, what am I doing here?'

'I need an independent witness.'

'What do you want me to do?'

'I'm going to walk down that track over there. After a while, I'll signal to you. Like this.' He held up his handkerchief, waved his arm in a twisting motion.

Amshel sniffed. 'Then what?'

'I want you to start calling out my name. As long as I can still hear you, I'll make the signal. Then I'll keep walking and you'll keep shouting. And when I can no longer hear you, I'll cross my arms above my head. Like this.'

'I still don't understand.'

'You don't need to understand. Just do what I've told you.'

'And when you can no longer hear me?'

'You can go back to sleep.'

Lev set off briskly along the track on its serpentine descent towards the Bedouin encampment. The sun was so hot now he could actually feel it blistering his scalp, scalding his already cracked lips, burning up his brain, making him dizzy. He held up his handkerchief. Amshel called out twice to him. He kept on walking, repeating the process, until he could no longer hear his name. He twirled the handkerchief in the air again just to make sure. Nothing. He crossed his arms above his head, scraped around in the dirt for some stones to mark the spot. Any land further on from here was *Mewat*. Dead land according to the ancient laws. He kept on walking. As expected, his exploits had caused alarm at the encampment. Two horsemen were now riding out to meet him. He recognized both of them. Zayed and Ibrahim.

'*Assalaamu aleikum*,' Lev said.

Zayed stayed back while his son approached. '*Wa-Aleikum Assalaam*,' Ibrahim said.

'Do you remember me?'

Ibrahim nodded. 'What do you want?'

'I want to talk again about your land.'

'There is no more to say.'

'The situation has changed. Let me speak.'

Ibrahim turned to his father, who dipped his head.

'Say what you need to say,' Ibrahim said.

'There is a way we both can have what we want.'

This time it was Zayed who spoke. 'You promise we can still come and go as we please?'

'There are legal matters to settle. But yes, I can promise.'

'Forget about the legal matters,' Ibrahim said. 'How much will you pay?'

They began to clap as Lev entered the *kibbutz* dining room. It started slowly, then gradually the noise built so that cutlery was tapped against cups and plates, palms slapped on the table-tops, until the whole performance soared into raucousness. And then everyone was singing '*Lai, lai, lai, lai, lai, mazel tov*' as if he were a groom entering his own wedding reception. He had no idea what was going on. His first thought was that he might be hallucinating. He was exhausted, battered by the heat all day and had just drunk two glasses of *arak* down in the Bedouin camp. Then he feared it might be something to do with the negotiations with Zayed and Ibrahim. But how would anyone know about that? And then he realized that what had started as a simple gesture of appreciation had quickly escalated into one of irony among the members, mocking themselves for the fact they could be so hopelessly grateful for a simple gift.

Lev looked around among the hot, laughing faces until he was able to locate his brother.

'The great hero…' Amshel said. 'Comrade Lev and his tins of sardines.'

'I'm glad I didn't take Mickey's offer of the false teeth.'

'I'm glad I did,' Amshel said, pointing to his mouth. 'Once I'm in America, I'll have these rotting beauties taken out.' He pushed a plate of food at him. 'Now eat.'

Lev forked up a portion of sardines. They really were tasty.

'How was your afternoon with the Bedouin?' Amshel asked.

'I can't discuss it.'

'I've heard people talking here. I know it's about their land in the valley.'

'Perhaps.'

'Just take it. That's the only way you'll get on in Palestine. Forget about all this shouting and handkerchief waving. Take what you can get, Lev. Snatch it up. Because nobody's going to give you anything.'

'That's not PICA's policy.'

'To hell with PICA. I don't know why you listen to that Sammy.'

'Sammy is a decent man. He looks out for the *fellaheen*. He's looked out for me ever since I came here.'

'Well, good for Sammy. Clap your hands together for Sammy. And give him your undying loyalty.'

'It's not just loyalty. I agree with him.'

'Listen, Lev. You always were the good son. Looking after Papa...'

'I was the only one left—'

'And now you're looking after the Bedouin. Making nice little property deals, trying to satisfy everyone. Well, that way of thinking doesn't work here. You need to be tough. You need to be more like the Zionists.'

'And be... what?'

'Realistic. We're never going to get on with the Arabs in one big happy family.'

'You should know all about that.'

'What do you mean?'

'Making a mess of families.'

'What?' Amshel was all riled up now, his dark eyes flashing, his throat flushed. 'I'll tell you something,' he said. 'My life was miserable back then. In that stinking hellhole of a village with that drunken bastard for a father. It wasn't a difficult decision to make. To get the hell out of there. You can't blame me for that.'

Lev remembered this was how Amshel could be. These explosions of anger, then the sudden calming once the damage had been done. He was just about to get up from the table when a hand pushed him down.

'I know you're here in a private capacity,' Rafi said. 'But I thought you might like to meet this gentleman.' Lev looked up at the stocky, cream-suited figure standing next to Rafi. Square face with a dark shock of hair, small moustache, round glasses, expression etched into a fierce scowl. 'Lev. This is Gregory Sverdlov.'

Sverdlov bowed his head slightly. 'You work with Sammy?'

'I do.'

'Gregory is an engineer,' Rafi said.

'From Russia,' Sverdlov added.

'He is on a survey mission of the region.'

'Surveying what?' Lev asked.

Sverdlov looked vaguely around the room as if he had already lost interest in the conversation. 'Different sites. For different potential projects.'

'Such as?'

'If I am more specific, the price of land would double – no, treble – overnight.'

'Then what is there to talk about?'

'I heard your Anonymous Donor is due to visit Palestine.'

'There is a rumour.'

'You cannot say for definite?'

'If I were to tell you, the price of land might treble overnight.'

Sverdlov laughed, turned to Rafi. 'Ah so, we have a smart one here.' Then the laughter stopped, and Sverdlov's gaze was back on Lev. 'You tell Sammy that Gregory Sverdlov has a very interesting proposition to make to his employer if he should happen to sail into port in the next week or so. A proposition that will benefit not only the entire population of Palestine, but also your Anonymous Donor's own commercial interests. I, of course, will make my own approaches. But any mention of Gregory Sverdlov's name in PICA's circles can only be of mutual benefit.'

Nineteen

Kfar Ha'Emek, Jordan Valley, Palestine

My dear Charlotte

It was so good to receive a letter from you this morning. I kept it unopened all day until I had some free time and then I walked down to our small cemetery to read it. Yes, we have already lost two dear souls in our little settlement. Before I came, a young man was killed when a paraffin lamp spilled over and set his tent on fire. Only last year, a baby was stillborn. They have a beautiful resting place here overlooking the valley. There is a bench where I can sit and contemplate (and read letters), young eucalyptus trees that will grow to provide shade. In the spring, you can see wild lupins here and anemones. Lavender and sage. Also, some plants I only know the names of now in Hebrew, for we never see them in Scotland.

I so enjoyed hearing about your holiday in Rothesay with Maggie and Big Bessie. I remember when we made the same trip ourselves, just the two of us, going down the Clyde in the paddle steamer from Glasgow. We took the temperance boat, of course. No drunken singing and vomiting on our vessel, or fighting couples on the way back home. We stood on the deck up against the railings, gazing out through the mist in wonder at the giant ships in their docks, as we sailed out passed Greenock and Dunoon, the sailors unloading the crates and milk churns at the pier as we got off the boat. It was so busy. It must have been the Glasgow holidays. We had to share a room and a double bed with two strangers. I even remember their names, Eileen and Lizzie. One of them snored and the other wore a nightgown with cigarette burns all over it, I can't remember which one was which. It rained the whole time except for the one day we could walk along the esplanade without our umbrellas. Everyone and their grannies must have been out that day. I don't know what was worse, the crowds or the rain. We could hardly move or eat our ice creams for want of someone jostling our arms. And then there were these two young lads from Edinburgh having a lark with us, making us laugh at their stupid jokes. Do you remember them? I can't remember laughing so much in my whole life. I hardly laugh at all now.

I would love a holiday, even if it were two weeks of rain down in Rothesay! We pray for it to rain here. It is strange how our needs are so opposite in these different parts of the world. I was sick for a few days with a very high fever and stomach cramps. I am all right now but I feared it was malaria. The thought of getting that disease terrifies me, never getting rid of it, always suffering the return of its fits and fevers.

Do you remember that young man I told you about? Lev. The one who said he might come to visit. Well, he did come. Along with his brother, who is going to build us a children's house. They came when I was sick. I wonder what Lev thought of me, this sweaty young woman smelling of vomit and antiseptic? He was kind to me. He held this poor patient's hand and told me his life story when he thought I wasn't listening. He has now invited me to visit him in Haifa. I may go. One of the members here has a relative with a house in Haifa so I have a place to stay. As I said, I would love a holiday even if it were only for a day or so. Just to see the sea. To breathe in the salty air. To feel the sand between my toes.

I saw your Arabian prince today. Or I thought I saw him. When I was sitting reading your letter, looking down at the valley, I could see the Bedouin camp. I saw two horsemen riding out with their hounds. The dogs are called salukis. They are like magnificent greyhounds, not bare and skinny like those we might see running around the streets of Glasgow. They have this long hair on their limbs and faces that flows back when they run. Anyway, I am sure one of these horsemen was your prince. He is such an elegant rider and really does sit perched on his mount like royalty. Of course, I cannot ride well although you would be surprised to learn that I am quite good with a horse and wagon these days. But you, Charlotte, with that fancy upbringing of yours, I remember you grew up with horses. I can imagine you and this handsome Arabian prince riding out together into the desert with your two salukis running alongside. I told you before that his name is Ibrahim. I still don't know if he has any wives. Perhaps he is waiting for you.

I must finish this letter now if it is to make today's post truck. I must also go to the kitchen to help prepare the evening meal. I am sure you are also busy with your campaigning. If you keep getting women to sign up their husbands on these temperance pledges, the divorce courts will soon have to shut down.

I apologize for such a brief letter but I promise to write more soon.

All my love, as always

Celia

Twenty

ALONG WITH HER COMPLAINTS, Madame Blum served up a Polish breakfast. Eggs (soft-boiled or scrambled) accompanied by copious amounts of bread as beds for the white cheese, slices of *vursht*, honey and various jams laid out across the table. There was no place for the bitter green olives of the region, the yoghurt cheese dripped with oil, the warm flat bread, the tomatoes and the cucumbers. When Lev first arrived in Haifa, he had appreciated Madame Blum's steadfast refusal to adopt the local fare, for her meals reminded him of home. But after over five years of Madame Blum's Eastern European cuisine, he would have preferred the lighter breakfast, the one that sat easier on his stomach during these hot, hot days. Although that still did not prevent him from calling out 'Scrambled' to Madame Blum's question from the kitchen. A response Lev knew would cause Mickey to look up from his copy of the *Ha'aretz* newspaper purchased solely for the English language supplement of the *Herald Tribune*.

'Scrambled?' Mickey said. 'Scrambled? Every morning for, I don't know how many years, you have said: "soft boiled". And now you say: "scrambled"?'

A perplexed-looking Madame Blum emerged from the kitchen to confirm the request had indeed come from her Polish rather than her English lodger.

'Yes, Madame Blum, you are right to be confused,' Mickey continued. 'Lev is having scrambled eggs.'

'What's wrong with that?' Lev protested.

'Nothing, nothing at all,' Madame Blum muttered in a retreat to the kitchen. 'A man has a right to choose whatever he wants. Even if it means choosing a worthless young harlot over a wife who gave him years of devotion. Otherwise I would not ask. But I may have to go out for more eggs.'

'It's all right,' Lev called out. 'Just the one soft-boiled. I was only joking.'

'*Gott sei dank*,' was the murmured response from the kitchen.

'Your trip north has certainly improved your humour,' Mickey said.

'It was productive.'

'What's that supposed to mean?'

'My PICA business went well. And I planted some date trees.'

'I'm sure PICA and palms weren't responsible for your present cheerful disposition.'

'Go back to your newspaper.'

'News of your romantic endeavours is far more important than an article on Tutankhamun's inner tombs.'

'There is nothing to tell.'

'Are you saying your second visit to this den of collective lust has not produced the desired result?'

'Kfar Ha'Emek is not a den of collective lust. It's a proper *kibbutz*.'

'Aha! Now I see what has happened here. Now I see. Not only has some Jezebel captured your heart. You have been corrupted by the socialist dream. Soon you'll be marching out to the fields to plant trees with your comrades, a spade over your shoulder, singing the *Internationale*.'

Lev stayed quiet.

Mickey put down his paper, nodded thoughtfully, assumed a more serious expression. 'Tell me something then, about this proper *kibbutz* of yours. Is it a border settlement?'

'It's close to Trans-Jordan.'

'And are the neighbours friendly?'

'Not really.'

'What about security?'

'Nothing much from what I could see.'

'Did the members carry out guard duty?'

'Not in any formal way.'

'Dogs?'

'A few strays picked up as pets.'

'Revolvers? Rifles?'

Lev shook his head.

'Are you sure? Nothing to defend themselves with? No guns?'

'No guns.'

'I don't want any talk about guns in this house,' Madame Blum warned, as she entered with a plate of cold meats, which she placed centre-table. Lev noticed the brushing of her ample cleavage against Mickey's cheek as she did so.

'Lev has decided to live on a *kibbutz*,' Mickey said.

'Don't be ridiculous. Why would he do that?'

'He has fallen in love with a young woman of the Revolution.'

'Oh, Lev. Is that true?'

'Of course it is true,' said Mickey. 'Can't you see from the colour of his cheeks?'

'Finally, Lev, you have found someone.'

'Nothing has happened, Madame Blum. I am staying here in Haifa with you. Mickey is only joking.'

'What's with all this joking this morning? This is no time for joking.'

'Why is that?' Lev asked.

'You weren't here yesterday. When the terrible thing happened.'

'What terrible thing?'

Madame Blum wriggled herself up to her full height, stroked the base of her throat, now flushed with what Lev assumed was her indignation. 'Well,' she said. 'I walked into town early to Koestler's Bakery. Just as I do every morning and have done for all the many years I have been here. To fetch the bread for breakfast. They do such a fine rye with caraway seeds, the taste always reminds me of home. And just as I was coming out of the shop, this man he spat at me. Just like that. Right at my feet. Isn't that true, Mickey?'

'I don't know, Madame Blum. I wasn't there.'

'Whether you were there or not, you could still back me up.'

'All right, I am sure it happened just as you said.'

Madame Blum scowled back at him. 'Just as I said.'

'Are you sure he was spitting at you?' Lev asked. 'Perhaps he was just clearing his throat at the very moment you came out of the bakery.'

'Of course he was spitting at me,' Madame Blum shrilled. 'Because he said the word "Jew" after he spat at me. "Jew, Jew, Jew." As if he were talking to a dog.'

'What kind of man was he?'

'A young Arab. Perhaps in his twenties. Spitting at me. A respectable widow. It is a disgrace.'

'There is a lot more tension here,' Mickey said. 'I can feel it myself.'

'Tension?' Lev said. 'In Jerusalem. But surely not here in Haifa?'

'What do you know, Lev? You keep to yourself. You only work with Jews. But in the coffee houses, the Arabs are talking.'

'What are they saying?'

'Too many Jews. That's what they're saying. Too many Jews. Poland's taxing them out of business. And America's toughened up on immigration. So they're coming here in their thousands.'

'I think you're wrong,' Lev said. 'We're not seeing any more land applications than usual.'

'These new Jews aren't interested in farming. They're not pioneers. They're not socialists. They're opportunists. They start off with a soda stand in Tel Aviv. Then a small business. A cobblers, maybe. A café. Or a bakery. And the next minute they're building hotels and factories. With jobs for their own Jewish workers. Soon they'll be moving into Haifa too. The Arabs feel it. They feel they're being hemmed in or pushed out. Fifty thousand Jews arrived here in the last two years. It could be Jaffa all over again.'

Lev remembered the Jaffa riots. They had happened not long after he had arrived in Palestine. Forty-seven Jews killed, a similar amount of Arabs. He couldn't even recall the actual incident that caused the flare-up but the overall reason was the same as what Mickey was talking about now. Arab fears over increased Jewish immigration. The fighting then hadn't spread from Jaffa as far north as Haifa but the British had sent in a warship just in case. He remembered watching the grey destroyer with its twin guns fore and aft trained on the harbour. He wasn't sure if it was there to defend or attack him.

'That's the way it goes here,' Mickey said. 'More Jews come in, the Arabs riot in protest, the British introduce quotas, the Zionists pressure the government in London and the quotas are lifted. Then it starts all over again. Soon it will be time for the riots again.'

'I don't know why these Jews want to come here in the first place,' Madame Blum exclaimed. 'Nothing works. The electricity is off and on. The water is off and on. A person could suffocate to death in the heat. I never understood why that adulterer of a husband, may his soul rest in peace, brought me here. To a place where they spit at a widow in the street. Why would a Jew come here?'

On his way to work that morning, Lev thought about what Mickey had said. Were there really tensions here? Were those knives being sharpened on that grinding wheel meant for Jewish hearts? What kind of plot was being conjured up by those old men sitting outside the coffee house? Was that joyful or mocking laughter he heard behind his back? What was inside the basket that woman carried on her head? A revolver for the Arab nationalist movement? He had almost forgotten those old feelings of fear he had been brought up with. The Catholic farmboys chasing him home from the forest, the pig-like snorting that followed his walks through the town, his father's hushed talk about pogroms in Russia. The few years spent here had been more or less peaceful ones. The deep-water port was being built. There was talk of a pipeline bringing oil from Iraq. A new olive oil and soap factory had opened. Surely there was work for everyone, Jews and Arabs alike?

He went straight to Sammy's office. Sitting behind his desk, head in hands, his boss seemed wrapped up in a tension of his own.

'A heavy curtain has come down on my brain,' Sammy said.

'You should lie down,' Lev suggested. 'Or go home.'

'Lie down? Go home? That is the opposite of what I should do. This visit from our Anonymous Donor. So many accounts and reports to prepare. So many meetings.' Sammy rubbed his fingers vigorously into his temples. 'What do you want to tell me?'

'That land at Kfar Ha'Emek. The piece that doesn't exist on any map. You were right. It is *Mewat*.'

'Are you sure?'

'I checked it myself. It is definitely out of earshot of the nearest settlement. I have a statement signed by myself and corroborated by an independent witness.'

Sammy peered at the document. 'Who is this witness?'

'My brother.'

'Then he is not independent.'

'The surnames are different. He is still a Gottleib. No-one will know.'

'And the Bedouin?'

'I made a deal with them. We will register the title in their names under *Mewat*. Then they will sell us what we need, keep the rest.'

'How much are we paying?'

Lev told him.

'A little high for a slice of swampland. But I suppose it is not unreasonable in the circumstances. At least we will have a clear and legal title. Otherwise, we could be fighting in the courts with the British, the French, the Arabs and even Those Bloody Zionists for years to come.'

'I will make up the necessary documents, take them to Jerusalem.'

'Before you do that, I will need the office of our Anonymous Donor to sign off on the purchase price.'

'How long will that take?'

'As long as it takes to get an appointment.' Sammy turned his attention back to the accounts on his desk. 'Now leave me alone with my headaches.'

'There is something else.'

'What is it now?'

'I met Gregory Sverdlov.'

'You met Sverdlov? Where was this?'

'At Kfar Ha'Emek.'

'What was he doing there?'

'He said he was surveying the region for potential projects. He wouldn't tell me exactly what.'

'Of course, he wouldn't tell you. Sverdlov gives nothing away for free. Yet he wants you to tell him everything. Did you notice his eyes? The way he looks at you?'

'Yes. Very unsettling.'

'Some say he hypnotizes people into giving him information. Like some kind of Rasputin. Did you tell him anything?'

'Nothing. No-one, apart from my brother, knows why I was there.'

'Good. With Sverdlov sniffing around, we need to act secretly. And quickly.'

'He says he has an important proposition to make to our Anonymous Donor. Something to the benefit of the whole of Palestine.'

'He means something to the benefit of Gregory Sverdlov. Go on.'

'He will make his own approaches to our benefactor. But he wanted you also to know.'

Sammy shrugged. 'To know what?'

'That was all.'

'See. He tells you nothing. Just stirs things up. That's what Sverdlov does. Stirs and stirs away. Like Rasputin. No wonder I have a headache.

Twenty-one

It was as if Julius Caesar himself had landed. Or King George of the Great British Empire. Or even the Messiah. The Anonymous Donor had arrived in his yacht just a few miles south of Haifa, at the Arab fishing village of Tantura. Lev had gone down with Sammy to witness the great man's disembarkation, managing with much pushing and elbowing to find a viewing point from a hillside overlooking the bay. Lev had never seen such crowds before with their bunting and their banners, their picnics and their good cheer. A longboat was rowed inshore from the yacht, manoeuvred expertly through a space in the rocks, then tied up to a jetty bedecked with flowers. The Anonymous Donor stepped out first to stand on the wooden platform alone. With his white pith helmet, (reminding Lev of the High Commissioner, Herbert Samuel), a full white beard, spectacles reflecting the sunlight, dark suit, bow tie and cane, the man still trim and spry despite his almost eighty years. The crowds were held back to allow this solitary figure, this 'Sultan of the Jews', as the Arabs called him, to find his shore-legs, to quietly express his gratitude for being able to return to this blessed land, to look up to the hillsides where his vines were planted and now thrived.

A band of horns and trumpets broke the spell with a martial melody that Lev had never heard before. 'The French national anthem,' Sammy told him. It was followed by *Hatikvah*, the Jewish song of hope. A young girl was ushered forward to present a bouquet. The Anonymous Donor knelt to her level to receive the gift, a gesture greeted by affectionate cheers and clapping. This was a sign for senior officials to move into action, to surround their esteemed guest, who became no more than a bobbing white helmet as he was guided to the waiting automobile that would take him the five miles of bumpy road to the settlement that several years ago had been named in his honour. Built on a former rock-strewn, malaria-ridden plateau overlooking the Mediterranean, this colony had been financed by the Anonymous Donor until it not only boasted vineyards but also main streets, a hospital, a bank, a makeshift fire station and one of the finest synagogues in the land. But most importantly, a venture always close to his heart as well as to his sophisticated palate, it had its own winery. With its cool underground cellars carved deep into the mountainsides. Of course, the wines produced here could not match those of his own famous French vineyards but he was looking forward to a glass nevertheless.

A few hours later, Lev sat with Sammy in the upper hallway of the Anonymous Donor's administration building set at the edge of the colony. It was a spacious room with ceiling fans and tall windows that framed a veranda, then beyond to the sea and the stately yacht anchored in the bay. Within the building, all was busy now the Anonymous Donor was in town. Side-doors opened and closed, secretaries clipped by from office to office, their heels tap-tapping their code of efficiency across the tiled floor, message boys came and went. But outside in the streets all was quiet. The eager crowds had followed their grand visitor on his inspection of the colony, then filed into the synagogue to hear his address to the citizens. There, he would exhort them to work harder, admonish them for their idleness, inspire them to be good Jews, reflect with them on the remarkable achievements of the last thirty years. However, their munificent benefactor, one of the richest men in the world, would not listen to their complaints, their petitions for endorsements, their pleas for loans and investments or even their requests for a blessing. That was the job of Chaim Kalisher, outside whose office Lev and Sammy now waited.

The fans struggled to do the best they could with the warm air but it remained hot, very hot. A dampness hung over everything, making even more slippery the polished wood of the bench on which they perched. Lev longed to take off his jacket, wrench open his shirt collar. Sammy sat next to him, his panama hat covering one knee, the other knee vibrating nervously. The plants across the windowsill sagged in their pots. A secretary brought out a tray of glasses and iced water. They had been waiting for over an hour.

Perhaps it was the heat mixed in with the clack-clack-clacking of typewriter keys coming through an open door but Lev began to think of Ewa Kaminsky. On a summer's day not unlike this one, her body close up beside his on the piano stool they used for his lesson, her bare arms with their fair down, the wonderful tingling sensation caused by her nearness, something almost animal about her, her heat, her smell, the way she hovered over him as if she could turn round at any moment and bite or scratch. He could almost hear the precise 'ting' of the carriage on the Kanzler 1B as it came to the end of a line, that same clack-clacking of the keys. He wondered what had happened to her. What had happened to his father. And whether they had received Amshel's letter requesting an invitation to come to stay with them in America.

He leaned forward for a glass of iced water, gulped down the cool liquid, and was just about to return it to the tray when the door to Chaim Kalisher's office swung open. But it was not Kalisher himself who stepped out but a stocky figure already familiar to Lev. The empty glass slipped out of his hand to smash on the tiled floor. A splash of sound echoed around the room, then silence.

'*Mazel tov*,' Sverdlov shouted in his commanding voice, like the hearty greeting of some operatic tenor to his fine stage-fellows. '*Mazel tov, mazel tov, mazel tov*. To break a glass is to bring good luck.'

This was surely not the thought of the secretary who ran out from one of the side offices, held a hand to her mouth, then raced away again. It was not Lev's thought either as he crouched down to pick up some of the larger pieces. Sammy was brushing off tiny shards from his suit trousers as Sverdlov strode over to greet him.

'Sammy, Sammy, Sammy,' he said. 'Why am I surprised to see you here?'

Sammy rose from his chair. 'It is I who am surprised to see you. After all, Gregory, this is the organization that employs me.'

Sammy shook an outstretched hand that boasted a large gold ring strangling one thick finger. Sverdlov wore a cream suit, a pink flower in his lapel. His thick hair remained untamed by whatever cream he had applied. Lines of moisture sat in the troughs of his permanent scowl. He glanced at Lev, then ignored him as he went on talking. 'Still the idealist, Sammy? Believing this can be one happy homeland for both Arabs and Jews.'

'I remain optimistic.'

Sverdlov chuckled, threw a confiding arm around Sammy's shoulder. 'There is no use trying to save the Arabs from their unhappy fate. PICA will soon align with the Zionists, you'll see. Your Anonymous Donor is becoming more and more sympathetic to the nationalist cause as he gets older. That's what happens to all of us, Sammy. The closer to death, the more determined we become to leave a legacy. And what better legacy than a Jewish state, eh? Isn't that right, Lev?' Sverdlov turned on him with his fierce eyes. 'Or are you too young to possess such fears in the face of mortality?'

Lev was surprised to hear that Sverdlov remembered his name, never mind the question directed towards him. 'I think I am too young,' he stammered. 'And I cannot speak for our Anonymous Donor.'

'Well, I can,' said Sammy. 'I sincerely believe he has never wanted one people to triumph over another for this land.'

'Ah, Sammy. How I envy your naive faith in the righteousness of human beings. Great struggles lie ahead. I can feel the strains already, can't you? I can even smell it. It's in the air. And it stinks like… like what? Like petrol. One match and "pouf" it will all go off.' Sverdlov blew out an imaginary candle with his fat, rosy lips. 'And then where will PICA and its settlements be without the protection of the Zionists? Do you think the British will look after you, eh?'

Sammy shrugged off the question. 'And where does Gregory Sverdlov fit into all these struggles?'

'Hah! Me? I am an engineer. I have no interest in your ideals or your politics. I am only interested in great projects. Yes, projects on the grandest scale.' And with that last remark, Sverdlov slapped Sammy on the back and walked out of the hall, careful to avoid the kneeling secretary in her search for pieces of glass.

Chaim Kalisher was an extremely tall, broad-shouldered, solid-looking man. Like a giant wardrobe, Lev thought, dwarfing the room and the rest of its furniture with his massive presence. Not surprising really for the person who was the Anonymous Donor's second-in-command in matters concerning Palestine. His protector, his gatekeeper, the human shield behind whom the Anonymous Donor could be hidden from view. But despite his size, Kalisher was an elegant man with his grey hair sleeked back from a thinning widow's peak, the clipped moustache, the shimmeringly expensive suit, the white cuffs, the trimmed nails. He moved smoothly and effortlessly as he came out from behind his desk to greet Sammy like an old friend. He shook Lev's hand too, the clasp soft and smooth as if Kalisher had powdered his palms in advance of the meeting. Lev was motioned to sit down, as was Sammy. Kalisher returned behind his desk, pinched the cloth of his suit at the knees, then sank down into his leather chair. The window was open yet the smell of cigars lingered.

'*Schnapps*?' Kalisher asked. 'Our patron's finest brandy.'

Sammy nodded, as did Lev. Kalisher filled up three shot glasses from a crystal decanter, pushed two of them towards his guests. '*L'chaim*,' he toasted, knocking back the drink in one gulp, then slamming his glass down on the table. Sammy did the same. Lev, who initially had only taken a sip of this smooth, warm liquid, was forced to imitate the gesture. Kalisher poured out another three glasses but left them on the desk.

'It is good to see you, Sammy. You look… you look anxious.'

'Our Anonymous Donor's presence always makes life a little more intense here, don't you think?

'Perhaps.'

'All the extra paperwork.'

'You prefer the feel of the soil between your fingers, Sammy. That we know. How are our settlements here in Palestine?'

'I have prepared the usual report,' Sammy said, handing over a file he had extracted from his briefcase.

Kalisher took the documents, placed them aside. 'Anything special I should know about?'

'It is still early days. Conditions are harsh. Always the demand for more money. But seeds are being sown, shoots are sprouting. It will all take time. But I think we are moving in the right direction.'

'Ah, Sammy, as usual, you tell me nothing.'

'The figures speak for themselves.'

Kalisher lifted the front leaf of the file, let it drop again. 'You have to admire these settlers for their courage. Their tenacity. And their beliefs.' Kalisher brought his fingers together in a steeple, sighed as he looked out of the window. A small black-and-white bird was pecking at some dried-up dates that had fallen onto the veranda. 'I wish I knew the names of birds. Do you know this one?'

Sammy leaned forward on his chair to get a better look. 'It is a white wagtail. It's very common here.'

'A white wagtail, is that it? I've just started to notice the birds, Sammy. Strange, isn't it? All these years they have been sharing this world with me. And I was hardly ever aware of them. What about you, Lev? Are you a bird man?'

'No. I am like you, sir. I rarely notice them myself.'

'What do you notice? Girls, I suppose. The female of the species. With whom we also share this world.'

'I saw Sverdlov in the hallway,' Sammy said.

'Yes, yes. You know what Gregory's like. He is in and out of here like… like what? Like the tide, I suppose. Full of grand schemes and bluster.'

'What did he want?'

'The usual. Land and money. Money, mostly.'

'What are his plans for the Jordan Valley?'

Kalisher swivelled his chair away from the window, back to his visitors. 'You know about that?'

'Lev met Sverdlov up there on one of his survey missions. Let me guess. He wants to build a hydro-electric power station.'

'That would be a good guess.' Kalisher opened up a wooden box on his desk. 'Cigar? Sammy? Lev? No? Well, if you don't mind, I might just indulge myself…'

'What do you think, Chaim?'

'It's a very exciting proposition,' Kalisher said as he snipped the end off his cigar. 'As Gregory says – it will be for the great benefit of

127

Jews and Arabs alike. As if the Arabs are going to take kindly to the Jews damming up their rivers and controlling the water. Are you sure that I cannot tempt you? These are specially made for our esteemed employer. All the way from the Dominican Republic. And who needs a humidor in this climate? Sammy?'

'No, thank you. Tell me about Sverdlov.'

'He showed me all the plans. You have to hand him that. He's very well prepared. The Zionists are extremely interested, so he tells me. But I personally know money has dried up for them here. Ever since our Jewish friends in America began channelling most of their funds to our poverty-stricken communities in central Europe. As for the British, they would be delighted to see electricity in the north of the country. But they can't be seen to favour a Jew over an Arab in this respect. They would prefer a joint venture. Which Sverdlov does not.'

'What does he want from PICA?'

Kalisher lit his cigar with a long match. The first wisps of smoke floated out of the window. Lev watched them go. 'He wanted to know our land holdings in the area. And if we are prepared to invest.'

'And are we?'

'I need to speak to the great man himself. But I'm sure he will be interested. In theory, he loves these grand projects. The mills. The glass works. The wineries, of course. He is even talking of an airstrip. Putting them into practice is another matter. Sverdlov's proposal could be years in the making. What are our land holdings in the Jordan Valley, around the rivers?'

'We have just the one settlement. A young *kibbutz*. Kfar Ha'Emek.'

'I thought there would be more.'

'That is actually the reason for this visit. There is another area I want to bring to your attention.'

'Which is?'

'We have discovered a parcel of land, a few hundred dunams in total, that doesn't exist on any map.'

'Of course it must be on a map.'

'We've checked. And checked again. There is definitely no official documentation. Lev, show him.'

Lev got up from his chair, took out a hand-drawn map from his files, laid it on Kalisher's desk. 'This area here,' he said, pointing to the segment shaded in red. 'It borders the Yarmuk River. And it's not on any map.'

'So who owns it then?' Kalisher asked, flicking away a block of ash that had fallen on the paper.

'As far as we know,' Lev said, 'no-one.'

'What about the British? Surely they could claim it as land captured from the Turks.'

'They probably could,' Sammy said. 'If they knew it existed. That's why we need to move quickly. Before they find out.'

'What do you suggest?'

'There's a Bedouin tribe living there. I want to register it in their name as *Mewat*.'

'*Mewat*, Sammy. Are you sure it's *Mewat*?'

'We've done the distance test. All other conditions apply.'

'The British won't like it. You know what they think of *Mewat*. Why don't we just take it for ourselves? If no-one owns it.'

'Because we'll end up in legal disputes with everyone else who thinks they have an interest. It could go on for years. It could be like Kabbara.'

'Ah yes, Kabbara.'

Lev noticed Kalisher visibly flinch at the mention of the name. Kabbara. The ten thousand acres of land only a few miles south from where they sat which the British had conceded to PICA almost ten years ago. The legal wrangling over its ownership with the local Arab population was still ongoing. The draining of the swamps was at a standstill, no development at all had taken place, huge sums of capital were in limbo.

'Well, we don't want that to happen, do we? So what's your plan?'

'Lev can explain.'

'As Sammy said, we register the title with the Bedouin who have agreed to sell us on–'

'…at a very fair price,' Sammy added.

'…that part of the land we need for our own settlement, Kfar Ha'Emek,' Lev continued. 'Swamps will need to be drained but in the end the *kibbutz* will have much-needed access to the river. And a few extra dunams for farming. The Bedouin meanwhile will have gained proper title under *Mewat* to their part of the land. Everyone is happy.'

'What about Sverdlov? That area would be absolutely crucial to his power station. He could dam the river from there.'

'As you said, even if his plans get the go-ahead, it could take years to put into action,' Sammy noted. 'So let him deal with the Bedouin when the time comes. At least they will be the legal owners. If they want to sell it to him, that's up to them.'

Kalisher sat back in his chair, almost concealed by a large cloud of smoke. 'But if we decide to invest in Sverdlov, we will be the ones buying this land from the Bedouin at a later date. At some exorbitant price, no doubt.'

'Better that than another Kabarra.'

'Hmmm.' Kalisher savoured the taste of yet another puff of his cigar. 'Or we could just buy all of it now before anyone gets a sniff of any plans for power stations. Can't we persuade the Bedouin to sell the whole lot, Lev?'

'No, sir. I tried but they insisted. They're not shifting.'

'Do we have a comparable site to offer in exchange?'

'Not in that part of Palestine. With both water and grazing.'

'I see. And if we increased our offer?'

'The elder of the tribe, Zayed, is determined to stay.'

'Everyone has their price.'

'It's land they've used for generations, sir.'

'You know how it is,' Sammy added. 'Land is land is land.'

Kalisher ground his cigar into a large glass ashtray. 'And when do you need the money for the section we want?'

'As soon as possible. And no bank drafts. They want cash.'

'I will need a few days then.'

'It is a fine plan, Chaim,' Sammy said. 'I am sure of it.'

Kalisher rose from his chair, walked to the window. He looked out at the sea, then turned his attention southwards. Towards Kabarra. 'Well, I hope you're right,' he said. 'I hope you're right.'

Twenty-two

LEV INVITED SAMMY for Friday night dinner. He thought Madame Blum had taken his request quite casually but he noticed she was wearing a pair of sparkling earrings when Sammy came to dine. An unfamiliar fragrance of rose and jasmine floated in the air.

With or without Sammy, the Sabbath eve meal at Madame Blum's was always a lavish affair. A white tablecloth freshly starched, a braided loaf from Koestler's Bakery, warm, ready and waiting under cover of an embroidered silk cloth. Centre-stage, a pair of silver candlesticks gifted by Madame Blum's late mother-in-law. There would be a freshly cooked chicken, not the tough old hen Lev had been reared on. And on special occasions like this one, a rack of roasted brisket soaked in a rich sauce which both Lev and Mickey guessed involved large spoonfuls of brandy. Sammy had brought a bottle of the finest *kosher* wine, courtesy of Chaim Kalisher and the cellars of the Anonymous Donor.

Madame Blum fussed over her three men, the conversation was lively but did not erupt into argument. Mickey and Sammy might disagree on most things, but their opinions were not so entrenched as to prevent either of them from listening to the other. Lev sat in the middle, enjoying their entreaties to enlist him to their side of the discussion on the usual topics – the tensions in Jerusalem over the Western Wall, the visit of the Anonymous Donor, the immigration quotas, the difference in wage levels between the Arab and Jewish labourers working on the port project. But Lev didn't really care for taking sides this evening – for his thoughts were with the letter from Celia tucked into his jacket pocket. He drank the last of the Anonymous Donor's full-bodied wine, stretched his legs under the table, let the conversation drift out of his consciousness. The windows were open to the warm night, the room shimmered with a wine-red candle-lit glow, the smell of coffee drifted in from the kitchen. He realized that for these few moments he was joyously happy.

'Oil,' Mickey said, pointing at Sammy. 'That's where the future lies.'

'Mickey, Mickey, Mickey.' Sammy burped, patted his belly. 'You are dreaming. It's all about the land. Isn't that right, Lev?'

'What did you say?'

'Forget about Lev, Sammy. His head is in the clouds. And forget about the land too. Or even the water. It's all about the oil. We need to push the British to build this pipeline from Iraq all the way to Haifa. And then we'll be rich. Oil is the future. You'll see. That's what you need to tell your Anonymous Donor to invest in. Not your damn flour mills and pear trees. But oil tankers and refineries.' Mickey rose from the table. 'Now, if you will excuse me, I am going for a walk.'

Lev looked at him suspiciously. Mickey was not a man for exercise or a breath of fresh air. This was either a business meeting or a rendezvous with some girl from Kiev. Mickey grimaced back at him. 'Tell Madame Blum for me,' he said.

As soon as Mickey had left, Sammy leaned across the table. 'How well do you know him?'

'Mickey? We've been friends ever since I came here.'

'What about his business interests?'

'Take a look around. That's four boxes of false teeth in the corner. There are sacks of rice in the kitchen. He's got crates of watermelons in his bedroom, boxes of vodka in the hallway. There are three European-style toilets stacked behind the house. He deals in anything to make a quick profit.'

'Has he ever said anything about guns?'

'Guns? What are you suggesting?'

Sammy tapped his ear with his index finger. 'One hears things. Around the card clubs.'

'What have you heard?'

'Rumours Mickey has been trading in handguns and rifles.'

'With the British?'

'That's one possibility. The other is he's importing them from overseas. From Zionist supporters. You haven't seen anything?'

'Boxes come in and out of here all the time. I don't know what's in them. I think he has a small storehouse somewhere in the town. But I don't think Mickey would get involved in guns.'

'I thought he used to be in the British army. Here in Palestine.'

'He also told me he liberated Jerusalem with Allenby. He was just a boy then, not even eighteen. The British had to release him in the end because he wasn't old enough to enlist.'

'He could still have good contacts with them.'

'That's without doubt. He uses these contacts to trade in all kinds of ex-Army goods. But guns? I would be very surprised.'

'Let's assume for a moment he is dealing in them. What are his political leanings?'

'Mickey? Politics? His only interest is in himself.'

'Well, it might be useful if you keep an eye on what he's up to. I think PICA should be aware of these matters.'

Madame Blum swung in from the kitchen with a tray full of coffee cups. 'What are you both whispering about?' She looked around. 'Where's Mickey?'

'He had to go out,' Lev told her.

'On the Sabbath? Without a word of goodbye. I don't know what's going on with that man.' She laid down the tray, returned to the kitchen.

'Come,' Sammy said. 'Let's take our coffee on the veranda.'

It was a balmy evening, the cicadas had started to sing, the smell of frangipani and lemons scented the air. They sat in silence for a while, drinking coffee, cracking sunflower seeds with their teeth, spitting the shells out onto the tiny square of grass Madame Blum proudly called her garden. The crows would fight over the husks in the dawn. Lev took off his jacket, loosened his tie, slipped off his shoes, the stone floor of the veranda still warm underfoot. He could see sets of Sabbath candles burning in the windows of other houses in the neighbourhood. Then across the rooftops to the bobbing lanterns of the fishing boats anchored in the black water of the bay. Here it felt like it was always summer. When he thought back to his life in Poland, he only remembered the winters. Yet there had been glorious summers there too. But it was always the coldness and the bitterness that lingered in his memory.

'What's the progress with our non-existent piece of land?' Sammy asked.

'Everything is ready. As soon as Kalisher comes up with the money, I'll register the documents, tie up our purchase from the Bedouin.'

'It seems I'll have to scour the docks for a new typist.' Sammy leaned forward, patted Lev's knee, looked at him with watery eyes. 'I am proud of you.'

'Thank you.'

'Ha!' he said, drawing back. 'I remember when I found you. A poor, skinny, heart-broken youth at Haifa docks. And now look at you. A man. A *mensch*. A land agent.'

'You have been a good teacher.'

'Perhaps. But a good pupil is like the soil. He needs to be prepared to suck up the nourishment to make things grow. You and me together, eh? A good team?'

'A good team.'

Sammy seemed to retreat into himself for a moment as if there was something else on his mind. 'Yes, that is what we are. A good team. And of this transaction I am equally proud. It shows we can still be fair to everyone, Jews and Bedouin alike. This is the PICA way. Remember that.'

'What about Sverdlov?'

'Ah, Sverdlov,' Sammy sighed. 'Don't worry about him. A power station is just another of his grand schemes. Next time we meet, he will probably be enthusing over oil and Mickey's refineries.' Sammy cracked a shell, spat it out over the veranda. 'But Sverdlov was right about one matter.'

'What's that?'

'Our Anonymous Donor is beginning to align himself more with Those Bloody Zionists. I had a long talk with Kalisher about it. All the usual reasons – the need to coordinate our policies, our capital and our security. I fear the days of PICA as an independent organization are over.' Sammy stared out into the night. 'It breaks my heart,' he said wearily. 'I could never work with the Zionists.'

'So what will we do?'

'I will do nothing. But you… you should give them a chance.'

'Me?'

'Yes, you. You are young. You have more energy to resist their ways.'

'They would walk all over me.'

'I don't think so. They need good land agents. You would be a great asset to them.'

'I don't understand why you're giving up so easily.'

'I'm getting old, Lev. Inside I am still young, but my body thinks otherwise. Everyday is such a struggle just to get up in the morning. I have no strength left to fight the Zionists as well. All my life I have helped others with their land. Now it is time for me to look after my own property. My roses are dying as we speak. As soon as there is any announcement of an official coordination of policies, I shall retire.'

'I think there is something you are not telling me.'

'What do you mean?'

'Your health?'

'I am perfectly fine. I am just being realistic. If our Anonymous Donor is not on my side, what can I do? The Zionists are determined. They know exactly what they want. A Jewish state. And nothing is going to stop them. They will wait and push and wait and push for as long as it takes.' Sammy spat the last of the sunflower husks into the garden. 'Without any concern for those who get in their way.'

Twenty-three

'I CALL IT THE SHOPKEEPER'S LUNCH,' Uncle Moustache told him, probably with a smile on his face although it was hard for Lev to see the man's lips under the enormous moustache. But the eyes gave away the café owner's amusement as he watched Lev eat his famous fava bean stew. It was the addition of a boiled egg sprinkled across the top that turned the standard dish into the renowned 'shopkeeper's lunch'.

'I've been looking forward to this all morning,' Lev said between mouthfuls.

'You came all the way from Haifa to eat this? That is nothing. Emir Abdullah rode in from Damascus for some of my *ful madammas*. General Allenby himself stopped by for a plate. He was told in Cairo – if you are ever in Jerusalem, you must have the *ful madammas* at Uncle Moustache's. And so he came. I even gave some to his horse.' Uncle Moustache slapped his towel over his shoulder, went back into his café, leaving Lev to the dust, the noise of the alleyways. And the tension.

Lev could feel it in the brittle air. He could see it in the strain on people's faces. The way they avoided his eyes as they trundled past with their donkeys and their push-carts. He could see it on the competing slogans painted on the ancient walls. On the half-ripped posters in Hebrew beseeching the Jews to unite. Over what? The cause had been torn away but Lev knew the reason. The Jews now wanted to bring chairs to the Western Wall so the aged and infirm could sit while they prayed. The Grand Mufti and Jerusalem's Islamic Trust would not allow it. First there would be chairs, they said, then benches, then screens, then canopies and soon the Jews would take over the whole site. That was the Arab fear. It applied to Temple Mount. It applied to the whole of Palestine. Lev sipped at his mint tea, took out Celia's letter from his pocket.

He didn't really need to read it, he knew what it said by heart. But it was good to have the sheet of paper spread out on the table, a distraction from the tight atmosphere around him. She would arrive in Haifa next week, for a couple of days of rest with the relatives of one of the *kibbutz* members. A Mr and Mrs Greenspan. He had gone round to take a look at the house already, it was not that far away from Madame Blum's. He imagined himself walking up the pathway to the door. Should he bring flowers? For Celia? Or for her hosts? He would linger in the doorway to catch his breath, smooth down his hair, wait for his heartbeat to subside. There was a brass knocker, a ring grasped in the mouth of a lion. A British household. He would give it a good rat-tat-tat. Not too firm as to be aggressive, just enough to sound confident. His imagination grew hazy after that, he wasn't sure if it would be Celia or which of her hosts – the man or woman of this couple – who answered the door. It didn't matter. For she wanted to see him. It said so in the letter. *It is important I use my time in Haifa to sleep, to rest, to regain my strength. I am so tired these days. But if you can find time for a short visit, I would be pleased to see you.*

He sipped at his tea, sat back in his chair with a certain degree of satisfaction. Life was changing. Or as Mickey would say, things were on the up-and-up. This land deal was about to go through as soon as he went round the corner to register the necessary documents. He might be taking over shortly from Sammy at PICA. Celia had written to say she would be pleased to see him. He leaned forward to read yet again these same words when a body clattered against his table, sending his bowl and glass of tea to smash on the ground. Lev only managed to stop himself from falling off his chair by grabbing one of the canopy poles. An Arab boy had stumbled into him off the alleyway, had turned, clutching at his knee, only to be confronted by his assailants, four Jewish boys, skullcaps pinned to their heads. Not seminary students with sidelocks. Just ordinary boys. One of them held a cricket bat. The others bricks and stones. Lev moved quickly, inserting himself between the injured youth and his pursuers.

'Leave him,' he said, holding up one hand, palm flattened against the advance of the four boys.

'Why do you protect the Arab?' the one with the bat called back.

'Just get out of here,' Lev said as calmly as he could. 'Go on. Away.'

'His mule shitted all over the Wall,' one of the other boys called out. He tossed a stone from hand to hand as he spoke. 'Shit, shit, shit. Over our holy place.'

'It was not my mule,' the lad on the ground countered. 'Not my mule. I did nothing wrong.'

'He chased us too.' Cricket bat boy again, advancing a step. 'That Arab dog and his friends. They started it. Ran after us. But we lost them.' He inched forward again, his three cohorts with him. This ringleader could have only been about fourteen, Lev thought, but he seemed to possess all the anger and aggression of a hard-bitten adult. 'Let us past.'

Lev held his ground. 'Leave him alone. He is just one boy.'

'Not my mule, not my mule,' the Arab insisted, kicking out futilely with his feet.

Lev felt a hand on his arm, Uncle Moustache gently pushing him aside. He saw the large club in the restaurant owner's grasp. The Jewish boys could see it too. They retreated a few paces. One of them lobbed a stone at Lev. Then they ran. Shouting: 'Arab lover. Arab lover.'

Lev turned to the injured youth, held out a hand. The boy flicked it away. 'I don't need your help,' he said, his eyes all flared up, not with anger but with a kind of hatred that made Lev shiver.

Uncle Moustache shouldered his club. 'Bah,' he said. 'Every day it is like this. One thing or another. It is not good for business.'

The youth scampered off as best he could with his injured leg. Lev returned to his table where Celia's letter lay sodden and stained with tea.

The thin figure of Douglas Raynsford, the chief clerk of maps and surveys at the Department of Land Registration of Palestine, slowly emerged from a dim corner of the map room.

'Ah, Mr Sela. Our friend from PICA. It is so nice to see you again. Come in, come in.'

They sat down at one of the map tables, Lev on one side, Raynsford on the other. Raynsford laid out his hands in a clasp in front of him. 'Are you all right, Mr Sela? You look a little pale.'

'There was a fight in the street.'

'Were you hurt?'

'No, no. I'm fine. But it seems every time I sit outside in the Old City, there is always some incident.'

'Ah yes. That is the nature of Jerusalem. Here we are in this holiest of places where one might expect a little – how can we say? – spiritual decorum. And instead, we see the basest of human instincts. Greed, jealousy, intolerance, violence. It is shameful. But at least you did not suffer an injury. Now, what can I do for you?'

'I would like to register the title to some land.'

'PICA has purchased some more property?'

'We are merely acting as agents on someone else's behalf. We would like to register this land as *Mewat*.'

Raynsford sat back abruptly in his seat. '*Mewat*, Mr Sela?'

'Yes, *Mewat*.'

'You are aware we British passed the *Mewat* Land Ordinance several years ago prohibiting the further use of land registration via *Mewat*?'

'I am aware of that law.'

'I am sure you are. Sammy the King certainly keeps himself up to date with all the most recent developments in the legal arena. So you will be aware then that all potential claimants were required to register their title within two months of said legislation being advertised in the *Official Gazette*.'

'I am also aware of that, Mr Raynsford.'

'And that those two months obviously passed several years ago.'

'Yes, I am aware of that too.'

'The law is very clear, Mr Sela. Two months to register one's claim. That was all.'

'You know as well as I do, Mr Raynsford, that the time limit was seen as unfair in the case of the Bedouin. Given the unlikely event they would ever be able to obtain, never mind read, a copy of the *Official Gazette.*'

'And your client is a Bedouin?'

'He is.'

'And can he read?'

'He is illiterate.'

'And was his tribe in possession of the land in question prior to 1921?'

'Yes.'

'And can you prove the land in question is outwith the earshot of the nearest settlement?'

'I have here a statement signed by an independent witness and myself declaring this to be so.'

Raynsford looked at the document and sighed. 'I have always been impressed by PICA. Because PICA is precise. PICA submits the proper documents. PICA respects the process. And where precisely is this land you would like to register?'

'I'm afraid this land does not appear on any of your maps.'

'I see. And is this land in the Jordan Valley by any chance?'

'It is.'

Raynsford stood up. 'One moment, please.' He went over to his desk, returned with a rolled-up map, which he spread out on the table. 'Show me.'

'I'm sorry, Mr Raynsford. I just told you this land does not appear on any map of the area. I saw this for myself when I was last here.'

'And you didn't point this out to me at the time?'

'I'm sorry. I wasn't sure about…'

'Even though you saw that the land did appear on the reconnaissance photographs I made available to you during your visit?'

'Yes, but…'

'As I said, show me.'

Lev looked at the map. The course of the Yarmuk River had been crudely altered to show how it now travelled in reality. Within the grasp of this new version of the river was the Bedouin land shaded in yellow. Lev pointed to it. 'That's it there. Between the PICA settlement of Kfar Ha'Emek and the river. That's the land we'd like to claim on behalf of the Bedouin. By *Mewat.*'

'Well, I'm afraid you are too late,' Raynsford said triumphantly. 'That land has been registered to someone else.'

'What? That's impossible. No-one knew about this land. Who has it been registered to?'

'I'm afraid I cannot tell you.'

'You have to tell me. This is a public register. These details are open to everyone.'

'That is true. But only after such details have been published in the *Official Gazette.*'

'When will that be?'

Raynsford shrugged. 'Oh, I don't know. As you can see, I am very busy. There are so many applications and registrations and disputes concerning land in this tiny part of the world it beggars belief. Now when I served in Tanganyika, I had time to attend to all the necessary paperwork. And, of course, I had assistants as well. Three of them, as a matter of fact.'

Lev stood up. 'I insist you tell me who registered the land.'

Raynsford sat back in his chair, gave the twitch of a smile. 'It is of no matter, Mr Sela. For the land has already been sold on.'

'Sold on? To whom?'

'Again, I cannot tell you until these details are formally registered. And then you would have to wait until they are published in the *Official Gazette.*'

Lev thought he had witnessed enough violence for the day, but he could easily step forward and punch Douglas Raynsford across his smug little mouth. Instead, he controlled himself, asked as calmly as he could: 'Was there a land agent involved in this sale?'

'Yes.'

'You can at least tell me his name.'

'I could do that.'

'Well?'

'First, I think you owe me an apology, Mr Sela.'

* * *

'Khaled Al Hamoud,' Lev said.

'Ah yes, Khaled Al Hamoud,' Sammy repeated softly. 'Khaled the Broker. That would make sense.'

Lev expected Sammy to be furious. To be pacing up and down on a carpet already well worn from previous rages. To be swearing at the injustice, the selfishness, the deceitfulness, the opportunism, the lack of appreciation, the sheer ingratitude. Instead his employer just sat slumped in his seat, his face crumpled in disillusionment, his chair half-turned to the window so he could look out to the harbour and the sea. The fishing boats were in. The market-traders were shouting out their prices, gulls screeched and squawked over the scraps from the catch. A large ship stationed far out in the bay raised excitement levels even higher as tourists arrived, ferried onshore in longboats. A line of fresh passengers waited to be taken out to the vessel.

'I used to pity them,' Sammy said, more to himself than to Lev. 'Those poor immigrants turned emigrants, queuing up to leave. Waiting for that ship to take them… where? Back to where they are hated? Across to an America that won't let them in? Yes, I used to pity them. Now I am as disillusioned as they are. Perhaps I should purchase my own ticket out of here.'

'Who is Khaled the Broker?'

Sammy continued to stare out of the window. 'Every day brings something else to eat away at my faith in human nature. Like a rust. Like a cancer. When I was younger, I had the strength to bounce back from all of this, Lev. But now, I feel myself being crushed by this greed. And I don't have the vigour, the optimism, or even the desire to fight back. It is time for me to pay attention to my roses.'

'Can you please stop all this talk of retirement? Who is Khaled the Broker?'

'He works out of Damascus. I used to deal with him a lot in the past. He acts as a middle-man, especially when Arabs want to transact with Jews. The Arabs are frightened the Zionists keep secret lists of all of their compatriots who sell land to Jews, lists they will use later to expose them as traitors. So they sell to Khaled first. That way it's his name on the deed.'

'It had to be Zayed's son, Ibrahim. Zayed would never have given up his land to anyone. But Ibrahim? He wanted the money. I could see it in his eyes when I was negotiating with him. He was already spending it.'

'And no-one else knew about our intention to use *Mewat*?'

'Just the Bedouin.'

'So you think this Ibrahim stole our idea about *Mewat*, registered the land in favour of himself, then sold it on to Khaled?'

'I don't see who else could have done it.'

'Well, your Ibrahim has outsmarted us.' Sammy plucked a cheroot from his shirt pocket, struck a match to it but the breeze through the window blew it out.

Twenty-four

LEV BROUGHT FLOWERS. Freshly cut roses courtesy of Sammy's garden. They were in full bloom, all that Sammy could give him at this end of the season, which meant he had to tread carefully with his bouquet otherwise the petals dropped off too easily. The flowers were Mickey's idea.

'Not for Celia,' Mickey had advised, 'but for the woman of the house. Who is she staying with?'

'The Greenspans. I think they're British.'

'Perfect.'

'Why is that?'

'Because we British like our gentility, our politeness, our protocol.'

'So why would I bring Mrs Greenspan the flowers?'

'As we say in English: it would be killing two birds with one stone. You have this expression in Polish?'

'We say: cooking two meals over one fire.'

'Two meals, two birds, two women, it is all the same.'

'What do you mean?'

'Well, if you brought the flowers for Celia, this would be too obvious an expression of your affection.'

'But I do like her.'

'Of course you do. That is why you must give the flowers to Mrs Greenspan.'

'I still don't understand.'

'If you give Mrs Greenspan the flowers, it will immediately soften her heart towards you. And there is nothing better than to soften the heart of the chaperone.'

'It is Celia's heart I want to soften.'

'Celia, of course, will see the flowers on your arrival, assume they are for her, will feel flattered but will also feel that, as the object of attention, she has the upper hand. Then when you pass the bouquet to Mrs Greenspan, Celia will feel surprised, perhaps embarrassed by her initial assumption, but then impressed by your consideration for her hosts. You will therefore not only have won the good favour of this Mrs Greenspan, but also impressed Celia and gained the advantage all at the same time. In fact, three birds with one stone.'

'You make it sound like a battle strategy.'

'Not a battle. A war.'

And so, with petals falling all over the place in his nervous grasp, Lev used his free hand to raise the brass ring gripped by the lion's mouth of a door-knocker, and struck three times. He was surprised when a young housemaid in full uniform answered the door. In his imagination, this was not how he had planned his entrance.

'Yes?' The maid looked down at his petal-covered fist and smiled.

'I am Mr Lev Sela,' he said, feeling the flush to his cheeks from this young woman's attention. He wanted to turn around and flee.

'If you are here to sell flowers, Mr Sela, then I suggest you–'

'I am here to see Miss…' He realized he didn't know her family name. '…To see Celia.'

'Is Miss Kahn expecting you?'

'Not exactly.'

'Well, she is or she isn't?'

Before he had time to answer, a large, elderly woman with a full bosom and bustle appeared behind the maid. 'Who are you?' she demanded.

'I am Mr Lev Sela.'

'And what do you want?'

'He wants to see Miss Kahn,' said the maid.

'Well, what is he doing on the doorstep? Come in, come in.'

Lev stepped over the threshold. 'These are for you, madam,' he said, handing over his bouquet.

'Oh,' she said, looking down at his gift with a mixture of surprise

145

and disdain. 'Don't give them to me. Give them to Ruta. She will put them in a vase. Now what did you say your name was?'

'Lev Sela.'

Mrs Greenspan turned to her maid. 'Please find Miss Kahn and tell her a Mr Sela is here to see her. Then add one more for our afternoon tea. We'll take it in the front room. And bring a broom for all these petals.'

The room was heavily curtained, filled with dark furniture, the walls hung with several paintings of landscapes that Lev assumed were representative of a longed-for English countryside. He was sunk down uncomfortably in a giant armchair of soft cushions and loose upholstery. Mrs Greenspan had taken up her position opposite in a similar chair. He wondered if she was in mourning, given her black finery, the lack of any jewellery and the scowl on her face. She tapped away with her fingers on a wooden inlay within the arm of the chair. Through the half-closed drapes, he could see the rooftops of the houses of the German colony all the way down to the sea. It would have been a magnificent view had most of it not been sealed off by the curtains. The windows were closed. The ceiling fan remained motionless. Mrs Greenspan tapped away. He wondered whether he should begin a polite conversation although he had no idea what a polite conversation should be in such circumstances. The door opened. Ruta entered with a vase filled with his much denuded roses. She was followed by Celia.

Lev was so stunned by the sight of her that he forgot to stand up. He had only ever seen her dressed in well-worn work clothes, her hair mussed up and dry. Here she stood quite beautiful in a sleeveless knee-length summer dress patterned with tiny yellow flowers, her hair all shiny dark curls, the tiredness gone from her face so that her skin glowed with a sun-kissed radiance. The sound of Mrs Greenspan noisily clearing her throat made him realize what he was supposed to do. He stood up, gently took Celia's extended hand, the skin so cool in this hot room. He found himself snapping his feet together, bowing his head slightly, something he had seen the Polish officers do, never having done it himself until now.

Celia laughed. Not with a mocking tone, but happily as if she actually might be pleased to see him. 'My, my, my,' she said. 'We have become all gentlemanly.'

'I-I-I… It is so good… I am pleased to see you.'

'And I am pleased to see you.' She turned to her host. 'That was thoughtful of Mr Sela to bring flowers.'

Mrs Greenspan reluctantly dipped her head then snapped her fingers at Ruta. 'Tea.'

Ruta exited the room and quickly returned, rolling in a tea trolley that must have been standing outside the doorway. Mrs Greenspan ushered her guests to a large, oak dining table in the corner of the room. 'Sit, sit,' she instructed.

If Lev had been nervous before, he was even more anxious now by what confronted him. He had never partaken of afternoon tea before. The china cups with their delicate handles, the various silver pots, jugs and bowls, the tongs for the sugar cubes – and where to start on this three-tiered stand of cakes and sandwiches? Even though he liked his tea sweet, he decided against the perils of tackling the tongs. He waited instead until Celia had made her selection from the cake stand then followed her lead. Meanwhile, Mrs Greenspan asked him what he did for a living.

'Ah yes, PICA,' she said. 'Your Anonymous Donor was here only recently.'

Lev didn't know if she meant here in Palestine or here in this house. 'That is correct,' he said, immediately regretting such a banal comment.

'Of course it is correct. Mr Greenspan had some business dealings with him. My husband is in printing. There was talk of his firm producing labels for the winery. Are you connected with such matters, Mr Sela?'

'I am a land agent for PICA, Mrs Greenspan. That is how I met Cel… Miss Kahn.'

'Nothing to do with labels then?'

'No.'

'Or the winery?'

'No, madam.'

'Or the glass bottle factory?'

'Only land.'

Mrs Greenspan went quiet after that, selected a piece of apple strudel from the top tier, sipped on her tea. Celia had produced a fan from somewhere and was gently cooling herself. Lev felt the tea beginning to make him sweat. A few more minutes passed in silence but for the clinking of tea cups on saucers until Celia stood up and announced: 'I thought Mr Sela and I might go for a walk.'

Mrs Greenspan shuddered herself into alertness. 'I shall go and get ready then.'

'There is no need, Mrs Greenspan. I am sure Mr Sela is quite knowledgeable about where to take a young woman for a stroll.'

'I cannot possibly let you go unescorted with someone you hardly know. With someone I do not know at all.'

'Mr Sela was kind enough to bring you flowers. Surely that speaks for the propriety of his nature.'

'You are a guest in my house. I must insist on my responsibility to chaperone you.'

'I reassure you, Mrs Greenspan, I am a modern woman quite capable of taking care of herself.'

Mrs Greenspan pushed herself up from her chair so that she stood face to face with Celia. Lev decided this was an opportune moment to tackle the tongs and sweeten his tea. Mickey was right. The matter of courting was indeed a war.

It was a war that Celia won, for within a few minutes the two of them were walking together down the garden path, the door closing perhaps a little too loudly behind them. Celia blew out a sigh.

'Thank God for that,' she said. 'I thought I was going to die in there.'

'She did seem rather overbearing.'

'The whole place is overbearing. Did you see that furniture? And the darkened room? It is as if they are trying to shut out the outside world. Keep themselves within their little England.'

'What is her husband like?'

'A fussy mouse of a man. I am so glad you came to rescue me.' She linked her arm in his. 'Now, where shall we go?'

Lev took her down to the beach. It was a delightful time to be there, in the light breeze that always rose with the setting sun, the fishermen out on the rocks with their rods and line, the seabirds frantically searching out their night-time nests among the cliffs and the trees. They took off their shoes, the sand crunchy and warm, a salty tang in the air, their skin glowing, the pressure of her arm on his, feelings of affection unspoken, a sense of wholeness. Was this only his reality? Or did she feel the same? He looked across at her, her lips bitten into a thoughtfulness. A few grains of sand powdered her cheek, he would like to kiss them away. The fabric of her dress against the bareness of his lower arm, the sense of her body swaying beside him, he could walk on like this forever.

'Let's go up there,' she said, pointing to the very same dune where he had once raced Amshel. 'We can have a view.'

They had their own kind of race to the summit, she dragging him back whenever he moved ahead, he doing the same to her. This physical boisterousness between them getting him all worked up, making him want to do things with her he had never wanted to do with a woman before. By the time they reached the top, he was hot, breathless, his skin tingling, his senses alive to everything around him. She sat down, motioned for him to sit beside her. Which he did. He took her hand, clasped it to him, her fingers folding around his own. They stared out to sea. The sun reddening now as it slotted down towards the horizon.

'Scotland is out there somewhere,' she said.

'And so is Poland.'

'Do you miss it?'

'Not at all.'

'There must be something, surely?'

'We were hated there.'

'What about family?'

'There's no-one left.'

'You are lucky to have Amshel here then.'

'Yes. Amshel.'

'He is doing well on the *kibbutz*.'

'I am glad to hear that.'

'He works hard. The members like that.'

'He was always good with his hands.'

'He is a good storyteller too. He makes me laugh. Which is not easy these days.'

Lev watched as a male bather swam in on the surf, scrambled to his feet, then raced along the beach. It was as if he had just witnessed the evolution from fish to man in the space of several seconds. He thought about sharing this observation with Celia, he thought about trying to make her laugh the way Amshel did. Instead, he asked: 'Do you miss Scotland?'

'I do.'

'What do you miss?'

'It's a beautiful country. Very lush and green. Even in the city there are lots of parks.'

'Do they hate the Jews there too?'

'The Protestants and Catholics are so busy hating each other, there is no hatred left over for us. The Jewish community is prospering.'

'So why did you leave?'

'I told you once before. I wanted a new life.'

'With Jonny?'

'Yes, Jonny was part of my reason. But I was also attracted to the idea of communal settlements.' She squeezed his hand. 'Let's just sit for a while.'

The sun melted away before their eyes, tainting the bay and the villas on the surrounding hills with a coral hue. The palm trees rustled their farewell to the day and a coolness entered the air. Lev remembered when he had been up here with Amshel, how they had called out to the camel drivers on their march up the beach. Where had they been going? Acre? Damascus? Beirut? Such exotic places. It was hard to believe this was his world now. He didn't miss Poland at all. With its dark forests and harsh winters. He had never seen the ocean until he had set sail for Palestine. And now he had the Mediterranean Sea on his doorstep, this wonderful light that made everything shimmer with an unearthly glow. Celia sitting by his side.

'I always feel sad when I watch a sunset,' she said. 'Sad but grateful.'

He didn't know what he felt about the sunset. All he knew was that he had never felt happier.

Twenty-five

LETTER 13

Haifa

My dear Charlotte

I am writing to you from the seaside town of Haifa. You would love it here. It is such a pretty place settled around a sandy bay with white-washed villas and palm trees. I wish I could properly describe to you the blue of the Mediterranean, for I do not think such a colour exists in Scotland.

I had forgotten what it was like to be by the sea, to have my lungs fill up with that invigorating air, to walk barefoot on warm sand. I have only been here one night and one day and I feel so much better already. I slept so soundly last night on a proper bed with freshly starched sheets and a pillow filled with down. I am staying with an elderly couple from London, Mr and Mrs Greenspan, who have a nephew on my kibbutz. They are pleased to host his comrades like me who are in desperate need of some rest. They do try to be strict with me, however, and the atmosphere in their house can be quite oppressive but it is only a small price to pay for clean bed linen and a soft mattress.

I am so glad to be away from the kibbutz. The situation has become very tense in the Jordan Valley. Gangs of Arab bandits have been crossing into the area from Trans-Jordan, attacking Jewish settlements. Only last week, a man was killed in the fields at a kibbutz near the Sea of Galilee. All for a wooden pick and some binding ropes. All of the members of my settlement must do guard duty now to cover four-hour shifts during the night. We have one rifle and one Webley revolver to protect ourselves, leftover relics from the Great War. We don't even know if they work properly as we don't want to waste the little ammunition we have in order to find out. Can you imagine me walking up and down our perimeter with my rifle staring into the darkness for sight of a marauder? To be honest, I am both scared and excited at the same time. We also have acquired an Alsatian dog that barks at every fieldmouse and spider, so we are always on constant alert.

Here in Haifa, the situation does not seem so bad. There are many building projects going on here. Both Jews and Arabs have work. Where there is work, there is money to spend, people are happier. It is the same for Haifa, it is the same for Glasgow. Despite the lack of tension, Mr Greenspan has still warned me off wandering into the Arab neighbourhoods of the town.

Lev, the land agent, came to visit me today. Do you remember him? He lives in Haifa so I asked him to call on me. His brother, Amshel, is presently living on the kibbutz, building a children's house. He has done a good job. It is nearly finished with space for twelve children sleeping in bunk beds. We only have five children at the moment so this extra space is a symbol of our optimism. He is quite a character, this Amshel. We call him Amshel the Storyteller as he has so many tales to tell. I don't know if half of them are true but I love the ones about the salt mines in Poland where the miners have carved buildings and statues into the salt. I asked Amshel why he didn't stay on with us as he is a hard worker and the members obviously like him. He asks me why we should think ourselves such proud socialists when we live on land bought for us by our Anonymous Donor, one of the richest men in the world. It is a good question for which I have no ready answer. He wants to go to America as soon as possible to make his fortune. How he will manage to do this I do not know.

I was telling you about Lev. We went for a walk together on the *beach. Mrs Greenspan wanted to chaperone me but I told her I was a modern girl who did not need an escort. She was not happy about this arrangement and has scowled at me in disapproval ever since. I wonder how she thinks we men and women live together on the kibbutz. I also wonder if I should tell her about her precious little nephew. He is sharing a tent with a Hungarian girl who in the last week looks as though she could be carrying the sixth child of our settlement.*

Lev took my hand as we walked along the shore. He is not nearly as confident as his brother, who comes to my tent, stretches out on one of the other cots, reads his newspapers and smokes his cigarettes as if he owns the place. I could actually feel Lev trembling as we strolled together, which in turn made me quite excited. Oh, Charlotte, we women are such fickle creatures sometimes. It certainly was not unpleasant to be reminded what it is like to be desired as a woman. However, I do not want to fill Lev with hope, for him to fail to realize that a woman's need for tenderness can be confused with love.

The bad news is that Lev told me the land we so needed for access to the river has been sold to someone else. My comrades will not be happy. I am not happy. The failure of this land deal will have a huge impact on morale. I wonder if our little settlement will be able to survive in such circumstances. No water, no money, so much work, and now bandits as well. It is a very hard life.

I must finish this letter, Charlotte, so I can take it to the Post Office before I catch the train back to the kibbutz. I fear I could be spending the entire morning there as I have a whole pile of letters and parcels to send on behalf of my comrades. No doubt there will be a huge amount to collect as well. Perhaps even one from you. Letters from home. They are the nourishment of our existence out here. Perhaps even more important than water. Please write back soon.

All my love

Celia

Twenty-six

THE SHUDDERING WOKE LEV from his dreams, almost tipped him out of his bed. He heard Madame Blum screaming: 'We're all going to die. We're all going to die.' He looked under the bed. Nothing there. Another judder. Another cry from Madame Blum: 'Armageddon. Armageddon is here.' Books fell out of shelves, a framed watercolour of Haifa swayed on its hook, crashed to the tiled floor. He jumped out of bed. The ground shook. Where was there to run to when the whole world was in spasms? Madame Blum again: 'Where are my candlesticks?' Mickey's voice: 'Get under the table. Under the table. It will pass.' Lev at the doorway to his room, hands placed against the jambs for balance, under the lintel for protection, watermelons rolling around the hallway. Another tremor. Screaming coming from outside now, the smash of tiles off roofs, a glimpse through the window of palm trees swaying and bending, bunches of dates breaking, dropping to the earth with a hiss and thud. Then everything settling, rocking back into place. Lev held his breath, waited. Silence except for Madame Blum sobbing in the kitchen. An automobile horn. A generator starting up. Lev waited. Voices in the street. Mickey coming through to the hallway, saying: 'It's over. Don't worry. It's over.'

Haifa escaped relatively unscathed. Madame Blum lost some dishes, picture frames, a lamp; Mickey some watermelons, a few bottles of vodka. Elsewhere, news of damage caused by the earthquake arrived sporadically. Communication systems were down in many places, only a few telegrams and telegraphs getting through.

Landslides were being reported. The Jordan River was dammed up. Reports of many deaths in Nablus, also in Jerusalem and Trans-Jordan. Buildings collapsed everywhere. The famous Winter Palace Hotel in Jericho gone. 'God is punishing us,' cried Madame Blum, but for what she wouldn't say. Mickey was more pragmatic: 'What do you expect? The hotel was built with mud.' Lev worried about Celia. The Jordan Valley had split in places. There had been casualties in Tiberias. But no information had seeped through about any incidents in the settlements.

The next morning, Lev went down to the beach on his way to work. There were a few topless palms, trunks snapped, bunches of dates scattered across the sand like dead bodies, armies of ants carrying off the spoils. Other than that, everything appeared as normal. Yet, he still felt shaken, unsure, disorientated. The ground for his footsteps, once so secure, could no longer be trusted. His world, once so fixed and solid, was now a fragile place. If he could not rely on this Earth, what could he rely on? Who could he rely on?

He certainly could rely on the Haifa Central Post Office. For here it was business as usual. The building could not afford to be otherwise, hosting as it did the daily sackloads of letters and parcels arriving on trains from Damascus, on boats from Egypt and England, in post-vans from Jerusalem and Jaffa, in the saddlebags of horses from outlying villages. Sammy, in particular, took advantage of this postal hub, collecting international stamps in several albums, carefully steaming them off the correspondence that arrived at the desks of PICA from all over the world. As for the domestic stamps of Palestine, the Arabs and Jews argued fiercely over their design and wording just as much as they argued over Jerusalem and everything else.

On this day, the postal halls were particularly busy. As Lev waited in line, he watched the anxious customers crowding outside the few telephone booths to check for news of loved ones. Celia's settlement had no telephone, he didn't even know where the nearest one might be. But he had just seen the morning's newspapers – still no reports of any casualties in the Jordan Valley. He collected the usual healthy stack of letters for PICA, flicked through the bundle, these postmarks from far-off places still giving him a thrill. There was even one from

Australia, two or three from the United States. It wasn't even seeing his own name that first caught his eye. But the slightly raised letter 'v' in the word 'Lev'. It was a typewritten tic carried deep in his memory, the one flaw in that magnificent machine of his youth with the name 'Kanzler' scrolled in gold across the top. There could be only one source for this letter which he now held in his shaking hand.

He ignored it at first. Buried the letter deep in the pile which he carried back to the office. He was surprised not to find Sammy already there, waiting eagerly for the correspondence that would begin his day. Lev left the bundle on Sammy's desk, extracted the letter addressed to him, went and sat in his own room. He took up his usual posture with his chair swung round to face the open window, his feet resting up on the sill. He looked at the envelope in his hands. 'Ewa Kaminsky,' he said to himself. 'How is life treating you in America?'

New York

My dear Lev

So many years we didn't communicate. It was a great mistake. Your father and I thought you wanted a fresh start, that it was best for you to get on with this life of yours with Sarah in Palestine without the burden of all our previous tragedies. We were wrong. It was not good for a father and son to be apart like this, but Amshel broke your father's heart by leaving, then the death of the two boys in the war, he thought it was best to let you go. And now this. Your letter. And this change of name. From Gottleib to Sela. How would we ever have found you?

Your father is dead, Lev. He was killed more than two years ago in a stupid, stupid accident. He was run over by an automobile just outside our apartment. I heard it happen. The window was open, it was one of those hot New York summer evenings, still light outside. Your father never did get used to those automobiles. Horses and donkeys was what he knew. I rushed outside. He died in my arms. I am so sorry I have to write to tell you this.

I want you to know we had a good life together here in America. For these few years, he was happy. We were happy. He had stopped drinking. Even if he had wanted to continue, it would have been difficult as it is forbidden to buy alcohol here. He was working in construction. There is so much building going on in this city. Bridges. Roads. Office buildings that scrape the sky they are so tall. Your father was a strong man, he worked hard. I also had work. As a secretary, of course. We had a nice apartment with electricity and an inside toilet. Outside in the streets, the sewers are buried underground in pipes. What a wonderful place this is.

New York is a good city to be a Jew. We are surrounded by Jews. I believe there are more Jews in New York than in Palestine. There are newspapers in Yiddish, theatres in Yiddish, gossip in Yiddish, barrels of pickled herrings in the street. People leave us alone. They do not call us names, they do not desecrate our tombstones. I am happy to be in America. To speak in English. I took your father to the movies. We went to hear jazz. We even went dancing. Can you imagine, Lev? Your father dancing. We also started to save some money. We had big plans for the future. And then this stupid accident happened.

What about you, Lev? What is life like in Haifa? Are you married to Sarah now? Do you have children? Your father would have been so happy to be a grandfather. You tell us nothing about yourself, only about your brother Amshel. I try to keep up with the news about Palestine. Always there seems to be some kind of trouble. Jews are going there, Jews are leaving there. I have a pushke on my sideboard for money I give to the Zionists. Every time I put my nickels and dimes in the slot, I think of you, Lev, and that summer we spent together before you went away. Tell me, how is your typing?

I am glad that Amshel has found you. I never knew him, of course, but it must be good for you to have a brother with you. To be with family is a fine thing. Unfortunately, I am not in the situation to help him. To tell you the truth, after a time of terrible loneliness, I met someone else. He is a kind man, he looks after me. But he does not want to know of my previous life. I am a new woman for him, with no past. So I cannot help Amshel with any letter of financial support. If it were you, then maybe it would be different. But with Amshel I have no connection. I am sorry. I realize a Jew cannot just turn up in America any more without the proper papers and sponsors. Perhaps Amshel should go back to Poland? Your grandfather left some property there, the cottage in the wood – you must remember? There was land around it too. Your father tried to sort it out from here but then he died and it is not my business anymore. Amshel should attend to this – after all, he is the oldest son.

I hope you are well, Lev. I hope you have found happiness with your Sarah, and your children give you many blessings.

With warmest regards
Ewa Kaminsky

Lev put down the letter, dropped his feet from the sill, turned his back on the sea. His father was dead. Such a remote figure in his life, why should it matter to him? He remembered how Amshel used to say: 'Look at him, Lev. Look at him.' And here his brother put a circle of thumb and index finger in front of his eye to help him focus better on the stooped figure plodding up the street. 'He always looks like he's *schlepping* a piano.'

It wasn't a piano his father was *schlepping* in America. Or crates of liquor as he used to do in Mr Borkowski's store. But bricks and planks and girders. Building bridges and roads and office buildings. It seemed America had straightened his crouched frame so that he even went dancing. Lev tried to imagine the two of them, all dressed up in evening wear, gliding across a shiny, empty floor in each other's arms, his father's trousers just a little bit too long for him. Smiling. Szmul Gottleib, happy in America.

Lev went back to the post office, sent a simple telegram to Amshel, asking him to come to Haifa immediately. He then went home for lunch.

Twenty-seven

THE EARTH MIGHT HAVE STOPPED SHAKING but Lev could see Madame Blum was still trembling as she served him cold *borsht* and a salad of raw vegetables at the kitchen table. She then sat down beside him. Her hair was pulled back into a headscarf, dragging up her thin eyebrows over the stretched, powdered skin of her forehead. Her eyes, usually black-lined, were devoid of any make-up.

'What's the matter?' she asked.

'Nothing.'

'I can tell something is wrong.'

Lev shrugged, slurped on a spoonful of beetroot soup. That sweet, earthy taste, it was delicious.

'You are holding something in, Lev. I see it written in the lines of your brow. It is not good. You will get indigestion.'

Lev relented. 'I received a letter this morning. From America.'

'From your father?'

He told her what Ewa had written.

'For the death of your father, I wish you "long life",' Madame Blum said, then asked: 'How do you feel?'

The question surprised him. Nobody had ever asked him that before. About anything. He didn't have an answer.

'To lose a father is never simple,' she said. 'Even one who was so far away.'

Lev thought about the last time he had seen him. On a station platform in Warsaw, together with Ewa Kaminsky. As his train departed. Ewa was blowing kisses, his father's head was bowed, his hands deep in his pockets. Lev knew then he would never see him again.

Madame Blum patted the back of his hand. 'You and Mickey, you are like my own children.'

'I know that.'

'My late husband and I… we couldn't have children. We wanted, but we couldn't have.'

It was the first time he had heard this. It was unusual for Madame Blum to say anything about her husband without cursing him. He and Mickey still wondered what had really happened to him that day he fell in front of the Haifa-Damascus train.

Madame Blum went on. 'Yes, having you and Mickey here has been a blessing.' She stared at her ringless fingers. 'You are not lonely here. A woman my age knows how it feels to be lonely. But you have me. And you also have Sammy. He has been like a father to you.'

Sammy lived in the German colony. Straight rows of detached houses set in their own gardens stretching from the Abbas Effendi Garden in the hills right down to the sea. The properties tended to be two-storey, red-tiled affairs with wonderful views of the Mediterranean. They had been built by some German religious group Lev knew nothing about. But then there were so many religious groups in Palestine, it would have been hard to keep track of them all. At least this one built fine houses.

Sammy's home stood out from the rest. It had been designed by a German architect who had worked for the Turkish administration but loved all things English. As a result, Sammy lived in a compact, one-storey cottage with exposed internal beams, all hemmed in by cedar trees and a garden overgrown with imported rose bushes. 'A house fit for Shakespeare,' was how Sammy described his dwelling. Lev had no idea what Shakespeare would have looked like but he imagined him to be rather short given the low height of all the cottage's doorways.

A dead dog lay on the road close by Sammy's gate, the second one Lev had come across on the short walk over from Madame Blum's. Flies hovered over its skinny frame, burrowing into the ears and eyes. He gave the lifeless animal a wide berth, covered his mouth against the stench for fear of catching rabies. He pushed open the gate, glad of the dim and cool of Sammy's garden with its shade of cedar trees, its scent of roses.

The tremors had shaken a couple of tiles off the roof into the flowerbeds, pots of succulents lay broken at the entrance doorway. Other than that, no damage. Lev scraped the pot shards and loose earth into a heap with his foot, knocked on the front door. No answer. He searched for the spare key in its usual spot on top of the lintel. Nothing there. He tried to peer through a few of the windows but it was too dark or the glass was too dirty for him to see inside. Sammy must have gone away on some field trip. As he turned to walk away from the house, he saw Mickey standing at the gate, one arm resting on a two-wheeled trolley loaded up with wooden crates.

'This is a bit of luck,' Mickey said. 'I could do with a hand.'

Lev grabbed one trolley handle, Mickey the other, they tipped up the crates, pushed the load forward.

'What's inside?' Lev asked.

'*Tchatchkes.*'

A typical Mickey answer. Yiddish. Vague. Trinkets. 'Why can't you just tell me?'

'My business is my business.'

'People are talking about your business.'

'Really? What are they saying?'

'That you're dealing in guns.'

Mickey laughed, stopped pushing the trolley. 'Who told you this?'

'Rumours. In the markets. The coffee houses. The card schools.'

'Gun smuggling is a serious accusation.'

'I'm just telling you what people are saying.'

'Is that what you think is in these crates? Rifles? Grenades?'

Lev shrugged. 'As you said. *Tchatchkes.*'

Mickey pulled a screwdriver from his back pocket, set about levering the lid off one of the crates. A splinter cut into his hand, forcing him to pull back, suck at the wound. 'I'll show you fucking guns,' he said.

'Forget it, Mickey. I believe you.'

It was too late. Mickey was back attacking the crate, prying off the lid. He held up a small, green, metal container with a red cross on it.

'See?' he said. 'First Aid boxes. Not hand grenades. First fucking Aid.'

They didn't talk after that. The going was a bit tougher anyway, pushing the load uphill, Mickey reduced to one arm as he sucked away at his cut, trying to stem the flow with a piece of gauze from one of the First Aid boxes. Back at the house, Madame Blum took him away to bandage up his hand, leaving Lev to prepare some fresh orange juice in the kitchen. But Mickey was soon back in the room.

'Why didn't you tell me about your father?'

'I was going to,' he said, squeezing down hard on an orange. 'But the contents of the crates got in the way.' He felt himself closed up over his loss anyway. For years he had lived as if he had no father. Ewa's letter might have upset his balance for a few hours, but now he was back to his orphan life.

'For God's sake, Lev. I am your friend...'

'...The news is just terrible,' Madame Blum exclaimed as she burst into the kitchen. 'Terrible, terrible, terrible.'

'What news?' Lev asked.

'I've just spoken to Ida. She says the area around Nablus is like... like Armageddon.'

'How does she know?'

'Her husband Max works in the mayor's office. They have telephones there.' Madame Blum sat down at the kitchen table, fanned the worry on her face with her fingers. 'Ida says they are talking about over one hundred dead. Many buildings collapsed. People still buried under the rubble. Children crushed. A tragedy.'

'Did she say anything about the north?' Lev asked. 'The Jordan Valley?'

'What do I know about the north? I am talking about Nablus.'

'Celia will be fine,' Mickey said.

'What makes you so sure?'

'If Nablus is the centre of the quake, the Jordan Valley will be like here. No deaths. No casualties. No buildings damaged. Just a slight shaking.'

'Yes, yes,' Madame Blum said. 'A shaking. A shaking up of everything.'

Twenty-eight

EVEN AFTER LEV'S MANY YEARS in Haifa, the feverish babble of the station terminus on Faisal Street continued to thrill him. The bursts of steam, the whistles, the shouts for assistance, the cries of the porters, the tea-sellers and the trinket vendors. As did the sight of the wealthy tourists stepping off the longboats from a recently arrived ship moored out in the bay. Those whiskered men suave and confident in their top hats, their stylish wives wrapped in their minks despite the warmth. Those American and European visitors who had enough money not only to come here but also the freedom to return happily from where they came. Awaiting these first-class passengers, over on a siding away from the main tracks, uniformed guards stood by a special train with its luxury coaches, shiny dining cars and sleeping saloons soon to be covered in flies and dust. Destination: Sea of Galilee and the religious sites of Tiberias.

The train from Damascus via the Jordan Valley was only twenty-five minutes late, the engine crew marking this unusual triumph with huge, pink smiles on their coal-blackened faces as the train hissed breathless to a standstill by one of the station's tall palms. And there was Amshel, first off, with a stampede of passengers following in his wake. He looked well, Lev thought, muscled and lean, sun-tanned, smiling, something different about him, he couldn't quite work out what. Amshel upon him now, hands grabbing him by the shoulders, shaking him affectionately, then raising his arms out to the side, presenting himself with a grin. 'Well?'

'Well what?'

'What do you think?'

'About what?'

Amshel pointed repeatedly at his own mouth. 'Are you blind?'

'Your teeth,' Lev said. 'What happened to your teeth?'

'God give thanks to your friend Mickey. He told me he was giving me a special set. I could see they were top quality myself. Vulcanised rubber plates with a good set of porcelains attached.' Amshel tipped his head up and to the side, mouth opened wide so Lev could get a good look. 'Uh, uh, uh,' Amshel grunted, pointing to his shining dentures.

'What are you saying?'

Amshel closed his mouth. 'I don't even have to take them out when I eat. They fit perfectly. Where is Mickey? I want to thank him. I want to kiss him. I am a new man.'

'Who took out the old ones?'

'A blacksmith in Tiberias.'

'You went to a blacksmith?'

'Nails out of hooves, teeth out of mouths, it's all the same to me, that's what the man told me. Although I drank half a bottle of *arak* before he started. I hardly noticed the pain after he'd taken out the first three or four. It was good he was strong, held me down with an arm across my throat, a knee on my chest. He did a fine job too, didn't break one tooth. Not one tooth. Or my jaw. I still spat up enough blood to fill the Sea of Galilee though. Then these dentures Mickey gave me, a perfect fit. It was like a miracle, Lev. A miracle. It has changed my whole life.'

'You look good, Amshel. I was worried about you after the quake.'

'We suffered a few tremors.'

'How about Celia?'

'Everyone is safe. And my children's house is still standing, not a brick or beam out of place. But further south, there were enormous cracks in the ground. A few of us went to have a look. It was as if God Himself tried to tear Trans-Jordan away from the rest of Palestine.' Amshel waved the single page of his telegram at him. 'You've heard from America?'

'Yes.' Then slowly, he added: 'Papa is dead.'

'What?'

'Killed in an accident.'

Amshel grasped his head in his hands, closing up his elbows so as to conceal his face. Lev could hear the sniffing, the sudden gulping for breath. He hadn't expected this, his brother's instant dissolution into tears, especially compared to his own dry reaction to the news. But soon it was over. One last gasp. Amshel brought his arms down, wiped the back of his hand across his nose.

'Borkowski wrote you?'

'No. Papa's wife. Ewa.'

'Show me.'

Lev extracted the letter from his satchel, gave it over. Amshel peered at the typewritten address, then at the stamp printed with the map of the country of sender. 'The United States of America,' he mouthed, before handing back the envelope. 'Read it to me.'

'We should sit down and talk somewhere.' Lev had thought about going over to the German Colony, to sit in Sammy's garden, but now he realized he wanted to be up high, a place where there was space and a view, room to say what needed to be said. 'We'll go up there.' He pointed to Mount Carmel. 'Up by the monastery.'

'Just tell me what's in the letter.'

'We can talk as we go along.'

Amshel chased after him. 'What did she say?'

'I'll tell you soon enough.'

'Will she still sponsor me?'

'Is that all you care about?'

Amshel stopped asking questions, dropped back as Lev walked on, moving faster, kicking out at stones, concentrating on the view. This would be a good place to build a house, he thought, if there was a proper road rather than this dirt path to the monastery. There had been much talk of constructing one, with a hospital or even a university at the end of it. It would be wonderful to live up here, looking out to the sea, not only north along the bay but also south to the famous vineyards of the Anonymous Donor.

He came to a simple bench a few hundred yards short of the monastery gates. It was a good place to stop, the path twisting away from the direct blaze of the sun, the ancient branches of an olive tree wrapping the seat in some shade. Perhaps this was where the Carmelite monks came for some solitary contemplation away from the monastery itself. He sat down, damp with sweat, waited for his heart to slow, for his breath to settle, for Amshel to arrive. Which he did, a minute or so later, to sit beside him on the bench, stretch out his legs, fold his arms and ask: 'What happened to him?'

'He was run over by an automobile. In New York City.'

'Read it, Lev. Read out the letter.'

Lev did as he was told.

'She is my stepmother,' Amshel said when he had finished. 'Yet she won't help me.'

'She doesn't even know you. What do you expect?'

'I don't expect anything. I have had no luck in my life. Not one little piece of *mazel*. Nothing.'

'It's Papa who was unlucky.'

'Papa wasn't unlucky. He was just stupid enough to get hit by an automobile. Leaving me to that heartless wife of his.'

'She was kind to me.'

'You're the lucky one then.'

'What about our *zeide*'s land? You could go back, claim your inheritance.'

'Go back to Poland? Go back to where they hate us? Grandfather's house is probably a pig-pen by now.' Amshel stood up. 'I'm going back into town.'

'What for?'

'To thank Mickey for my teeth.'

'Wait.' Lev played with the pages of Ewa's letter on his lap. 'There is something else.'

'More bad news?'

'What happened between you and Sarah?'

Amshel sniffed hard. 'What do you mean?'

'You know what I mean.'

'It was years ago.'

'Answer me, Amshel.'

'You know something, Lev. You were always like this. Even when you were a child. Like a little dog snapping, snapping, snapping away at my ankles. Refusing to let go. Tell me this, Amshel. How do you do this, Amshel? What do I do now, Amshel?'

'I want to know about you and Sarah.'

'What difference will it make?'

'I just want to know.'

'She was sleeping with everyone. They all were. The situation was unusual. Conditions were primitive.'

'Answer me.'

'All right then. Yes. Something happened between us. Are you happy now?'

Lev got to his feet, faced his brother. 'I want you to leave Celia alone.'

'Has the sun boiled your brains?'

'You heard what I said.'

'I wouldn't do that to you.'

'It didn't stop you with Sarah.'

'I didn't consider Sarah forbidden fruit.'

'Swear it then.'

'I can't believe you don't trust me.'

'Swear it.'

Amshel spat into the dry earth, turned his back, started to walk down the path away from the monastery.

'That's just like you, Amshel. Always leaving.'

Without turning round, Amshel gave a dismissive wave, continued down the track.

Lev didn't make any conscious decision, his actions just came from pure emotion. He ran after his brother, flew at him, grabbed him around the shoulders, forced his knees into the back of his legs, so that the two of them fell forward on to the ground. 'Swear it!' he shouted as he pummelled his fists into Amshel's back. 'Swear it.'

He had Amshel pinned down face-first but still his brother managed to twist his head around. He saw his mouth open and close in a gummy emptiness, his dentures knocked out from the fall. He kept beating on his bucking back as Amshel tried to push him off. But somehow Amshel found the strength to turn himself round, forcing Lev over and on to the ground. And before he knew it, Amshel was on top of him, one hand against his throat, the other scraping around in the dirt for his teeth. There was blood on Amshel's forehead, a gash across his nose, his lips white with dust. He was mouthing toothless words Lev couldn't understand.

Amshel didn't seem to know what to do from his position of strength. He faked a punch, then grabbed a handful of loose dirt, smeared it across Lev's face. Lev felt the scratches across his cheeks, the loose stones being forced into his mouth. It was his turn to buck and heave but Amshel was too strong for him. Always had been.

Suddenly, where there had been blue sky and raw sunlight, there was now shadow. Lev saw a set of hands grasp Amshel's shoulders, pulling him back. Then a voice that was not his brother's. A gentle, soothing, coaxing tone. Amshel calming, gradually lifting his weight. Lev wriggled free, pushed himself up onto his feet. Amshel opposite, held back in the loose grip of a man dressed in simple brown robes. Lev spat out the dirt from his mouth, stared at his brother. Amshel gulped in air, wiped his wrist across his lips, was about to say something but the man intervened.

'Walk away,' the monk told Lev firmly. 'Walk away.'

Lev half-walked, half-ran down the track. He had somehow hurt his knee in the fight and his left leg kept buckling under him. There was an ache in his chest that could have been a physical injury or just all the hurt that had arisen inside of him. He found it hard to breathe. But he kept going, walking off the pain, down off the hill and back through the residential streets of the German Quarter, ignoring the looks from those he passed, until he reached PICA's offices. There at an outside tap in the back court, he flushed the dirt out of his mouth, drank away his thirst, cleaned himself up. His cheeks were grazed, the back of his shirt torn and bloodied. He would tell Madame Blum he had got into a fight with some Arab youths.

He went upstairs to the empty offices, sat by the window, looked out at the sea, stayed there for hours until the light started to go out of the day, and his anger with it. He rose from his chair, switched off the fan, passed by Sammy's room, the unopened letters still on his desk. He thought of the shut-up cottage, the broken plant pots, the missing key on the lintel.

Twenty-nine

IT WAS DARK BY THE TIME Lev arrived at the cottage. He knocked on the door. No answer. He eased himself around the side of the building, stepping in sandy beds, through low bushes, tapping on the window-panes. Still no answer. He returned to the front. On the entrance step, the small pile of earth and pot shards he had scraped together on his previous visit remained untouched. He tested the door again. He would have to break in. But he would do so through one of the side windows where the cedars stood thick and tall, concealing his entry from any neighbours. He picked up the broken base of one of the plant pots, slid back around the outside wall, the branches of the trees scraping against his already torn shirt, treading carefully until he came to a small window. Sammy's bedroom. He tried to push it open but it was snibbed shut. He wrapped his knuckles in his hand-kerchief, inserted his fist into the pot base. He was lucky. It was a snug fit. He didn't have much space to arc back his arm but he did what he could to gain some leverage before giving the pane a short sharp jab. The glass shattered easily. He waited to see if any noise came from inside. Or even if there might be a shout from a neighbour. But all he could hear was his own breathing. He twisted in his arm, released the catch but the window wouldn't budge upwards. He had no choice but to tap the pot against the remaining window shards until the area was clear. He then wriggled himself through into the darkness.

It was the stench that hit him first. He unwrapped his handker-chief from his fist, placed it over his nose and mouth. He waited for his stomach to settle, his eyes to adjust to the very little light that crept into the room from the outside. Sammy's was one of the first properties in the town to have its own electricity. Sometimes it worked, sometimes it didn't. He prayed that it would, if he could only find the switch. He felt his way around the bed, then over to the doorway, where he searched blindly for the nipple of a switch. He clicked it on. He had light.

He pushed open the low door into the hallway. The fetid stink was too much. His stomach turned and he choked up the bile into his handkerchief. He ran back to the broken window, sucked in the clean air, steeled himself to try again. He crossed the bedroom floor, out into the hallway, trying not to breathe. He had three doors to choose from. He found it hard to focus on them. His face burned, his eyes stung from his sweat as he tried to concentrate. It had to be Sammy's study. He moved towards the door, turned the knob. It was locked. He shook it again, and again. He took a few paces back into the bedroom, then ran shoulder-first at the study door. The wood around the lock snapped away easily and he was inside.

Thirty

Kfar Ha'Emek, Jordan Valley, Palestine

My dear Charlotte

As always, it was so wonderful to receive your letter and to hear all of your news. I want to thank you for visiting my parents. I am pleased to hear that while they may be frail they are still in good health. I worry about them so much.

I worry about you too. I fear you may be getting far too involved in the temperance movement. I can understand your campaigns against the demon drink but is it necessary to want to close down other venues of recreation as well? What is wrong with the ice-cream parlours? I am sure you remember those sunny days when we walked through Queens Park together for an ice-cream and some confection at that lovely Café Moderne on Pollokshaws Road. Surely that wonderful parlour cannot be considered a den of iniquity in the same breath you speak of Glasgow's public houses? I am surprised you hold such extreme views these days against public entertainment when I remember you as a young woman so full of outward joy and mischief. Has something happened to you, Charlotte? What are you not telling me? As for me, ice-cream parlours could not be further from my daily existence. The raids by bandits from across the border are becoming more frequent up and down the valley. Although we have not experienced any direct attack ourselves, we must remain very vigilant and our all-night guard duty continues.

Since our land deal with the Bedouin has fallen through, we can no longer draw any water from the river, even in emergencies. Our crops are dying in the fields and water for our personal use is being severely rationed. The first priority is for drinking purposes. Water for cooking is next priority. We may wash our hands prior to eating but full body showers are now restricted to once a week. As for our laundry, well there is little chance of that. My skin constantly itches from the lack of a good wash and from the dirt and sweat on my clothes.

On top of these problems, we have suffered great conflict among ourselves. We are so lacking in manpower and the extra guard duty has only added to our burden. The citrus fruit needed to be picked or it would die on the branch but we had so few people to do the work. We usually ask the Bedouin to help us in exchange for some produce and medical services but as we are not on speaking terms this was not possible. Consequently we had to hire Arab workers from the nearby village of al-Dalhamiyya. This arrangement did not sit well with the most fervent Zionists among us who demanded we should hire only Jewish workers from Tiberias to carry out Jewish labour. This was not a financially viable option as Jewish workers want higher wages than the Arabs. (The reason this is so would require another letter altogether.) This inequality was not acceptable to the socialists among us. In the end, after endless meetings, meetings and more meetings, necessity prevailed and we brought in the Arab workers. That caused a fight to break out in the fields between our Zionist and socialist members as the Arab workers watched on. I was so embarrassed and disappointed I could have raced back to Haifa and taken the first boat back to Scotland. I really don't know why the Arabs worry about the Jews. They should just leave us alone until we end up killing each other. Then they can walk back in and take back all the land they want.

If this was not enough, we experienced an earthquake here a few days ago. The centre was in Nablus which is about fifty miles away, and many people were killed there. Here, we felt only the tremors. It is a frightening experience when all the ground around you is shaking and there is nowhere to run. Even when it finishes and everything settles down again, the world doesn't quite feel the same as it was before.

I stole away from the kibbutz after the quake with Amshel the Storyteller. He had heard there were huge splits in the ground further south in the valley and wanted to see them for himself. It was quite a little adventure and I felt as if we were children running away from school but it was good to get away for a while, even for just a few hours. Amshel is good company too, with all the tales he has to tell. He is also much more handsome now he has had his teeth fixed. On our little day trip, we came across these great cracks in the ground and were told that some cattle had fallen into the chasm. We could still hear one poor beast bellowing from down below but there was nothing we could do to help the farmers pull it out. In the end, someone had to shoot the animal.

As for Amshel's brother, Lev, I have not heard from him since I returned from Haifa. Perhaps that is just as well as I worry he might have over-estimated my feelings for him. He did send Amshel a telegram asking him to go down there immediately and that is where Amshel is now. He hopes Lev has heard from their father in America. That is all Amshel ever talks about. America, America, America. It is very good for the Jews there. Amshel says there is so much empty land you can buy an acre for the price of a postage stamp.

Men. It is hard to know how to deal with them these days. I live here together with so many of them in such close proximity yet the relationships do not seem to be intimate in a man-woman kind of way. Perhaps it is because we are just so tired and busy all the time. It is almost as if we are sexless, just relating to each other as human beings where gender does not seem to matter. I know this should be a good thing, a socialist ideal. But I do miss the excitement of being as a woman to a man. It would be so good to talk to you about these things.

I must go now. It is late and I have guard duty to do.

All my love
Celia

Thirty-one

THE VERDICT FROM the British police doctor had been straightforward. Suicide by a bullet through the mouth into the brain. Cold words on a medical certificate that did not mirror in the slightest the scene Lev had encountered when he shouldered open the study door. At first, he wasn't even sure what kind of tableau he had been looking at. A body and head flung back in a chair, it was almost as if Sammy had been laughing at something uproariously funny. But the top of his cranium was gone, blood and brain and bone matter spattered against the wall, down the sides of his face, his mouth a burnt and blasted mess. The flies. The smell. Lev dry-retched then collapsed to his knees. 'Oh no,' he mouthed over and over again. 'Oh no.'

He managed to drag himself away from the study to sit outside on the front step, his head in his hands, he did not know what to do. He was aware there were duties he should attend to, people he must speak to. The police, a doctor, a rabbi, Chaim Kalisher at PICA. He lacked the strength to do anything. A neighbour found him sitting on the same spot an hour later. Lev recognized the face looking down at him. An ex-British officer who had decided to retire to the warmth of the Middle East rather than return home. A military man, Colonel George Henderson, he was just who Lev needed. Someone to take control, someone to give orders, someone who was used to death. Mrs Henderson helped take Lev back to Madame Blum's. A tall, fragile, considerate woman, who wore a wide-brimmed hat, moved gracefully, spoke beautifully and smelled of roses. He wanted to hug her, cry into the shoulder of her silk blouse. Instead, he allowed her to support his arm with her spindly fingers as they walked slowly together along the lanes to his home, she guiding him around the dead dog lying in their path, both of them feeling awkward at the sight of the maggot-infested flesh. She deposited him into the care of Madame Blum who unfortunately was hopeless for the task. She had screamed at the news, retreated to her bedroom, leaving Lev to sit silently with Mrs Henderson, side by side on the sofa, until Mickey arrived home.

The Jewish cemetery in Haifa was close to the sea, a breezy enclave set back from the cranes and the diggers working on the new port. Sammy had picked out a plot many years before, located on a slight westward-facing slope that would allow him to look out to the wide, blinding-blue horizons of the Mediterranean. Young palms close to his site would grow tall over the years to provide much-needed shade as Sammy never really liked the sun. Lev thought it was an unusual choice for Sammy not to look back at the land that had so defined him. After all, Sammy was king of the soil. Land is land is land. Why not look on it in death as in life? But perhaps Sammy was sick of all the squabbling over territory. Better to find peace in the elusive incorporeal nature of the sea.

Even with the delay caused by the autopsy, the funeral remained a small affair. Sammy had no family in Palestine. Apart from Lev, only Mickey, Chaim Kalisher from PICA, Colonel and Mrs Henderson, a few other neighbours and some shop owners were in attendance. Madame Blum was too stricken with grief to make the short journey to the cemetery though she was keen her home should host the reception that would take place afterwards.

It was a beautiful day for a burial, if there could be such a thing. The sky was cloudless, the temperature not too warm, a pleasant onshore breeze gently lifted the palm fronds, if not the mood. Even the usual sound of metal gouging out earth for the port construction suddenly ceased for the ceremony. The local rabbi reluctantly conducted the service, muttering a few hastily prepared words about a man he didn't know, trying to conjure up something good to say from the one fact he did. A sin according to the *Talmud*, for it was up to God to put to death and to make to live. There was even discussion that Sammy's dedicated plot could not be used and he would have to be buried at some remote corner, far away from those who had died properly at God's will. Lev insisted other scholars should be consulted to argue the point but in the end the rabbi agreed Sammy's sin could be forgiven on the grounds he was suffering from some kind of mental illness at the time of death.

Sammy was not a religious man anyway, attending the synagogue only when he felt like it. He was not an atheist, he just considered religion as being for the most part some kind of personal vanity. 'I believe God has better things to do with His time than look after the private interests of Sammy Ziv,' he often declared. Sammy had a lot of wise words to say. Lev would miss him terribly for that. *Sammy was the father I never had,* he thought, as he stood over the open grave. For that reason he accepted the honour of being the official mourner in the absence of any son or other male relative. But as he recited the Prayer for the Dead, he felt regret for the death of his real father too, that sad figure whose demise was symbolic of a man so out of place in the modern world. He slowed down his recitation, fixing it in his thoughts that his words were intended for both of their departed souls. He then scattered a shovel of earth onto the thin-wooded coffin. The gravediggers did the rest.

Back at Madame Blum's, it was the neighbour, Ida, the one with the husband that worked at the mayor's office, who ended up hosting the small reception, happy to hand out the *blintzes,* the *strudel,* the black tea and the brandy along with a bit of gossip. Madame Blum herself was back in her bedroom, too overwhelmed with grief to carry out her duties. Lev, who was just emerging from his own shock at the tragedy, was surprised she had taken the news so badly.

'She really loved him,' Mickey told him.

'She hardly knew him.'

'They were lovers, Lev. Had been for many years.'

'Lovers? Don't be ridiculous.'

'Look how the poor woman grieves.'

'Remember when he was over here for Friday night dinner? It was the first time he had been in the house.'

'That may have been true. Madame Blum preferred to conduct their affair at Sammy's residence. That way, she felt she wasn't betraying the memory of her dead husband.'

'She hated her dead husband.'

'Women have strange loyalties,' Mickey said knowingly as he helped himself to another piece of cake. 'This *strudel* is delicious. Did Ida bake this?'

'Forget the *strudel*. You knew about this affair all along?'

'She knew I could keep a secret.'

'And I couldn't?'

'No. With you, I believe she was embarrassed.'

'I wouldn't have cared.'

'With you and Sammy working so closely together, she felt it might be complicated for you.' At this remark, Mickey drifted off, leaving Lev to contemplate what had just been said. Sammy and Madame Blum. It seemed so obvious to him now, how had he missed it? He wondered if Sammy had other lovers as well, one to suit each occasion, just like his different hats.

He felt a touch to his arm, then the softly spoken words: 'A great loss to all of us.' Lev looked up into the grey eyes of Chaim Kalisher. Lev had noticed him before. His large, elegant frame sliding effortlessly around the room from one knot of mourners to another, shaking hands, bending forward to provide an appropriate comment, the Anonymous Donor's representative in Palestine handing out his largesse. There was a benign smile on Kalisher's lips, no doubt perfected for the beggars and the bereaved, as he went on to say: 'How hard it is to know the soul living inside every one of us.'

'What do you mean?'

'It appears I was the last person to witness Sammy alive. After he left my office, he returned home and then… well, to be honest, I didn't notice anything unusual. He had been so agitated recently.'

'Enough to make him go off and kill himself.'

Kalisher sighed. 'These things build up over time. As you know, Sammy had an immense trust in the overall goodness of human nature. A misguided trust perhaps. But a noble virtue all the same. When he came across others who didn't behave according to his expectations, he became very depressed.' Kalisher withdrew a cigar case from his inside jacket pocket, snapped it open. 'Can I interest you?'

Lev shook his head.

Kalisher looked around the room. 'Perhaps I should go outside. Come and see me, Lev, when all this has settled down.'

'And join an alliance with the Zionists?'

'PICA has to move with the times. Even our Anonymous Donor recognizes that. There is so much tension these days with the Arabs. What the Zionists can offer in the way of security cannot be ignored. They have weapons. They have trained fighters. They have influence. PICA by itself is no longer in a position to protect its investments.'

'It was the Zionists and their policies that caused all the tensions in the first place.'

'That may be true. But pragmatism rather than idealism will always prevail. Sammy thought very highly of you. Let us at least have a friendly chat at a more appropriate time.'

There was no time to respond, for Madame Blum had emerged from her bedroom. She wore a dressing gown she had cut and slashed in places, a torn garment in the tradition of a mourning wife. Her grey hair, rather than stretched tight in a stylish bun, hung greasy and loose over her face, down to her shoulders.

She clutched her gown tight with one hand, pointed at Kalisher with the other

'It was you,' she screamed. 'It was you who betrayed Sammy.'

Mickey rushed towards her, clutched at her sobbing figure, tried to lead her away. But she was able to wriggle free. 'You betrayed him,' she shouted again. 'You and your Anonymous Donor.' And with that final remark, she slapped Kalisher hard across the cheek.

The sound split the room, all eyes centred on Kalisher. The man's face had hardly flinched from the blow although red blotches were beginning to form on his check. Madame Blum collapsed back into Mickey's grip.

'All this talk of betrayal,' Kalisher said calmly, lighting up his cigar. 'I am afraid the woman is deranged with grief.'

After the reception was finished, Lev went over to Sammy's office. A stack of letters remained on the man's desk which so far he had not been able to bring himself to open. He swivelled in Sammy's chair, the leather singed in places from the burnt ash of his cheroots, then rolled over to the filing cabinet, a bland-grey, rusted unit inherited from the previous Turkish administration. There was no system or order to Sammy's filing which amounted to nothing more than placing a folder in a drawer, any drawer. No index, no alphabetic list, Lev wasn't sure where to start. But it didn't matter, for he came across the man's file in the first compartment he opened. The folder was named simply 'Khaled the Broker'.

He looked through the various papers, noted down the Damascus address. There was even a telephone number he could call to make an appointment. He then pulled out the bottom drawer of the desk, the one which held the small safe. He fiddled away with the numbers on the combination lock until he could open it. Inside, he found what he was looking for. An envelope containing the money Kalisher had given Sammy for the Bedouin land purchase. He slipped it into his satchel, shut up the safe.

Thirty-two

WHEN THE TRAIN STOPPED at Samach, Lev got off for a short walk while the Hejaz Railway crew took over from the British-run Palestinian Railways. The station wasn't the official border between Palestine and French-controlled Syria – that was technically further up into the Golan Heights at al-Hamma – but here at the southern tip of the Sea of Galilee, Samach served as a more natural hand-over point between the two crews for the journey on to Damascus. It was also where the first-class compartments emptied as the tourists descended for their boat-ride across the lake to the religious sites at Tiberias. Lev was watching the fishermen out on their boats, thinking how envious he was of their simple lives uncomplicated by land deals, when he heard a buzzing sound coming from behind him. He looked up to the sky and where he expected to see a swarm of bees, instead he found himself witnessing the arrival of a sea-plane. He wasn't alone in his astonishment. The rest of the passengers stopped and watched too, their hands held over their eyes against the sun, listening to the drone and the occasional cough and stutter of the engine as the plane dropped out of the sky then skidded across the water to a halt, a performance it seemed put on just for them. 'A miracle,' someone close to Lev said. 'Like walking on water,' was the whispered response, as Lev and the rest of the audience applauded spontaneously.

From the lake, the train travelled upwards through the Golan. But even with the release of its recent load of wealthy travellers, the locomotive gradually slowed to almost a standstill as the gradient increased. Some of the male passengers used the opportunity to open up the carriage doors, leap out onto the passing hillside to pick wild flowers, before grabbing the handrail of the last carriage to swing back on. There was much laughter and back-slapping at these feats, as well as shy gratitude from the women who became the recipients of these impromptu bouquets.

At the small, sun-baked town of Daraa, a junction on the line that ran all the way from Damascus to Medina, the carriages filled up again, this time with pilgrims returning from Mecca. Again Lev used the time to disembark the train, to have his shoes shined, to purchase some slices of watermelon and a yoghurt drink. He was just a few miles over the mountains from Palestine, yet he felt he had emerged into a vastly different land, a lone Polish Jew among a crowd of dusty pilgrims, armed Bedouin, clerks and businessmen in their tight suits and tarbooshes, the French language mixing in easily with Arabic. Yet he was glad of this feeling of alienation, for somehow it took him away from his grief.

Once back in his carriage, the rhythm of the track, the heat, the empty white plains of the Hauran plateau forced him to half-doze as others around him talked quietly, played cards or just stared out at the blank landscape. It was good to close his eyes, keep to himself. He almost wished he could continue on like this, trundling through unknown lands, with no particular destination, detached, suspended in time, a simple orphan.

When he awoke, the train was pulling into Al Hijaz station. He thought Damascus would remind him of Jerusalem, but even with its plethora of ancient domes and minarets, the city presented itself as a much more modern place. There was the usual traffic of camels and horse-drawn carriages but also electric tramcars and more automobiles than he had ever seen before. The streets were wider too, and tree-lined. There were squares with fountains and monument columns. There was even an opera house.

Mickey had given him the address of a travellers' hotel in the Jewish quarter, only a ten-minute walk away from the station. Darkness was already creeping in over the hills but many of the market stalls of the old city were still open. He spoke to one of the basket-sellers who gave him directions. The hotel of his destination had its own court-yard, weeds sprouting between the paving stones, the pillars cracked and worn, it would have been a grand place in years gone by. The old woman who answered the bell looked at him suspiciously until he gave her Mickey's name. She spoke of Damascus with the same bitterness Madame Blum spoke about her late husband.

'Why would a Jew come here?' the old woman continued as she showed him his room. 'When I was a little girl, they accused me of killing their babies. They burned our synagogues. Now they just let us dwindle away to nothing.' She moved over to the window, pushed open the shutters. Several of the slats were missing. She ran a sleeve across the dust on the sill, coughed, then turned to him. 'Most of the time, we are leaving. To America. Everyone wants to go to America. Do you want to go to America, Mr Sela?'

'I had my chance once. But I chose Palestine.'

She let out a rasping breath as if to scoff at the absurdity of his decision. 'My eldest son is in New York,' she said. 'My daughter is also in New York. Come, they say. Come see your grandchildren. Come see our Yiddish theatres and *kosher* restaurants. New York is the Jewish state we dream of. But what do I want to go to the other side of the world for, an old woman like me? Better I stay here until they murder me in my sleep, take over my home.' She grabbed his arm, pulled him in closer. 'Tell me, Mickey sent something with you? Something to ease the pain? A little brandy perhaps?'

'He gave me nothing.'

'Bah,' the woman spat as she handed over the key. 'You tell Mickey that next time, I will murder him in his sleep.' She laughed at that, then disappeared down the hallway, still cackling away.

Lev surveyed his accommodation. There was a spidery-cracked handbasin in the corner, a single bed covered with a torn mosquito net. He lay down on the straw mattress, his head against the coarse cloth of the damp pillow, listened to the noise of the street, the loud-speaker call to night prayer from one of the hundreds of minarets that populated this city, perhaps even from the Great Mosque itself. It was a comforting sound, a shepherd calling to his flock, a father to his children. 'Come, Lev,' the *muezzin* seemed to be saying. 'Come into the bosom of the temple. Come bow down to the Father. Come bow down to your father. Come pray with me.'

The offices of Khaled the Broker were located in the upper half of a two-storey building with tall windows and a narrow balcony in a side street off the main Marjeh Square. Lev had arranged an early appointment so he could catch the late-morning train back to Haifa, planning to disembark en route at al-Dalhamiyya to visit Celia. He chose to ignore what it would be like to see Amshel again. But in such a small settlement, it would be impossible to avoid the encounter.

On his arrival in the reception area, a severe-looking young assistant with goatee and spectacles informed him he would be seen immediately. In his mind, Lev had already formed an image of what Khaled would look like, a squat figure made fat from the profits of his various land deals. Instead, Lev discovered a short, nervous, bespectacled man with pointed features not unlike the secretary who had shown him in. Perhaps the two were brothers.

Khaled had been smoking outside on the balcony. He stepped back in to welcome Lev with a handshake, to direct him to a chair in front of his desk. The secretary returned with a tray of black tea and slices of sweet pastry. Khaled leaned against his desk, lit up another cigarette.

'So, you are from PICA,' he said. 'How is Sammy the King?'

'Unfortunately, Sammy is dead.'

Khaled's mouth twitched to the news. He then carefully placed his cigarette in an ashtray, took off his spectacles, rubbed each lens slowly with a handkerchief as he listened to what Lev had to tell him.

'I liked Sammy,' Khaled said. 'I liked him a lot. He was a fair man. But in this part of the world, to be fair is not necessarily good for your health.' He replaced his spectacles, retrieved his cigarette, went to sit behind his desk. 'Now. Tell me. Why are you here?'

'I believe you own a piece of land that is of interest to PICA.'

'Which land is that?'

'An area of about 250 dunams in the Jordan Valley. Situated along the west bank of the Yarmuk River.'

'What makes you think I have anything to do with it?'

'Mr Douglas Raynsford at the Department of Land Registration mentioned your name. Sammy also appeared convinced you were involved.'

Khaled smiled. 'I think I need to have stern words with Mr Raynsford about his loose tongue. But with regard to Sammy and his opinions, I shall be gracious to the memory of a departed colleague. I admit I do have an interest in this land that suddenly appeared from nowhere. As if by magic. A wonderful gift from God. What do you want with it?'

'I would like to buy back part of it from you. I can make you a cash offer right now.'

'And the reason for this purchase?'

'We need access to the river for the nearby PICA settlement of Kfar Ha'Emek. For general water supplies and also for irrigation.'

Khaled gave a short laugh. 'Your little settlement need not worry about water supplies. That whole area is to be flooded.'

'What do you mean?'

'I concluded the sale of that land only yesterday. You will have to deal with the new owner.'

'Who is that?'

'The Palestine Electric Power Company.'

'I have never heard of them.'

'A company newly formed for the purpose.'

'By whom?'

Khaled shrugged. 'Investors.'

'Sverdlov?'

'Yes. Gregory Sverdlov is involved. How do we say? He is the architect behind the deal. I believe he has grand plans to build a hydro-electric power station there. Good luck to him. I wonder at how a mere tributary of the River Jordan can possibly drive such a scheme. But it appears his watery charm has dazzled some careless and, no doubt, greedy investors.'

'His charm must also have persuaded the Bedouin to sell.'

'I don't know of any Bedouin.'

'The Bedouin who are currently living there.'

Khaled shrugged, stubbed out his cigarette. 'I am only interested in land, Mr Sela. I have no interest in those who choose to eke a living from it. In my experience, such concern only serves to confuse the issue.'

'If you don't mind me saying, I believe you are not being entirely straight with me. We both know it was the Bedouin who sold you this land.'

Khaled gave another short laugh. 'I am a broker, Mr Sela. The reason the owners came to me in the first place was so their identity should not be known. My discretion is of the utmost importance. My reputation and livelihood depend upon it. What does it matter to you who the previous owners were?'

'Because PICA had an arrangement with the Bedouin to buy some of that land. We even showed them how to register their title through *Mewat*. And somehow Sverdlov found out about it. Then persuaded them to sell to his Palestine Electric Power Company through you. Is that not what happened?'

'That is a very interesting supposition, Mr Sela. And one I am not willing to accept or deny. But why don't you speak to Sverdlov himself. I believe he is catching the same train as you back to Haifa.' Khaled squinted up at the large wall clock. 'Which is in…'

A strident, jarring sound ripped through the air, causing Lev to jump, Khaled to stop talking. They both looked at the source of the ringing, a small box on the wall, then to the shiny black candlestick telephone perched on the desk.

'A miracle of modern invention,' Khaled said quietly. 'It still surprises me.' He picked up the earpiece, listened to the operator, then spoke into the phone. 'Put him through.'

Khaled nodded as he listened, motioned with the palm of his free hand for Lev to wait. 'I see. Do what you can to ensure my interests are protected.'

He slowly replaced the earpiece on its hook, turned to Lev. 'That was my representative in Palestine. It appears there is serious rioting in Jerusalem.'

Thirty-three

LEV MIGHT HAVE OCCASIONALLY felt a tension with his Arab neigh-bours but he rarely feared them. Perhaps he had just become immune to such feelings of animosity. After all, he had been brought up in a land that despised him. Here was just another. Yet he felt a certain amount of trepidation now as he boarded the train at Al-Hijaz station along with his fellow passengers, many of whom carried daggers in their belts, bandoliers across their chests, rifles strapped to their backs. But his fear was unmerited as it appeared the news of the riots carried by telephone between Jerusalem and Damascus had not yet arrived by other means. For the mood aboard the train was calm, the talk not of uprisings but of pilgrimages, camel markets, the price of cotton. He looked for sight of the stocky figure of Gregory Sverdlov. But he was not to be seen. The man would no doubt be travelling first-class.

Lev waited until the train had left the outskirts of Damascus and was rolling across the empty, bleached landscape of the Hauran plateau before he decided to confront Sverdlov. He then pushed his way through the crowded carriages until he reached first-class where a uniformed guard took some satisfaction in blocking his progress. Lev handed over his business card, asked him to pass it through to Sverdlov. He was told to stand on the metal grid between carriages while the errand was reluctantly carried out. Lev was actually grateful for the pause, it gave him time to compose himself, to put into prac-tice what Sammy had long ago taught him: 'When you get a chance to meet a person who holds power, make sure you know exactly what you want.' He hung onto the metal rail, felt the rhythm of the track under his feet, thought about what he needed to say. A minute or so later, he was ushered into the first-class compartment. Sverdlov was seated alone at a table in a far corner, a silver tea-service before him. There was only one other passenger in the carriage – a pilgrim in full robes and head-dress muttering his prayers out of the window as he counted through his beads.

The Russian engineer put down his newspaper, scowled as Lev approached.

'I must warn you, Mr Sela, that I am not in good humour. My nose runs like the Volga.' To prove his point, Sverdlov blew loudly into his handkerchief. 'The dust, the pollen, I don't know. Perhaps I am just allergic to Damascus. Or to the French. I can order you something to drink. Coffee? Tea? Anything you like.'

'I would like a glass of water.'

Sverdlov nodded to an attendant who moved off to carry out the request. 'Now, what does PICA want from me?'

'Sammy is dead.'

Sverdlov shrugged, appeared to find more interest in the front-page article of the newspaper lying between them. 'I am sorry to hear that,' he said, running a fat finger along a column of figures. 'What happened?'

Lev waited until the attendant finished placing a glass of water on the table. It had ice and a slice of lemon in it. Lev clasped the glass, held his hand there, grateful for the coolness against his palm. 'He shot himself.'

Sverdlov looked up, the lines of his already furrowed brow deepening even further, squeezing out the moisture that lay on his forehead. 'What a waste.' He seemed about to return his attention to his newspaper when he changed his mind and said: 'As you know, Sammy was an idealist. A noble vocation, yet the world has no time for them, Mr Sela. I should know. For I used to be one myself not that long ago. Back in Russia, I helped support a revolution. And look what happened. We replaced one set of cruel, corrupt, power-seeking weaklings with another.' Sverdlov stopped, blew his nose. Lev sipped on his water, recalled what Sammy had said about this man, how he was like some kind of Rasputin who tried to mesmerize you with his eyes. But behind his glasses, Sverdlov's eyes were red and swollen, hopefully devoid of their power.

'I realized then, Mr Sela, that it is not possible to change the world unless one is prepared to change oneself. So either one must become a saint or admit defeat and become a pragmatist.' Sverdlov chuckled to himself. 'Well, I am certainly no saint. So I chose pragmatism. And here I am.' Sverdlov held out his arms to show that pragmatism travelled first-class. 'Sadly, Sammy, also a child of mother Russia, chose to remain an idealist. Unfortunately, idealists find it hard to cope with the disappointments they inevitably must face. Some tea?'

'No, thank you.'

'Which are you, Mr Sela?' Sverdlov took off his glasses, glared at him with a fierce stare. 'A realist? An idealist? Or perhaps even a saint?'

Lev sat looking back at Sverdlov as he pondered the questions. Idealism? Sainthood? Revolutions? Pragmatism? How had he even become involved in such a conversation? What was it that he wanted to talk about with Sverdlov in the first place? The train, which had been slowing down anyway, suddenly came to a halt, shunted forwards then backwards again. Lev grasped his glass. He didn't want to cause yet another breakage in front of this man. 'I'm sorry. What did you ask me?'

Sverdlov replaced his spectacles. 'It was of no importance. Is that what you came to tell me? That Sammy no longer resides in this wretched world?'

'I wanted to ask you about the land you recently acquired in the Jordan Valley.'

'It is the Palestine Electric Power Company that has purchased the land. I am merely its legal representative and a small investor. And, of course, chief engineer of a magnificent project that will bring electricity to the northern population of Palestine, both Arab and Jew alike.'

'How did you know this land was available, Mr Sverdlov? Up until a few weeks ago, it did not even appear on any map and its ownership was unknown.'

'It seems you know a lot about my business, Mr Sela. I assume therefore that you are aware I purchased this land through the services of the broker, Khaled Al Hamoud. I trust him entirely to deal with all the legal niceties of ownership. But as to how I knew about this land in the first place, your question surprises me.'

'Why is that?'

'Because your very own Chaim Kalisher organized the whole transaction. Kalisher is the principle investor in our little venture.'

Lev sat quietly in the standard-class compartment. In the centre aisle, two men had rolled out their mats and were now bowed down in prayer. Sitting opposite, a man with an eye-patch held onto a cage containing a leather-hooded hawk. Next to him, a Syrian businessman in a tarboosh who passed wind at every jiggle and bump of the train. Beside him, a young boy chewing on sunflower seeds, cracking the shells in his teeth, spitting them into his palm, looking over at Lev every time he did so. Lev stared through the dust-covered window slats at the empty landscape. Not a tree or bush in sight. Just miles of white, stony ground. He still couldn't believe what Sverdlov had told him. Perhaps he was lying. But there was no reason why he should be. Chaim Kalisher was behind everything. He was just like the hawk in the cage opposite. Unhooded, his eyes could see every little detail, every movement of his prey, long before anyone else. Then with talons hooked, he would swoop down on his target, gather it up in his clutches and return to perch quietly on the wrist of the Anonymous Donor.

The bird's one-eyed owner looked back at Lev, smiled through crooked teeth, laughed a throaty laugh, pointed to his patch.

'Wife,' the man said, then shook his finger over the cage. 'Not bird. Wife with knife.'

Lev nodded in pretended sympathy, returned to his thoughts. What he still did not understand was how Kalisher's actions had driven Sammy to kill himself. The Bedouin would have been paid off, Kfar Ha'Emek would have access to water and the north of Palestine would have electricity. Kalisher would no doubt eventually make huge profits but surely the man's greed and his underhand methods were not enough to make Sammy take his own life?

189

It was with such a question in mind that Lev watched the mass of pilgrims depart the train at Daraa station for their onward travel to Mecca. There was not a woman or child among them, just these predominantly older men, for it took many years to amass the wealth needed to afford this once-in-a-lifetime spiritual journey. To have such belief, such sense of purpose, both communal and private, how reassuring that must feel, Lev thought. For the Jews, their place of pilgrimage was the Western Wall, a site forever in dispute and no doubt the cause of the current riots. He stood up, leaned out of the window, let the air dry his face, watched the crowded platform disappear into the horizon as his own train churned westwards for Palestine and the cool breezes of the coast.

As with the outward journey, the engine slowed right down as it struggled with the slopes of the Golan. Once again, some of the male passengers jumped off on a flower-picking expedition and this time Lev decided to join them. He did so with a great whoop, landing safely on the soft, grassy earth, then grasping quickly at clumps of anemones, poppies, cyclamen and mustard before swinging back onto the rear of the train. As he walked back through the carriages, he could feel his whole body vibrant from the effort and the excitement. For the first time on this trip he was smiling.

'For wife?' his one-eyed companion asked.

Lev, still breathless, looked down at the hastily assembled bouquet. He didn't know how to answer. 'For a young woman,' he said eventually.

'I hope beautiful young woman,' the man said. 'Not wife with knife.'

They both laughed at that. It was the last time there would be any levity on the train, for at the Samach hand-over point Lev noticed it wasn't just the Palestinian Railways crew and a group of weary tourists awaiting the arrival of the train. There was a small unit of British infantrymen as well.

The soldiers came on board quickly, spreading throughout the train until there was one positioned at either end of each carriage. An officer followed, bringing with him news of 'certain disruption in the region'. Passengers were to be confined to their carriages but within that restriction many still moved to sit beside those they no doubt considered allies should the 'certain disruption' extend to the train itself. The one-eyed man and his caged hawk went off to a far-away bench. As did the Syrian businessman and his sunflower seed-eating son. Lev sat alone. As soon as the train pulled away from the Sea of Galilee, he went to find a railway guard. The soldier at the end of his carriage barred his passage.

'I need to get off at the next stop,' Lev told him.

'That's not going to happen,' said the soldier, a surly, red-haired youth with a sun-blistered face. Then, with a nod to the flowers: 'These for me?'

Lev ignored the comment. 'Let me speak to the guard.'

'You'll have to wait till he comes around.'

'It'll be too late. I'm getting off at al-Dalhamiyya.'

'al-Dalhamiyya? A nothing place in the middle of nowhere.'

'I have business there.'

'With your pretty little posy? I bet it's a dusky maiden you're after. Only Arabs live round al-Dalhamiyya.'

'Not just Arabs. There's a Jewish settlement nearby.'

'I'm sorry to break your Jewess' heart. But this train isn't taking special requests. It's going all the way to Haifa.'

'Please, let me speak to the guard.'

'Orders are orders. This train is non-stop. The Jezreel Valley Express. Sit back down. Enjoy the ride.'

It was late by the time Lev arrived back in Haifa but the light was still on in Madame Blum's bedroom. He tried not to make a noise as he moved around in the dark hallway but she called out: 'Is that you, Mickey?'

'It's Lev.'

She didn't reply. He tapped at her door, she told him to come in. She was sat up in bed, reading. And smoking. This was a new habit she had taken up since Sammy had died. Smoking his cheroots. She had found boxes of them. Her hair was tied up into a headscarf. She wore no make-up. Her eyes were rheumy and red. There was ash all down the front of her nightgown.

'I thought you were in Damascus,' she said without looking up at him.

'It was only for one night. I brought you some flowers.'

'That's very thoughtful.'

'I'll bring a vase.'

'No, no. Just leave them on the dresser.' She patted the bed beside her. 'Come. Sit.'

He did as he was told. She took his hand in hers. It was cold and greasy with cream.

'What am I going to do, Lev? I can't sleep.'

'I thought the doctor gave you powders.'

'Powders that can put elephants to sleep. But not me. How can a person sleep with all these terrible events happening?' She took a puff of the cheroot, blew out the smoke, then started to cough terribly. He went to bring her a glass of water but she waved him to stop. She banged her chest with her fist and the coughing stopped. 'First the earthquake. Then poor Sammy. And now these riots.'

'The riots are in Jerusalem.'

She gripped his hand tighter. 'No, no, no, Lev. The riots are spreading. That's what Ida told me. Her husband Max works in the mayor's office.'

'You shouldn't believe everything Ida tells you.'

'They have telephones there. They receive news from all over. Soon the riots will be in Haifa. Soon they will be murdering us in our beds. No wonder I can't sleep.'

'I keep telling you. Haifa is safe. There are no problems here with the Arabs.'

'What do you know, Lev? What do you know? Ask Mickey. He knows these things. Where is Mickey?'

'He must be out somewhere.'

'He is always out somewhere.' And then she started to sob. Her head fell forward, her back went into huge spasms, tears were dripping off her cheeks. He had never seen anyone cry in such a violent way before. He drew in closer to her, put an arm around her shoulder, felt the bones underneath the cotton fabric. She rested her head against him, stayed like that until the sobbing stopped. She then pulled away, wiped her cheeks.

'I miss him so much.'

'Why did you never tell me about the two of you?'

'We wanted to. We talked about it a lot. But we decided it was better that you didn't know.'

'But why?'

'We both loved you like a son. I still do. And then if Sammy and I stopped seeing each other, who would have you?'

Lev got up from the side of the bed, walked over to the window. He noticed the glow of a fire somewhere off on the beach. The local boys sometimes did that, sat up around the flames, drinking *arak*, playing music on strings and drums. It reminded him of when he and Celia had sat together on the same stretch of sand.

Thirty-four

Kfar Ha'Emek, Jordan Valley, Palestine

My dear Charlotte

I am frightened. The night is echoing with gunfire. The shots go off like firecrackers. One or two at a time. Then a pause. Then it starts again. Every time I hear one, I jump in my chair, my pen jerks on the page. You will know my fear from the quivering flow of my handwriting. But I need to keep on writing. It distracts me from my terror, it helps to calm me. I will try to send this on tomorrow's train if it chooses to stop. I tried to flag it down today, we had boxes of oranges to send to Haifa. But it just went flying past as if my red flag didn't exist. I saw British soldiers on board. Perhaps they feared I had a band of armed Jews waiting behind me ready to pounce.

It has been like this for more than twenty-four hours now. We hear rumours of riots in Jerusalem. Killings and rapes in Sefad and Hebron, massacres everywhere. We have no telephone or telegraph here but riders have passed by from Tiberias with the news. They tell us to take up arms, to guard our perimeters. But we only have an ancient gun and a few machetes. The men are carrying out all the sentry duty. The few women that remain are trying to keep our settlement going as best we can. I don't even know who we are defending ourselves against. Emir Abdullah in Trans-Jordan? The Arabs in Palestine? The Bedouins in the valley? Or just bandits after the few possessions we have?

The little news we have received tells us of fighting in Jerusalem over the right to pray at the Western Wall, that holiest of sites for both Moslems and Jews. But that is just the taper that lights the powder of all the fears and bitterness that exists between our two peoples. I wanted to feel that by coming here I could make a positive contribution to this land, that we could live in peace with our neighbours, benefit from each other's knowledge, culture and labour. Now all I see is hatred on both sides. I can't take it anymore, Charlotte. I want to leave. I want to return to Scotland, to tread on a land again without fear.

It has gone quiet now. Even in the silence my nerves are all shattered. Amshel the Storyteller will come by soon. He sleeps in a cot in my tent to keep me company during the night. I am surprised he still remains with us. After all, he is not an official member of our community. He also teases me, saying it is ridiculous a capitalist such as he should be defending us poor socialists. However, I am glad of his company. It is better we stay close like this during such terrible times. I fear for my life but where is there to escape to? It seems the whole of Palestine is in upheaval.

A child is crying. I must go. I have to take tea and biscuits out to the men. I will try to write more later.

All my love

Celia

Thirty-five

LEV WOKE TO A CHURNING, urgent wave of shouting from some-where in the neighbourhood. He had fallen asleep where he sat in an armchair in Madame Blum's bedroom, the intensity of the light pouring through the window showing him it was probably already mid-morning. Madame Blum still slept, sitting upright against the pillows, snoring slightly, the doctor's draught having done its trick. On the bedside table, his bouquet of withered flowers plucked from the hills of the Golan. Still drenched in sleep, he pushed himself out of the chair, stretched and straightened, walked through the house and out of the front door into the courtyard, trying to locate the source of the noise that had woken him. He went out into the street, looked down towards the alleyways that led through the old town to the harbour and the sea. About two hundred yards along the slight incline, he saw a mob of men and boys hemmed into the lanes, their raised arms holding clubs and sticks and knives and swords. Two riders on horseback were either trying to lead the crowd or hold them back from coming up the hill, it was difficult to know. He could now make out what was being chanted: 'Kill the Jews. Kill the Jews.' A vocal blast of hatred that fully awakened him from his somnolent state.

Close by, someone whistled. He looked up. Flat on the roof of a neighbouring house, a man with a rifle waving for him to get back inside. It was Ida's husband, Max Kaplan, the smug little clerk from the mayor's office. Max Kaplan with a gun, how could this be? Max whistled again. And then he felt someone beside him, pushing him indoors. Mickey. His head wrapped in a bandana, his face smeared with oil. He held a rifle in each hand.

'Get off the street, for fuck's sake.'

'What's going on?'

'The Arabs are trying to move into the Jewish Quarter. We need to hold them off until the Brits arrive with their warship. Stay here with Madame Blum. And take this.' Mickey handed over a rifle. 'It's loaded.'

'I've never used one.'

'I thought you Polish boys shot boar and bear?'

'My brother did. I wasn't allowed to.'

Mickey held up his own rifle as an example. 'Jerk back this bolt here, let the next cartridge slot in and you can fire again. Five cartridges is all you have, so make them count if you have to. With a bit of luck, just showing them your weapon will be enough to put them off.' Mickey stared at him straight, gave a quick smile of encouragement, then left him to manage a Lee-Enfield Mark III rifle for the first time in his life.

Lev went quickly back into the house, checked on Madame Blum. If she could just stay asleep like this for the next couple of hours, his life would be much simpler. He filled up a flask of water from the kitchen tap, picked up an apple, a pair of field glasses hanging on the door. He then went back out into the courtyard, took up a position crouched behind the stone pillars of the front gate. From there, he had a view down the hill to where the mob was still being contained, as well as behind to Max Kaplan up on the roof. He wiped the sweat from his eyes, tried to calm himself with several deep intakes of breath.

The Lee-Enfield had been well used, the wood cut and chipped in places, but the actual mechanism was polished clean and recently oiled. Without touching any levers, he tried to figure out how it would be to re-load it. He then rested the tip on the topmost of the ornamental ledges cut into the pillar. Using the binoculars, he had a good look round.

Down in the lanes, the mob had quietened and appeared no closer to him than when he had first seen them. Up on the rooftops, he saw that Max Kaplan was just one among several snipers. Then, focusing out beyond the bay, he was able to pick out the movement of a British warship bearing down on the town. He wondered if those in the crowd below had seen it too and that was what had calmed them. But just as he was feeling more relaxed, the 'Kill the Jews' chant started up again. He put down the field glasses, took a proper grip of the rifle, pressed the butt hard into the bed of his shoulder.

The two riders on horseback Lev had seen earlier had disappeared. That left a few of the more adventurous among the crowd to break loose and begin inching forward in a press against the walls of the lanes. The rest of the mob surged forward several yards in the wake of this advance party, then stopped. Lev looked back at Max who signalled with the flat of his hand to do nothing. The youths in the vanguard continued to move ahead, hugging the walls, testing the safety of the advance. The chanting was getting louder, more people were breaking away from the main group, spreading out across the lane, scrambling upwards, throwing stones at invisible targets. The mob began to move with them. A drop of sweat fell from Lev's nose onto his fingers where he gripped the butt of the rifle close to his chin. He realized he might have to shoot someone, to kill someone. Another drop of sweat on to his hand. He must not waver, he must keep his breathing even, his rifle steady.

The crowd drew closer. He could see some of their faces clearly now without the need of binoculars. The rage, the hatred, the whipped-up fervour. It was frightening. A young Arab broke through from the front, running ahead of everyone else, stooping, picking up a stone, throwing it, running again, this lone figure, Lev could see his eyes, the mouth twisted in anger, screaming: 'Kill the–'

The shot came from somewhere behind him, the shock of it causing Lev to pull on his own trigger, jerk back from the force of the firing. He saw the burst of dust and plaster as his bullet hit a wall yards from anyone. Where the previous bullet had gone he had no idea. But that crack-crack noise blew a hole in the fabric of the whole situation. It was as if the day had missed a couple of beats as the echoes of the shots faded over the town. Everything stopped. The Arabs might have armed themselves with sticks and knives and swords, but they didn't have guns. Guns were different. Guns were power. The youth who had moved forward on his own, turned and ran. As did the rest of the crowd, scattering, scuttling away. To leave, once the dust had settled, a single body lying on the ground. A church bell rang out from somewhere. Lev looked at his watch. It was eleven o'clock.

Thirty-six

MADAME BLUM WAS MAKING LUNCH. She was only too happy to do so, humming away as she fried the fish, boiled the potatoes. What was a poor woman to do in such a situation? Not just a woman, but a widow. Widowed twice – in her heart if not by legal document. What did she care about earthquakes and land deals and betrayals and riots and shooting in the street and guns in her house? Better that she just cook. For she was in high spirits. She had not slept so well for years, ever since she was a little girl, ever since she could remember. Until she had been woken so crudely at eleven o'clock by all these noises. She turned the fish in the pan, pleased to see the skin bubbled up all brown. She was lucky to have bought these fine sea bream the day before. For the markets were closed this morning, what with all the troubles.

Lev sat next door in the dining room with Mickey, their rifles stacked in a corner, a revolver lying between them on the table. Lev's whole body was still taut and tingling from the fear, excitement and sheer relief of the morning's events. His voice sounded louder, his eyes opened wider, his belly ached from the smell of fried fish.

'I was lucky it wasn't me,' he conceded.

'Damn right,' Mickey agreed. He had got rid of the bandana, wiped the oil off his face. 'The Brits went straight in and arrested the first person they saw.'

'Poor Max had just come down off the roof.'

'Bloody idiots. His rifle was fully loaded yet they still took him. If you hadn't nipped in to see our dear landlady, you were first in line. And you had a spent cartridge at your feet.'

'I told you. I fired by mistake.'

'Don't worry. I know exactly who the sniper was.'

'What'll they do with Max? Charge him with murder?'

'Attempted murder. The boy was shot in the thigh. But it's good the Arabs know someone has been arrested. It will calm everyone down.'

'Everyone except Max.'

Mickey laughed, gave the revolver on the table a twirl. 'We'll sort out matters with Max and the Brits later.'

'I always thought Haifa would be safe from all of this.'

'Not any more. The whole of Palestine has exploded. It's been waiting to go off for nearly ten years now. Since the last riots. And yesterday was the day. Jerusalem was always going to be the spark but now we're hearing terrible things from Safed and Hebron. To be honest, we also didn't think there would be trouble here. We were wrong.'

'Who is "we"?'

Mickey shrugged.

'It's the *Haganah*, isn't it?'

'The *Haganah* doesn't exist. The British are the military force in Palestine. It is illegal to have a secret army here.'

'A secret army everyone knows about.'

'I have to feed you the official line, Lev.'

'So Sammy was right. You are selling guns. You're selling guns to the *Haganah*.'

'My business is my business.'

Lev bit his lip, listened to Madame Blum cooking away in the kitchen. Then he leaned over, whispered: 'You sold Sammy the gun.'

Mickey didn't even blink at the accusation. 'He told me he needed it for protection. Money he kept in the house, something like that. I didn't think he was going to kill himself.'

'What are you two talking about?' Madame Blum said, as she emerged from the kitchen with a plate of fried fish. She placed the dish on the table after moving Mickey's revolver to make space. 'My two boys,' she said, patting Lev on the shoulder. 'I'll just bring the potatoes.'

With Madame Blum back in the kitchen, Mickey said: 'I'm sorry about what happened with Sammy. But don't expect me to have a conscience about it.'

'I didn't think you would have.'

Mickey leaned back in his chair, stretched out his arms in an exaggerated yawn. 'I think we should talk about something else.'

'I agree.'

'Haifa should be safe now the Brits are here with their destroyer.'

'And the rest of Palestine?'

'We have units in Tel Aviv and Jerusalem doing their best to protect the Jews there. But it's the settlements I'm worried about.'

Madame Blum was back with the potatoes. 'Now eat these while they are still hot,' she said. 'I am going to make a dessert. Do you think the markets will be open now?'

'Not a chance,' Mickey told her. 'It could be days before that happens.'

'I'll have to steal one of your watermelons,' she said, before disappearing once again.

Lev picked up a knife, topped and tailed the sea bream, pulled back the skin, cut himself a slice. 'I want to buy some of your guns.'

Mickey chuckled. 'What do you want with guns?'

'For one of the settlements.'

'Where Celia is?'

'And Amshel too. They've got very little protection up there.'

Mickey chewed on his fish, nodded thoughtfully. 'It won't be cheap. Bottom line, I'm a businessman. Even if it's you who's buying.'

'I have money.'

'Not that kind of money.'

'Don't worry. I've got the cash.'

'How much cash?'

'How much for the guns?'

Mickey smiled, named his price. Lev told him how much money he had.

'That'll give you six rifles like the one you had this morning. All oiled and primed, ready to go. Plus six hundred cartridges. It's all I have.'

'I'll need someone to take me and the guns to the Jordan Valley. That's part of the deal.'

'Quite the little businessman,' Mickey acknowledged. 'Yes, I can arrange that. When do you want to go?'

'As soon as I've finished this fish.'

Two hours later, Mickey returned with a flatbed truck, loaded up with strapped-down bales of hay and several jerry cans of petrol.

'Where did you get this junk heap?' Lev asked.

'The best I could find in a hurry.' Mickey poked at one of the bales. 'The guns and cartridges are hidden underneath. I've thrown in twenty First Aid boxes as well. There's a tarpaulin to cover it all.'

'Who's the driver?'

'I am. I'll take you there, then I'm coming straight back. I'll add the petrol to my bill.'

Lev stared out of the truck window at the warship sitting out in the bay, a dull-grey fearsome blight on an otherwise bright blue vista. Mickey had his nose close to the windscreen, trying to avoid the potholes, speeding up whenever he came across sight of anyone on the road, either walking or on horseback. The occasional truck passed from the opposite direction but they were almost all British Army vehicles carrying personnel back into Haifa. As soon as they cleared the town, the roads became devoid of man and mule, the villages were quiet too, everyone apparently holed up indoors until the tensions subsided. Mickey began to relax, enjoying himself as he drove around the holes in the road, speeding off to the side so the vehicle would run along at a tilt and back down again, Lev gripping the seat just to keep himself from sliding into his friend or falling out of a door hanging loose on a dodgy lock.

'Where did you learn to drive?'

'One of many skills acquired courtesy of His Majesty's forces.' Mickey ground through to a higher gear as if to prove his point.

'I always thought you made most of that up, your time in the Army.'

'Private Michael Rosenblatt. All information correct as stated.'

'What about the *Haganah*? How long have you been with them?'

Mickey swerved hard round a pothole then straightened the vehicle again. 'Right from the start. I was like a lot of Jews serving with the Brits who wanted to do something to protect ourselves once the war was over. Especially after the riots in Jaffa a few years back. We weren't ready then. We're better prepared now. You saw that this morning with our snipers on the rooftops. But we've got no money, few weapons, no proper training and we're illegal. Although all that might change now.'

'Why do you say that?'

'Fear is a great fundraiser. A great recruitment officer as well.'

The truck boiled over in the heat on the steep climb from the Jezreel Valley towards Tiberias, forcing Mickey to pull over. It was an anxious delay by the roadside waiting for the engine to cool. Any sign of an approaching vehicle or traveller had the two of them standing up primed in an alertness for rioters or bandits, their hands reaching for the rifles hidden at the back of the truck. Lev eventually went into the cabin to fetch an old newspaper, returned with a battered backgammon set instead. They climbed up on the bales, sat down on top of their load.

'The Garden of Eden is situated down there somewhere,' Mickey said with a nod down towards the Jordan Valley. 'If you believe in such a thing.'

Lev didn't believe in such a thing but he could see why God might have chosen this place. The outlook was spectacular, taking in the slopes of Mount Tabor, the stretch of the hills all the way down to Tiberias and the serene blue of the Sea of Galilee, shaped like a human heart.

They played on in quietness, falling into a rhythm with the rattle of the dice, the clip-clip of the wooden disks on the board, the fading light, the lessening heat. Until Mickey said: 'She must really matter to you.'

Lev didn't respond.

'Why go to all this trouble then?' Mickey persisted.

'It's a PICA settlement. I'm merely protecting our assets.'

Mickey picked up a couple of disks from the board. 'There's no shame in loving a woman,' he said in that world-wisely way of his.

It wasn't shame Lev felt. It was fear. He threw the dice against the board. Double six. What did that signify? 'I like her a lot,' he conceded.

Mickey smiled, Lev waited for the inevitable sarcastic remark. None came. 'I can see that,' was all his friend said.

Lev won the next couple of games, Mickey lost patience, deemed the radiator cool enough, then used up the last of their precious drinking water for the refill. They drove on to arrive at the make-shift guardhouse on the perimeter of Kfar Ha'Emek just as darkness properly set in, which was just as well as the headlights on the truck weren't working. Mickey switched off the engine. Lev made to get out but Mickey held him back.

'Better let them check us out first,' he said. 'A truck with no lights.'

Two men emerged from the hut, both holding lanterns, one armed with a rifle. The lamps swayed back and forth across the windscreen, making it hard to make out the men's faces until one of them was over by the passenger door peering in. Lev recognized him as Moshe, a farmer from Russia who had not only survived the Revolution but also a lightning storm that had killed both his parents on their family escape to Palestine.

'The man from PICA,' Moshe said, gripping the top of the sill with his thick, scarred fingers then looking in and around the cabin. 'What are you doing here?'

'I've brought guns.'

The other lantern appeared at Mickey's side. Jonny the doctor. 'What did you say?'

'I've brought guns.'

'Six rifles in the back,' Mickey added. 'Cartridges as well.'

'Who are you?' Jonny asked.

'Mickey Vered. *Haganah.*'

'*Haganah*? I thought you chaps weren't supposed to exist.'

'We crawl out of the woodwork from time to time.'

'Show me the guns,' Moshe said, standing back to let Lev out while Jonny dragged open the other door. Mickey went to the rear, unfas-tened the tarpaulin, shifted over the bales to reveal the crate of rifles. He pulled off the lid, passed one of the rifles over to Moshe who whis-tled and said: 'Lee-Enfield Mark III,' as if it were a rod of gold he was holding. Lev watched as he handled the reloading mechanism with an enviable expertise. 'PICA send them?'

'You could say that,' Lev replied.

'This is going to make a huge difference,' Moshe said.

'What's your current status?' Mickey asked.

'Fourteen of us,' Moshe told him. 'Unless someone else has deserted since this morning. Twelve men, two women. There are also four children. Until now, we had just this one rifle for the whole settlement. A few machetes, a scimitar. One nervous guard dog. That's about it.'

'Any attacks?'

'Bandits have been coming in across the border for two or three weeks now, raiding some of the other settlements. They tend to enter further north as we're protected here by the ridge. They haven't come this far south yet. But that's probably only a matter of time.'

'What about the Bedouin?' Lev asked.

'We're no longer on friendly terms,' Jonny explained. 'The worry is with all these riots going on, they might take up with the bandits as well.'

'To be honest,' Moshe added, 'we don't really know what's going on out there. We just want to protect ourselves the best we can. Rafi's set up a guard duty rota. Three shifts through the night.'

'Where is Rafi anyway?' Lev asked.

'Probably asleep. He's just come off two straight shifts.'

Mickey kicked at the front tyre with his heel. 'I can't get this thing back tonight with these broken headlights,' he said. 'Put me down for one of the later shifts. What about you, Lev?'

'What time's the next one?'

'You can come with me,' Jonny said, picking up one of the rifles. 'I'm going out in about half an hour. In the meantime, I imagine your brother will be pleased to see you.'

'Where is he?'

'You could try Celia's tent.'

Thirty-seven

LETTER 16

Kfar Ha'Emek, Jordan Valley, Palestine

My dear Charlotte

I don't know if this is a letter I am writing or just a death note to myself. These could be my last words, found here unfinished on this table by my enemies, whoever they are. I have no means of sending it to you anyway as the train no longer stops here. We have been abandoned. We are alone. We are without help and have only one gun to protect the whole settlement. Once we were close to forty proud souls, now hardly a dozen of us remain. Those who had come here for no other reason than having nowhere else to go were the first to leave. Then a man and woman with child left too – who could blame them? – the father taking one of the only guns we had. I suppose it is the true socialists who remain, those who still cling to the hope we can build a community here based on ideals and hard work.

I don't think I can go through another night like last night. The sound of gunshots from who knows where. Fires blazing across the borders. People shouting, children screaming, riders galloping here and there. Our own dog barking wildly until I feared it might collapse from sheer exhaustion. The scraps of news we hear tell of horrific stories – of rape and slaughter – on both sides. How can we do such things to our fellow human beings? I so much want to leave here. To return to Scotland, to walk in the Highlands, to pick berries, to bathe in the rivers. I should go right now while there is still a breath in my body but I cannot find it in me to abandon my community at this time of crisis.

Amshel the Storyteller is here with me now. He tries to distract me with amusing tales but I have no patience for such things and we argue. My nerves are on edge. My mother used to take powders at times like these. How I wish I could do the same. This is usually such a wonderful time of year, the warm evenings, the glow of a late summer's day. Instead I am frightened of the approaching night and the dangers it will bring…

Thirty-eight

It was Amshel who pulled back the flap. He wore a tattered grey vest and a pair of shorts, a cigarette hung damp from the corner of his mouth. There was the faint stink of aniseed about him too. Like a disinfectant, Lev thought.

'You,' his brother said. 'What are you doing here?'

'I want to see Celia.'

Amshel flicked his cigarette into the darkness, moved reluctantly to the side. Lev could feel his brother tense up as he squeezed by. A couple of candles lit the interior, the mosquito nets were rolled up. There was a stench of sweat and dirty clothes. Celia was seated at a small table, a sheet of writing paper in front of her.

'Lev,' she said, standing up to hover awkwardly in front of him. 'You came.'

He wasn't sure if he should embrace her or hold out a hand. It seemed she didn't know what to do either. In the end, he just smiled at her. She looked exhausted, her face thinner than he remembered, her eyes smudged dark and deep above the glow from the candle-light. Amshel had gone to sit on one of the beds. There were only two cots in the tent now, rather than the three he recalled from when he had last visited. Hanging off a peg on the centre pole, the jacket Madame Blum had given Amshel from her husband's wardrobe.

'Why did you come?' she asked.

'Yes. Why did you come?' Amshel added, his hands beating out a fast rhythm on his thighs.

'I brought guns.'

Amshel laughed, showing his once perfect dentures now stained and chipped. 'What do you know about guns?'

'Mickey and I. We've come with six rifles. Ammunition too.'

Amshel smacked his lips, then leaned under the cot to bring out a bottle of *arak*. He poured some into a glass on the floor, held it up to Lev. 'To my little brother. Our saviour.'

'That's enough,' Celia said sharply.

Amshel ignored her, knocked back his drink, poured out another.

'He does this to annoy me,' Celia said.

'I do it because I have guard duty.' Amshel put his glass down, started again with his palms drumming away on his thighs. 'All the men do. We never volunteered to be soldiers.'

Celia gave Lev an exasperated look. 'I'm glad you came,' she said. She started clearing away her clothes from the other cot. 'Two brothers together.'

'Our happy family,' Amshel said.

Lev turned to Celia. 'Is this where he sleeps?'

She stopped what she was doing, folded her arms against his question. 'Yes, he sleeps here. Where should he sleep? The nights are cold now.'

'But here? With you?'

'I don't want to be alone. I'm scared.'

'What about the other women?'

'There are no other single women here.'

Lev went over to stand in front of his brother. 'Why do you keep doing this?' he said.

Amshel stopped his drumming, looked up at him. 'Doing what?'

'Destroying everything for me.'

Amshel snorted a laugh. 'You just need to trust me.'

'How can I trust you when you do this to me?'

'I'm not doing anything to you. I'm protecting her, Lev. Don't you see that?'

'No, I don't see that.'

'I'm protecting her... for you.'

The crack of a rifle shot. Followed by the awful whinny of a terrified horse. Celia let out a yelp like a trodden-on puppy. Amshel, in his effort to get to his feet, knocked over the bottle of *arak*. Lev turned, ducked outside.

He ran and ran, sucking in the cool air, pumping his limbs as hard as he could, just glad to be out of that tent. He sped past the dining room, then along the avenue of young date palms he had once helped plant, until he reached the rear of the settlement. There he could see the cluster of lanterns, several figures standing by, others stooped around a body lying on the ground. A riderless horse pawed the ground, snorting and shivering.

Lev recognized the injured man immediately. Zayed's son, Ibrahim. Mickey was in a crouch beside him, Moshe was holding up a lantern, Jonny was pressing his hands over Ibrahim's body.

'What happened?' Lev asked.

'He rode out of the darkness straight at me,' Mickey said, then to Jonny: 'Will he be all right?'

'He's not going to die from any bullet,' Jonny said. 'It's the fall off the horse that's hurt him.'

'Thank God.' Mickey looked up at Lev. 'How was I to know? How was I to fucking know?'

'He came to warn us,' Jonny said. 'He says bandits are moving down here from the north. Let's take him inside.'

Lev helped Mickey and Jonny raise him, then they half-walked, half-carried him into the dining room, sat him down on a bench. Jonny stripped off the man's jacket and shirt, re-examined him again for any broken bones, asked him to concentrate on the pass of a finger in front of his eyes.

'Doesn't seem to be any concussion. Rib area is very bruised though. Could be a few fractures in there. I'll strap him up. Nothing else to do here.'

Ibrahim shook his head, tried to focus on those in front of him, pointed at Lev. 'You promised us...'

'I need you to sit still,' Jonny protested, pushing down Ibrahim's outstretched arm.

The Bedouin ignored him. 'You promised us the land would be ours. Why did you betray us?'

'What are you talking about?' Lev countered. 'It was *you* who betrayed us.'

'That is crazy talk.'

'You claimed the land through *Mewat*. Then you went behind our backs to Khaled Al Hamoud.'

'I don't know any Khaled Al Hamoud.'

'Khaled the Broker. In Damascus. You sold him your land. Then he sold it on for the power station.'

'We sold the land to no-one. It was the British. The British just came and took it.'

'The British?'

'Yes, the British.' Ibrahim grimaced as Jonny drew the bandage tight. 'A captain came with his men, read out the orders. Our whole tribe must move now, further south, south of Beisan. What do we know of such a place? It is not our land. We have lost our home. We have lost everything. Why did you do this to us? Our lives were fine until you came.'

Thirty-nine

DESPITE HIS INJURIES, Ibrahim insisted on riding back to the encampment. Someone then went to wake up Rafi who came rushing over, tried to placate the Bedouin before he rode off, to reassure him the *kibbutz* knew nothing of the British involvement in the displacement of his tribe. Ibrahim didn't respond. He looked like a man defeated as he turned away, galloped off. Lev and everyone else who was left on the settlement assembled to see him go, no-one straying from their watch of him until rider and horse were sucked up into the night. Lev felt as if all Sammy's hopes and ideals had ridden off with him.

'The bandits are coming tonight,' Rafi said to his depleted community. 'Thanks to Lev and Mickey, we have rifles. But if anyone wants to leave, they should go now.'

No-one moved.

The air was warm, clouds shaded the moon, only a few stars shone through. A baby was crying in one of the tents, the crackle of gunshot came from somewhere out in the darkness. Lev looked around at the others in the group, the lantern light hollowing out strange shadows on their anxious faces. How had he ended up here at this time, in this place, in this danger, with these people? Was it purely by accident? Or fate? Or was it because they were all Jews? Or was it because of their desire for their own land? Or for their ideals? Or for the love of another person? He found he had a desperate need to remember who they were, each and every one of them. His beloved Celia, his brother Amshel, his old friend Mickey. Standing across from him, Rafi, Jonny, Amos, muscle-man Barak. The cook Shoshana had gone to look after the children but her husband Yossie was there, a short bald man from Yemen with a huge moustache. Beside him stood Moshe the Russian farmer, Dudu a young Polish man from the Zionist Youth, Shlomo a former seminary student whose family had lived for generations in Tiberias. Then there were the Grün twins, also from Poland, who rarely spoke except to each other. Finally, Benny Matsas, a Greek Jew from Salonika, an expert in olive growing, who was always smiling, even now.

'Forget about tonight's rotas,' Rafi continued. 'Everyone is on guard duty. Except Shoshana who'll stay with the children. Celia, I want you to run the perimeter with the ammunition, anything else that's needed. And be ready to help Jonny with any wounded. Now who can handle a rifle?'

Amshel was one of those who stepped forward.

'Good,' Rafi said. 'Everyone else pair off with those who are armed.'

Lev stepped up to stand beside his brother.

They quickly built a rough look-out point at the side of the cowshed. Amshel tossed out the bales from the shed while Lev stacked them. It was just like old times when they used to construct hide-outs in the woods to spy on the boar, the memory and the combined effort of their task dissipating the tension between them. This look-out faced north. If an attack was going to come, it would be from there. The east was protected by the ridge, the west by the road from Tiberias to Beisan, the south was behind them. About fifty yards to the left was Amos and Barak. Mickey was off somewhere to the right. Lev sat down with his back to the wall of bales while Amshel peered over the rim with his rifle.

'What happened back there with Ibrahim?' Amshel asked.

'The British have taken his land.'

'I thought they didn't know anything about it.'

'Chaim Kalisher was behind everything. I thought he only tipped off Sverdlov but he must have told the British as well. He then put together a secret deal for a power station using a broker in Damascus as a middle man.'

'Why use a broker at all?'

'I imagine the British didn't want to be seen favouring the Jews over the Arabs for such an important project. So they used him to stay anonymous. Sammy must have discovered what happened. That's what drove him over the edge. Not just Kalisher going behind his back. But knowing the Bedouin had lost their land too.'

'How many times do I have to tell you, little brother? People are only out for themselves… What was that?'

'I didn't hear anything.'

'Shhh.'

Lev held his breath while Amshel stared out into the night. The moon and stars had clouded over, difficult to make anything out at all. Amshel gave the agreed signal, a four-note whistle that asked if everything was all right at the next guard post. An echo of the same notes came back at them from both directions. Lev could breathe again. Amshel checked his rifle. He had five cartridges already loaded. Lev held onto the clips holding the other twenty.

'Remember how we used to do this back home?' Lev said.

'The two of us hiding out in the woods, hunting for hogs.'

'I was just the look-out. You were the hunter.'

'Papa wouldn't let you use a gun.'

'It would have helped me now if he had.'

Amshel smiled. 'It's strange how life can bring you round in full circle like this–'

The sound of several gunshots strafed the night. Amshel was back at his post, Lev crouched low against the bales, ready with the cartridge clips.

'I can see flames,' Amshel said.

'Where?'

'North-east.'

'What's over there?'

'An olive grove.'

'The bandits must have set fire to it.'

'That's still a good half-mile away.'

They waited in silence for a few minutes, then again the exchange of whistled signals. They relaxed.

'What will you do after this?' Lev asked. 'If we survive.'

'I'm off to the United States.'

'Still with your dream of America.'

'I'll go back to Poland first, sell our grandfather's land. Then try to buy my way in. You could come with me. That stepmother of ours would probably sponsor you. What do you think? The brothers Gottleib in America. In the land of opportunity.'

Lev tried to imagine it. Buildings that scraped the sky, streets as wide as the broadest river, Ewa Kaminsky with carmine on her lips. What had that old woman in Damascus told him? New York is the Jewish state we dream of. With its *kosher* restaurants and stores run by Jews, Yiddish theatres and newspapers. He would ask Celia to come with him. He could buy and sell land, they could own an automobile, perhaps even an apartment. They could go to fairgrounds and dance halls and movie theatres.

'What time is it?' Amshel asked.

Lev peered at his trench watch. 'Nearly midnight.'

'If they come, they will come soon. In the deepest part of the night.'

'They won't know we have rifles.'

'That will make them confident. But careless.'

The sound of more gunfire. Lev felt the churn in his stomach, the tremors running down his legs. 'They're getting closer,' he said.

'It sounds like it.'

'Aren't you scared?'

'Of course I'm scared. I just hope it's a band of thieves we're looking out for. A few rifle shots should see them off. If it's an angry Arab population on the rampage, we'll have a proper battle on our hands.'

Lev thought they would come on horseback, riding out of the night like Ibrahim. But instead, they approached on foot, slipping behind whatever object might protect them. An olive tree. A wagon. A fence post. Through a space between the bales, Lev could see their grey shadows, ghosts in the night, swooping here and there. He wondered if all this compacted straw could stop the penetration of a bullet. Someone to his right – Amos or Barak – stood up, fired a shot into the darkness. Everything went quiet, only the smell of cordite lingered. Amshel slipped down beside him. 'I can't see a damn thing.'

A whistled request from Mickey, Lev barely managing to find the breath to whistle back. No-one hurt. Amshel creeping back up until he could look over the top of the bale.

Forty

Glenkura, Western Highlands, Scotland

My dear Charlotte

Well, here I am at my Uncle Mendel's tiny cottage just outside the village of Glenkura. A more remote place on earth you cannot imagine. From my table by the window I can see down to the enormous loch that reflects the high mountains in its glassy stillness. There is the rush of the icy cold stream passing by the cottage but otherwise not a sound to be heard. Early spring is the perfect time to be in the Highlands. The skies are so clear, there is still a sprinkle of snow on the mountain-tops, I can see a scattering of bluebells, the heather on the lower slopes and, of course, there are no midges to pester the life out of a person.

The cottage is just one room, a resting place for my uncle when he used to work as a credit draper, selling goods on behalf of the Glasgow warehouses to the crofters and farmers of the area. He hasn't been here for many months but I cleaned it out quick enough with a good sweep, a dusting and a beating of the mattress. There is still a good supply of dried-out peat for the fire, a stock of oats in the girnel, I bought some milk and a clutch of eggs from the local farmer. I have already put a vase of spring flowers on the window-sill, some lavender underneath the pillows.

I so enjoyed the time we spent together in Glasgow, catching up with all your news and gossip. It pleased me to hear you have a fine new suitor in John Armstrong McKenzie. He appears to be a wonderful gentleman, very gracious, a strong personality, someone well equipped to put up with your independent ways, a supporter of your causes... and a man of means as well! I am only sorry to have arrived at a time when the work of the temperance movement is not going so well for you both. Only a few years ago, you were so full of hope for the success of the various campaigns to create dry areas across the city. It is hard to believe that support for these campaigns is dwindling and the publicans are winning out again. Glasgow is such a wealthy city but it is swimming in alcohol. Drinks for the merchants, the commercial travellers, the sailors, the workers who would rather spend their wages in the public houses than on their wives and bairns at home. Alcohol is the cause of all the ills in the city. It puts such a wedge between man and woman, unless that woman is willing to put up with such drunkenness or go the way of alcohol herself. Dear me, there I go again, getting involved in these social problems when all I want for myself is this time for peace and quiet away from all the worries of the world.

I was pleased also to see my parents. They are elderly and frail now, each suffering from their own little illnesses. My father was suffering from heart problems and forgetfulness when I left for Palestine. I never expected to see him again, he whispered to me as much when he kissed me goodbye on the platform at Central Station. Yet, here he still is in this world, becoming more religious the closer he gets to death. As for my mother, she is so shrill and robust, I think that death itself is frightened to pay her a visit. My brother Nathan, I just saw the once, and only for a short time. He is such a successful businessman now, the finest tailor in the city, providing suits to the highest levels of society. He refuses to mention names but he tells me he boasts a duke and several of the richest merchants among his clientele. Perhaps even one John Armstrong McKenzie has had a suit made for him by Nathan Kahn. He remains unmarried and I have a sense he always will.

As for me, I feel that I started to recover as soon as I set foot in the Highlands. I cannot fully describe what it feels like to walk on a land that is free. The people of Scotland surely do not appreciate how lucky they are to have access to this space, this wildness, this beauty without worry or dispute. Who owns that loch down there? And those mountains? And that gorse? And that stream? That wild hare? I do not know. I do not care. Possibly some laird somewhere in his fancy house but he is not chasing me off his land unless I come armed with traps and a shotgun for the purpose of poaching. It gives me so much happiness to feel this liberated. I want to go outside and dance barefoot on the heather, to try and embrace this landscape in the gather of my arms. But I know I cannot grasp such beauty. For it is not there for the ownership but for the enjoyment and appreciation.

Palestine is such a different land to this one. It is a place so parched in places that every little patch of greenery represents a triumph of nature over adversity. Land and water, water and land. What a struggle we had to secure both. Yet here I can step out of the cottage door and drink cool, clear water from a mountain stream to my heart's content. I can bathe myself in it, launder all the clothes of the shire in it without a thought for its source or its availability. But what I miss about the Holy Land is the light. There was such an intensity in that light, Charlotte, I cannot describe. When I was bathed in it, I felt as if I were being kissed by God.

Yes, Palestine. It seems so far away now. It seems as though what happened that night in Kfar Ha'Emek happened to other people living in another world. You asked me my reasons for leaving Palestine but I was not ready to tell you. Now that I am here in the Highlands away from everything, I feel able to tell you that story. I will just get up and make myself a pot of tea before I begin.

Shoshana and I woke up the four children that remained and took them from their newly built children's house into the dining room. It was not the practice of our settlement or in true socialist principles for the women to be the only ones to look after the children. But we were under threat and all of our principles went out of the window that night. It was the men who guarded the perimeter with their knives and guns, and it was we two women who were left to be the child-minders and run the supply line. Two of the children were Shoshana's. The other two belonged to a woman gone to Tiberias for the day but unable to return for the fighting taking place all along the valley. We made beds for them underneath the tables then went about making coffee, tea and sandwiches to take out to the men. There were shots throughout the night, each one making me jump in my skin. Shoshana and I told the children it was firecrackers for an Arab festival. They seemed happy with that explanation and went back to sleep.

At midnight I went out with my provisions for the men on the perimeter. It had been a cloudy night with only a hazy moon and a few stars and I was thinking we were going to get some much-needed rain. I could see this reddish glow not that far off in the distance, it was only later I realized these were the flames coming from the burning of our ancient olive grove. It all started with just one shot, then a pause when my heart leapt up my throat and I dropped to the ground. After that, there was a frenzy of shooting just like Jumping Jacks going off all at once on a Guy Fawkes night. I covered my ears, put my head down, and waited. Waited for the noise to pass, waited for death, I did not know which. A stray bullet even whistled close by me and into the wall of the cow-shed. Just as quickly as it had started, the shooting stopped. That was when the shouting began.

We lost two men that night. Barak, a stocky little fighter of a man who had been with us from the beginning, was shot in the chest. He died a few hours later despite all Jonny's attempts to save him. The other was dear Amshel. He was killed instantly with a bullet to the face, dropped down dead right beside Lev. He wanted nothing to do with our socialism, he even used to mock us about it. In the end, he died defending it.

We don't know exactly what happened at our settlement that night. We don't know if we were attacked by bandits from across the border in Trans-Jordan or we were part of the general rioting that took place across Palestine. Our men claimed they shot at least two of our attackers but no bodies were found in the fields. The next day, we buried Amshel and Barak at the small cemetery we have close to the Centre of the World. It is a very beautiful spot, I am sure I described it to you once before. The rain fell as we put the bodies in the ground.

While we mourned for the passing of our two comrades, the news of what else had gone on in Palestine that night began to arrive on our doorstep as travellers passed through on the road between Beisan and Tiberias. There were stories of riots in Jerusalem and a massacre in Hebron. We heard of murders and rapes, the bodies of burned women, young children found with their heads cut off. We heard the riots were spreading to Tel Aviv and to Safed in the north. For one week, I felt we were living in a hell on earth, never knowing when our turn might come. Our only hope came from the six rifles Lev and Mickey brought us. With them, we felt we could fend off any attack. I promised myself though that if my future was to depend on the need for guns, there was no place for me in this land.

I know that you read the reports of what happened that week in your own newspapers. One hundred and thirty Jews and more than one hundred Arabs were killed. Many more injured on both sides. There were stories of hope too. In Hebron, for example, some Arab families did their best to protect their Jewish neighbours from being massacred. But in the end, it was all about the mistrust that exists between Arab and Jew here in Palestine. At first, Charlotte, I wanted to write the word 'hatred' but I don't think that is fair. After all, we are two great nations born of the same father Abraham. A brother should not hate a brother. It is not a hatred but a mistrust. A mistrust that I feel will never ever go away.

I was surprised by the attitudes of the few remaining members of our settlement after that week of riots. Most decided to stay. I don't know if it was because they had a stronger belief in what they were defending or because they had nowhere else to go. America is mostly closed to Jews these days unless they have money to bring with them and there is much talk of anti-Semitism in Europe. I was lucky. Scotland is not closed to me and I have rarely experienced any anti-Semitic behaviour here.

As for Lev, I think it will take a lot more time for him to recover, for the wonder of this place to seep into his soul, for the wilderness to heal him. The terrors of that night continue to plague him. I can see it in the heaviness of his heart and in the restlessness of his dreams. He is down at the loch now, trying to catch fish. I fear he has no clue what to do with a rod and a line, and that it will be porridge rather than trout we will have for our supper tonight. I need to remind myself to be patient and to indulge him when I can. It is not often a man sees his brother die in his arms.

So, Charlotte, that is the story of that fearful night now told. It feels so much better now that I have written down these words. I hope that it marks the end of one chapter in my life and the beginning of another.

I look out of the window of my uncle's cottage and see that Lev is approaching. My goodness, he carries a large fish in one hand which he is now showing off to me. He is smiling.

With all my love

Your friend, as always

Celia

Epilogue

Madame Blum never fully recovered from her grief over Sammy's suicide and died peacefully in her sleep soon afterwards. Her property was sold and turned into a guesthouse by the new purchasers who, for reasons unknown, called it after the name of the previous owner. In the 1960s, 'Madame Blum's' became well known as a hostel and message hub for travellers passing through the Middle East, alongside other legendary outposts such as Uncle Moustache's restaurant just inside Damascus Gate in the Old City of Jerusalem, and The Pudding Shop opposite the Blue Mosque in Istanbul.

Mickey Vered (originally Michael Rosenblatt from Manchester, England) continued to run a successful import/export firm in Haifa. However, his business was merely a front for his efforts in helping re-organize the Jewish underground defence force known as the *Haganah*. Mickey became instrumental in smuggling large caches of weapons into Palestine from Europe. He was arrested several times by the British security forces for his clandestine activities but never imprisoned. He was killed in 1947 from injuries sustained when a faulty grenade from one of his illegal shipments blew up in his face.

Rafi Melamud remained on Kibbutz Kfar Ha'Emek after the riots. He served three two-year terms as *kibbutz* secretary and was responsible for introducing modern farming and irrigation methods into the settlement. He returned to Poland in early 1939 in an attempt to bring back his remaining family members to Palestine. Unfortunately, he got caught up in the German invasion of Poland later that year.

Records show that he was shot (not gassed, as originally thought) in Majdanek concentration camp in December 1943.

Amos Tzedek remained on Kibbutz Kfar Ha'Emek for the rest of his days. His strong leadership and socialist ideals meant the settlement always kept to the political left of the wider *kibbutz* movement as it developed through the decades. Kfar Ha'Emek remained one of the few settlements where children were brought up separately from their parents. It also has survived entirely on the labour of its own members and has never employed workers from outside, whether Arabs or Jews. Amos went on to become the principle archivist at Kfar Ha'Emek and a small museum was built in his name to host his work. He died in 1994 at the age of ninety-two and is buried at the small cemetery alongside the viewing point known locally as the Centre of the World.

Gregory Sverdlov and the Palestine Electric Power Company went ahead with their plans to build a hydro-electric power station by damming up the River Yarmuk. The land that had never existed on any map was flooded and submerged in the process. For fifteen years, the power station supplied electricity to both the Jewish and Arab population alike until it was blown up in 1948 in a raid by pan-Arab forces in Israel's War of Independence or *Nakba* (the catastrophe) as it is known by Palestinian Arabs.

Zayed and Ibrahim Daraghmeh The British administration provided the Daraghmeh tribe with land just south of Beisan along with a certain amount of monetary compensation. The tribe elder, Zayed, died shortly after the move. It is thought Ibrahim was killed in the above raid to blow up the hydro-electric power station owned by the Palestine Electric Power Company in 1948. More recently, the Israeli Army has attempted to force the Daraghmeh tribe to leave its current site, destroyed many houses and outbuildings with bulldozers and cut off water supplies to the area. The confiscated land is to be used for the expansion of Jewish settlements in the region. The Israeli Supreme Court is currently considering claims by the Daragmeh tribe asserting their lawful right to remain on this land as granted to them under the British Mandate.

Jonny Levy remained on Kfar Ha'Emek for a number of years where he served as the unofficial doctor and medical adviser for the settlements in the Jordan Valley. He eventually went to work at the Hadassah University Hospital on Mount Scopus in Jerusalem. There he became a leading expert in trachoma and a relentless campaigner for its eradication throughout Palestine by means of improved sanitation conditions for both Jews and Arabs alike.

Chaim Kalisher returned to Paris in 1930 where he became one of many personal advisers to the Anonymous Donor. However, the more formalised nature of the work there did not suit his temperament and he retired soon after on profits made from his investment in the Palestine Electric Power Company. He took up ornithology and established a reputation for himself as an accomplished amateur with a particular focus on the red-footed falcon. He died peacefully in his sleep on the 13th June 1940, on the eve of the German occupation of Paris.

Sarah Lindenbaum and her friends from the Young Guard worked for two years on a road gang before becoming part of a seed group for a new socialist settlement in the Jezreel Valley. Sadly, Sarah contracted cholera and died before the project got off the ground. She was only twenty-three years old. Her grave can be found in a small cemetery near Tel Megiddo.

Charlotte Maxwell married John Armstrong McKenzie, later Lord McKenzie of Springbank. The couple remained strong campaigners for temperance in the city of Glasgow and opened the well-known Grand Temperance Hotel in the Dennistoun area of the city where alcohol was forbidden on the premises. The business of the hotel gradually declined during the 1930s and eventually closed down just before the beginning of World War II. The building took on various guises thereafter but was eventually demolished in 2009 to make way for the construction of sporting facilities in advance of Glasgow hosting the Commonwealth Games in 2014. Lady McKenzie died in 1950.

Lev Sela (originally Gottlieb) went back to Poland to sell his grandfather's land before returning to Scotland where he used the proceeds of the sale to support himself through a law degree at Glasgow University. He married Celia Kahn in 1934 and the couple had two children, Samuel and Daniel. Lev went on to set up the Amshel Property Company, an estate agency with branches throughout the city and West Scotland. Sammy and Danny took over the business on Lev's death in 1970. Their own children continue to run what remains a family business to this day.

Celia Kahn returned to Glasgow where she worked for a number of years in an administrative role for the Women's Welfare and Advisory Clinic, a birth control centre in the Govan area of the city. After she married, she withdrew from the workforce to raise her children but moved into political activism in the late 1950s and early 1960s when she became involved with the then fledgling anti-nuclear protest movement, the Campaign for Nuclear Disarmament. Celia died in 1980 in Glenkura, Western Scotland while holidaying with her family at her late uncle's cottage which she and her husband Lev had earlier expanded into a holiday home. Her memoirs *From Glasgow to the Galilee* are held in a collection by the Scottish Jewish Archive Centre, Garnethill Synagogue, Glasgow.

The land that didn't exist on any map. After being totally submerged as a result of the damming work by the Palestine Electric Power Company, this area of land later re-emerged after the hydro-electric power station was destroyed in 1948. The Kfar Ha'Emek *kibbutz* subsequently used the land for the cultivation of cotton as the years of flooding had reproduced to some extent the conditions of the Nile delta which are ideal for growing high quality cotton fibres. The land was later ceded to the State of Israel in 1958 when the son of the Anonymous Donor in a generous gesture agreed to transfer all PICA-owned properties to the State. There are now proposed plans between the Israeli and Jordanian governments to turn the area into a peace park.

The Anonymous Donor remains anonymous.

Author's Note

This is a work of fiction. While every effort has been made to accurately represent the general attitudes and policies of the various real life parties to the issues surrounding Palestine in the 1920s – the Jews, the Arabs, the Zionists, the Bedouin, the British and the French – many of the specific details concerning individuals, organizations, dates, places, geography have been altered to accommodate the narrative of the story.

To avoid confusion, however, the following are actual events but they may not have taken place at the exact time specified in the novel. These include the Jaffa Riots in 1921, the Palestine Riots in 1929 – also known as the 1929 Massacres (by the Jews) and the *Buraq* Uprising (by the Arabs). An earthquake did take place in Palestine in 1927 and the port of Haifa was constructed during the 1920s although it did not officially open until 1933.

A hydro-electric power station was established at the confluence of the Yarmuk River and the Jordan River at Naharayim (Arab name: Jisr al-Kajami) in 1932 by the famous Russian engineer Pinchas Rutenberg (on which the character Gregory Sverdlov is based only in terms of nationality and profession), partly using land leased from Emir Abdullah of Trans-Jordan in exchange for electricity. The power station ceased to be operational following fierce fighting between Israeli and Arab brigades in 1948.

In 1994, Naharayim was the site used for the signing of the Israeli-Jordanian peace treaty and became known as the Island of Peace. However, that peace was shattered three years later when a Jordanian soldier opened fire on a party of visiting Israeli schoolgirls, killing seven of them. It remains as the site of the proposed Jordan River Peace Park under the auspices of the Friends of the Earth Middle East (FoEME), a non-government eco-organization with offices in Tel Aviv, Amman and Ramallah. There are plans, endorsed by mayors and communities in both Israel and Jordan, to re-flood part of the area to create a bird sanctuary. For more information, please visit the FoEME website: http://foeme.org/www/?module=projects&record_id=123

The land that didn't exist on any map does in fact exist although about a kilometre to the north-east of Naharayim. It forms part of the land cultivated by Kibbutz Ashdot Ya'akov (Ichud) where the author lived and worked for six years during the 1980s. The land was, in fact, known as The Jungle by the members of the *kibbutz* and the author worked in the cotton and alfalfa fields there. It is overlooked by a viewing site known as The End of the World because of its vistas as described in this book. Adjacent to this point is the rather beautiful *kibbutz* cemetery.

The Palestine Jewish Colonization Association (PICA) did exist but all of its deeds and personnel as mentioned in this book are purely fictitious. *Mewat* is a properly documented land right under the Ottoman Code relating to 'dead land' but was outlawed by the British via the *Mewat* Land Ordinance of 1921.

Acknowledgements

The author is extremely grateful to both Creative Scotland and The Robert Louis Stevenson Fellowship for their support in the writing of this novel.

The author would also like to thank Ross Bradshaw at Five Leaves Publications for nurturing his first two books, *The Credit Draper* and *The Liberation of Celia Kahn*, then releasing them to be published alongside *The Land Agent* as part of a unified trilogy – known as the *Glasgow to Galilee* trilogy – all under the Saraband imprint.

About the Author

J. David Simons was born in Glasgow in 1953. He studied law at Glasgow University and became a partner at an Edinburgh law firm before giving up his practice in 1978 to live on a *kibbutz* in Israel. Since then he has lived in Australia, Japan and England, working at various stages along the way as a charity administrator, cotton farmer, language teacher, university lecturer and journalist. He returned to live in Glasgow in 2006.

Apart from his *Glasgow to Galilee* trilogy, he has also written about contemporary and 1950s Japan in his novel *An Exquisite Sense of What is Beautiful* (2013). His work has been shortlisted for The McKitterick Prize and he has been the recipient of two Writer's Bursaries from Creative Scotland and a Robert Louis Stevenson Fellowship.

The Glasgow to Galilee Trilogy

While *The Land Agent* stands as a novel in its own right, it is also the third part of a loose trilogy incorporating two other novels, *The Credit Draper* and *The Liberation of Celia Kahn*, also published by Saraband. The three books can be read separately and in any order.

An Exquisite Sense of What Is Beautiful

An eminent British writer returns to the resort hotel in Japan where he once spent a beautiful, snowed-in winter. It was there he fell in love and wrote a best-selling novel accusing America of being in denial about the horrific destruction during World War II. As we learn more, however, we realise that he too is in denial, and that his past is now rapidly catching up with him. A sweeping novel of East and West, love and war, truth and delusion.